Nowhere Land

Pamela K. Kinney

ISBN: 978-1-963928-14-3
978-1-963928-15-0 (open dyslexic)
978-1-963928-16-7 (e-Pub)

CHAPTER ONE

Carla Smith crossed over to the other side of the one-room historic building where her Electromagnetic Field Detector meter lay on the floor. It displayed all five colors, blinking in the same sequence over and over in a manic dance.

She called out to her fellow investigator and longtime friend, Jenny, who stood by the door, fiddling with her own digital mini camcorder, changing batteries. The ones in their equipment kept draining out.

Carla had just finished putting a new battery in her meter.

"Hey, Jenny, come over here and check this out."

The petite dark-haired woman walked over to her. She dropped to a crouching position beside Carla's meter. Her ponytail fell over one shoulder as she looked down at it.

"Your meter's going crazy."

"Yeah, whacked out like blinking Christmas lights," said Carla. "Let's do an EVP session with our recorders."

She switched her recorder on and placed it on the uneven dirt floor next to her meter. The lights did not stop blinking.

Jenny unzipped her bag and lifted her own digital recorder from inside. She clicked it on and set it right beside Carla's before sitting down beside the other investigator on the floor.

Carla crisscrossed her legs and waited while Jenny took her mini camcorder and switched it on, focusing down at the recorders and meter. She switched it to night vision.

Virginia Ghost Trappers had a stroke of luck when the new owner of the deserted village and the property called Burkett—but better known under the nickname, Nowhere Land—had contacted them to do a ghost hunt. The owner had problems hiring people to do any work on the historic structures, and those he did get didn't stay long enough to finish anything.

Carla fought the freaked-out feeling that she'd been experiencing ever since they'd arrived, struggling to not let it overcome her. The head of VGT wouldn't invite her on any more investigations if she chickened out.

That must never happen.

Before Carla joined VGT, her life had been a round of tedious work at Richmond Social Services and nights spent alone at home, except for her parakeet, Daisy. Nights she watched paranormal reality shows on television and on DVDs, eating coconut ice cream. Doing the real thing made her feel alive. She'd lost weight, too, as she quit buying ice cream and spent money on equipment for her new interest.

Carla blew out a breath and spoke. "Is there anyone of the spirit realm in here with us?"

No answer. *Not out loud anyway*, thought Carla. *I hope both recorders caught something.*

"Do you have a name? What is it?" Carla pointed at her partner. "This is Jenny, and I'm Carla."

Silence.

The meter's lights still flashed.

Earlier, Carla had made sure there was nothing electrical in the cabin that could be the cause of any potential spikes to the equipment, but the historical buildings appeared to not ever have electricity put in. She found nothing under 2.0 or over 7.0. Over or under meant spirit presence might not be causing the fluctuations in the electromagnetic fields detected inside the one-room domicile. She had even climbed up a rickety ladder and, using her flashlight, checked for any electrical outlets or anything else modern. The darkened garret had disturbed her for the short time she'd been there, so she'd scurried back down. She never told Jenny about those feelings; she just kept them to herself.

Her stomach cramping, Carla looked up at that shadowy area. Nothing moved, not even shadows. Not there, or along the ceiling, or elsewhere in the room. And yet, against all logic, a sensation of someone or something watching pricked at her. "Are you observing us from the room we can only access by the ladder?"

The perception of being contemplated intensified.

Carla licked her lips and rubbed her sweaty palms on her jean-covered legs. She spouted off more questions, pausing a minute after each to give any spirits time to answer before she asked the next one.

"How old are you?"

"Are you male or female?"

"Adult or child?"

"What year is it?"

"What year did you die?"

"What is your name?"

"Are you trapped in this spot, or do you go back and forth between here and the other side?"

She rubbed her hands together to warm them up; the air in the room had grown chillier. "I give you permission to touch me, so go ahead and do so. Or make a racket like two knocks on the wall or the floor to let us know you're here."

No voice answered her questions. No sounds like knocking, or anything else reached her ears.

There had been nothing but silence since their group had arrived around five o'clock that afternoon. No animal or bird calls breaking the stillness, just a strange heaviness. To tell the truth, she hadn't seen any sign of life at all. Only the team—and the only clamor came from the group's feet, voices, and equipment.

That bothered Carla all the way to a cellular level.

Knock it off, Smith. Quit being a wuss. It's just the paranormal in this place affecting you, nothing more.

The coldness grew more bitter. It seeped into Carla's bones.

Cold as a tomb in winter.

Okay, not a good thing to think in a place like this. Rubbing her hands together again, she noticed that Jenny did the same. *So, Jenny felt the chill, too.* It didn't help, though. She wished she'd brought gloves. As if woolen gloves could fend off arctic conditions brought on by something supernatural.

Honestly, this might be good. Personal experience. This is the first spot we've investigated that gave me bad-ass chills.

Jenny's voice boomed into the stillness. "I guess it can't do anything audible enough for our ears." Then...

Jenny squealed and jumped to her feet.

"Did you hear that?" Her friend screeched.

Carla frowned. "Hear what?

"Booted footsteps and something like a hard kick to the wall near us."

Carla could hear the panic escalating in Jenny's voice.

Not even waiting to hear Carla's answer, Jenny grabbed her bag with her free hand and, still clutching her camcorder like a lifeline, bolted from the place. The door slammed into the wall inside.

Carla, who hadn't heard anything, frowned at the open doorway. It was hard to see anything outside, only pitch blackness. A chill skittered up her spine like a spider up a web, even as she rationalized what had just happened in her brain. Her friend had taken off and violated a rule of all paranormal investigations: One did not leave their partner alone.

Jenny's never flaunted the rules before. Never.

And yet, her friend had scurried off like a frightened rabbit pursued by a wolf. Funny thing about that, Carla could not think of one investigation where anything ever scared Jenny before, not even during the poltergeist activity the group checked out last year in Norfolk. This place....

Along with the increasing frigidness, a thickened air enclosed her; it was like being stuck inside a dark closet. Her breath left her mouth in puffs of icy clouds. It shocked her that she could see them, that they luminated in the darkness. Hands trembling, she managed to gather up her meter, Jenny's recorder and her own, and her bag before she scrambled to her feet. Her heart hammered. She broke out in a cold sweat. The equipment she held almost slipped out of her hands.

"Thank you for any answers you gave us and any sounds you might have left on the recorder. I'm leaving now, and I ask that you do not follow me, Jenny, or any of the other investigators, home."

Shutting off the still-flashing meter, she tucked it and her recorder inside her bag.

The cold increased even more, and she slipped her flashlight out of a pocket inside the bag. She thumbed the switch on. The line of light flared and showed her— nothing. Relieved, she slung her bag over her shoulder and clutching Jenny's recorder with a death grip, she trailed the light to the open doorway.

Just as the beam reached it, the door slammed shut. A unbidden shriek left her mouth, her heart thudding, and she leaped back in time to avoid it. She walked back up to the door to open it.

It refused to budge.

Unlike modern exits, there was no lock on this Colonial version. She couldn't find a doorknob, either.

The acid in her stomach gurgled, and her heart sped into double-time, as she tried the door again.

A pressure rammed into her back and slammed her into the wood, holding her there. A splinter jabbed at her cheek. The recorder and flashlight slipped from her hands. She heard the thuds as they hit the floor. Carla found her hands freed and tried to pound on the door, but then something grabbed her hands and squeezed. Pain riveted through them, the bones under the skin cracking, a couple of fingers being forced up.

Nothing stopped her from screaming, though. "Help! Oh God, it's hurting me! I'm locked in here. Jenny? John? Anybody?"

The pressure against her back and on her hands vanished, although not the agony.

Carla turned around. The recorder clicked, which meant it had been switched on. The flashlight must have landed facing back into the room and its light lit up a few feet in front of her. Her bladder loosened, and she wet her pants. Her shrieks echoed as she was jerked off her feet, the back of her head slammed against the door before it hit the floor. Still yelling, she felt herself being dragged deeper into the room.

"Oh God, oh God, oh—" Her scream broke off in a gurgle.

The recorder stopped recording, and a deep, dark voice arose out of it. "Are any of the living left alive in this room?" A cackle rose from it, before the small box imploded as if something stepped on it with a heavy boot. The flashlight died.

***

John stopped talking to the other three members of VGT when Jenny skidded to a stop in the middle of them. John Peters, along with the rest of the team, Leonard Price, Bubba Booth, and Tom Jackson sat on canvas chairs on what was thought to have had been the village green.

Neglected for a decade or more, the grass sprang wild in the spring and summer, though now during the cooler fall, it had grown brown. The team had cut some of it down, making a central spot for the team members to return to. A battery-operated camcorder with night vision stood filming on a three-legged stand facing down the middle of the village.

Bubba held a thermal camera, and he panned it all around, at the five homes and the surrounding woods. He put it down at Jenny's disruption.

John took a swig from a bottle of water and shone his flashlight at Jenny's face, swallowing.

"Jenny, you're pale as the underbelly of a fish, and your eyes? Big black holes."

Jenny couldn't stop shaking. "Something happened. Back in the place that you told Carla and me to check out."

John, a bona fide skeptic, didn't believe in the paranormal activity he investigated, but tonight things had happened that he couldn't explain. It didn't mean he had no definable reason for them, just that he hadn't found anything justifiable at the moment. That troubled him. This whole area gave him the willies. He kept those feelings to himself. No need to freak out his team. This was the first investigation that made him question his skepticism in the paranormal.

"Where's Carla?"

"She's behind me...wait a minute, oh God, she's not." Jenny craned her neck around to peer through the night vision camcorder she still clasped. She whipped her wild eyes back at him. "God, I don't see her through the camcorder. I think she's still back at the building. I thought she was behind me when I ran."

John frowned. "You left your partner alone, Jenny. You know the rules."

"Yeah, I know, each investigation must have two people together always." A sheepish look replaced the fear in her eyes before the dread returned full force.

"There was something in that room with us. Something with heavy footsteps and it even kicked the wall. It frightened me, and okay, I bolted. I've never been scared before on any hunt we did—you know that—but there's a whole other wrongness to this area. Maybe the stories are true." She knotted her hands together; still clenching the camcorder. "I just can't understand why Carla didn't follow me."

Snorting, John screwed the cap back on his bottle and thumped it down beside his stuff on the ground. "Because she's not a chicken shit? Come on, we'll all go and get Carla."

Still trembling, Jenny put down her camcorder on a small plastic table. "Can I wait here? I like Carla, but I really don't want to go back inside that place." She fished her flashlight out of her bag and switched it on. The light barely pierced the darkness. "Oh, I left my recorder back at the building. I guess Carla has it."

John stood. "Great. No more investigations for you, Jenny. You're out. Permanently. But you're coming with us."

Jenny shook her head, her ponytail flying and slapping each side of her head. "No way. Since you just told me I'm out, I don't have to go back. I'd leave this Godforsaken place right now, but I came with Carla in her car. I'll stay here with the equipment and watch it until you get back with her."

John opened his mouth, only to close it. He nodded, feeling the slow burn of anger rising in him. "All right, fine. Just don't go anywhere. Leave the equipment, and I'll take your ass to court for anything missing or ruined." He stomped off, the other three guys trailing after him. The lights from their flashlights stabbed the trees along the trail.

***

Jenny watched until the night swallowed the men's lights. *Humph. Like I can go anywhere without a car. I don't know how to drive. Jerk.*

She clutched her bag to her breasts like a baby and directed her own beam of light over the trees. They appeared to have drawn closer and enclosed her in a tight circle, looming menacing predators. Ready to snatch her up and eat her. Her bag almost slipped from her fingers, but at the last moment she snatched it by the straps. She couldn't help it, couldn't stop the shudders. They just kept on coming like earthquake tremors. She hated being here and couldn't wait until they got Carla, and everybody left.

Even if John refused to go right away, she would demand that Carla take her home. Deep down, the former team member felt glad that John had told her no more investigating with the team. If she never had another paranormal experience, it would be fine with her. The closest she planned to see a ghost would be in a movie. Or read about them in a book. Of course, that might be a year or two from tonight.

I might need a glass of wine tonight. Several glasses, to help her fall asleep in her bed and not have nightmares.

No freaking noises. Where the hell are the commotions of the night? Not even a breeze, just eternal stillness.

That should have been her indication on arrival that this was not a spot to do a ghost hunt. The place acted wonky even in the daytime.

The blasted land is one big grave. She sucked in her breath. *Oh, God, why did I think that?*

Thinking back, she felt sure that Carla never locked her car when they first arrived. Yeah, the woman always left it unlocked in the parking lot at the shopping center. Maybe she should go ahead and check to see if Carla had done that. If it was open, she could climb inside and wait for the others. Lock all the doors and feel safe. John would be mad...hell screw him.

Ghosts and demons can pass through solid objects. Why the hell do I think a locked car could keep anything out?

Jenny licked dry lips. "Doesn't matter, I'm going to the car. Let anything try and stop me."

Without warning, something snatched her from behind. Her mouth opened, but nothing left it, not even a whisper. She watched as the ground below her feet grew farther and farther away. An invisible punch to her stomach knocked all the air out of her and tears rolled down her cheeks. She screamed, but only in her head.

A fetid odor blasted her sinuses and a giggle tickled her ear. "Gonna have fun."

***

The men reached the hand-hewn building. It stood dark and silent, the door closed and locked.

The hair fought and won, rising on the back of John's neck. He realized he didn't hear anything coming from inside or outside where they stood.

He rationalized in his head, as he always did. *It's night. Things are asleep.*

Except for owls. They hunt at night. There are other night predators, too.

He ignored those thoughts and banged on the door. Finally, sound, even if it came from his fist.

"Carla, open up. The investigation is done. We're leaving."

The door didn't open, nor did Carla call out.

Ignoring the tiny voice inside his head saying not to do it, his fingers clasped a leather strap hanging from where a knob would be on a modern door. He yanked, and to his surprise, the door swung in. He stumbled inside. The room gloomy as thick black ink, the light from his flashlight barely making a dent in it.

The other men followed him in.

They flicked their lights along the walls and floor, but they didn't find Carla anywhere in the room. All sent their lights up at the loft. The beams scarcely breached the darkness there.

Tom turned to John. "Maybe she's up there and out cold. Want me to check it out?"

John nodded. "Yeah, sure, go ahead. If she's not up there, we'll search the other buildings."

John and the others watched Tom disappear into the blackness. They couldn't see him ascend the ladder, only hear the creaks from it breaking the unnatural silence. That bothered John. No other noise of any kind—then they heard something.

Leonard had brought his thermal camera, and he pointed it up and toward where he assumed Tom had gone.

John gave it a quick glance and saw Tom's heat signature. Nothing else.

Bubba said, "Anything, Leonard?"

"No, nothing. Just Tom's body heat."

John never put claim to any psychic abilities. He hadn't even believed in his ex-fiancée's. But this land overwhelmed him. As always, he told himself that it couldn't have anything to do with the paranormal. That the stories he knew about it caused him to let the place get under his skin. Sweat dripped from his forehead, and he wiped it away before it stung his eyes. Several minutes later, agitated at the growing silence, he switched on his flashlight and waved its light up at the loft.

He called out. "Hey, Tom, did you find Carla?"

Tom didn't reply.

Leonard gasped, "Hey, Tom's body heat is gone from my thermal camera's screen."

John peeked at the thermal imager. No heat signature of anything. He called out again. "Tom?"

Something flew from the loft and the three men vaulted out of the way. It hit the floor with a thud. Light from their flashlights cut through the darkness and revealed Tom, his eyes and mouth open, blood leaking from his mouth and his skin porcelain white.

Leonard yelled, stumbling back. "Oh God, oh God! What happened? He didn't even scream. Did the fall kill him?"

John snatched the thermal camera from Leonard's hand and held it over the body. Tom's body held no heat.

Bubba dropped to his knees and placed his fingers where the pulse would be on Tom's throat. "I can't find a pulse. He feels cold as a corpse, too. Like he's dead. But maybe I'm wrong?"

Leonard screeched. "Dead? He was alive and talking and climbing up that ladder a few minutes ago. Are you trying to screw with us?"

Bubba stood. "You know me better than that. Like I said, I might be wrong."

John said, "Both of you grab Tom and let's get out of here. After we get him in the van, we'll collect Jenny and the equipment and get the hell out of here. We'll call the owner and the police when we arrive at the emergency ward at the hospital. Fuck finding Carla, let the cops find her. Somebody is playing nasty tricks on us, and I'll be glad to see the back of Nowhere Land."

But when Leonard and Bubba leaned over to pick up their fellow investigator, they were flung to opposite sides of the room. John heard the simultaneous thuds of their bodies smack the walls. Neither moved nor called out.

Somebody, or maybe more than one person, had to be messing with him. Ghosts don't do harm to the living. That's what the experts always said. Experts he always thought of as idiots before because they believed in phantoms. Now it looked as though those experts might be wrong about what ghosts could do. Two grown men who weren't lightweights had been thrown across the room. Had whatever did that, killed them?

John's heart pounded as he sent the beam of light from his flashlight around the room. Nothing. Except for him and maybe three bodies.

Possible bodies. They might be all alive, just unconscious.

Sweat stuck his clothing to his skin. Not sure what to do, he pressed a foot forward to go to one of the men, but fear kept him from moving.

Maybe it wasn't a ghost or ghosts. By the shade of Linda Blair....demonic presence?

Forget the freaking paranormal.

John wanted to grab Jenny and get the hell out of there. Get drunk. Get out of the ghost-hunting business. Leave the mystical to the unknown. That made perfect sense, now.

He turned to leave. The fading light from his flashlight exposed the white features of Carla. She wore a psychotic grin, standing in front of the opened doorway. Her eyes were no longer green, but gleamed crimson. Like blood.

"Going somewhere?" she asked. Her voice had dropped several octaves, more mannish than feminine. "I don't think so."

She grew taller and thinner until her head barely touched the ceiling. The door swung shut behind her without a sound.

John's flashlight died. The darkness suffocated whatever bravery he still had.

John Peters had never believed in the paranormal all of his life. A horrible smell brushed against the hairs inside his nose, and freezing cold seeped into his bones, and Carla ripped the heart out of his chest.

At the last moment of his life, he believed.

CHAPTER TWO

Parker Burkett stopped his rental jeep next to one of the investigator's trucks. His sister, Lisa Polivka, sat in the passenger side and climbed out after he did. The early morning air felt crisp, the smell of rain and rotting leaves aromatizing it. He walked around to the front of the jeep to stand beside Lisa.

It began to drizzle.

Misty droplets ran down Parker's face and slipped beneath his long-sleeved T-shirt. Shivering from the cold wet, he wished he'd worn his jacket before he left home.

"This place always creeps me out, Parker," said Lisa, her breath visible in the air. "Since the first time two months ago when we stepped on the property, I never hear any sounds, only here and there." She glanced at her brother. "Just like this morning—still as a graveyard."

He shrugged and headed for the area in the middle of the buildings. His sister sighed and trotted after him. It was hard keeping his feelings to himself—he didn't want to alarm her about the thick oppression he always felt here and how it filled the air even now. It made his hair rise off his skin, and he had to tamp down the urge to turn tail and run back to his jeep. He walked over to the equipment in the middle of what one archaeologist told him would have been the village green.

Looking around, there was no sign of the paranormal team he had hired to do an investigation in the village last night.

He agreed with Lisa. No noise. There should have been some kind of bird noise at the least. Funny…he didn't see a bird, not in the sky or in any of the trees, some still costumed in their colored autumn leaves. The color that appeared lackluster, haggard.

Parker and Lisa searched each shack, but they didn't find a body, much less anyone alive. No sign of mice living in any of the walls, spiders or spider webs decorating a darkened corner. Parker would have assumed the investigators hadn't waited for him, and left, but their vehicles were still parked on the other end of his property.

When they stepped inside the last place, light from Parker's flashlight lit up dried blood painting the walls. Not much, but enough to indicate something had happened. He tightened his jaw. A touch at his back nearly had him jumping out of his skin and he let loose a curse word.

Lisa's soft voice at his ear settled the jerking of his heart. "What do you think happened to them, Parker?"

He shook his head and waved his flashlight around. Something glinted from up in the loft and, tucking the flashlight in the pocket of his jacket, he climbed the ladder. When he reached the top, he shone the light around and caught sight of what had made the glint. He cursed again.

Lisa called out. "Parker, what is it?"

"It's a finger with a ring still attached." Shock had loosened his tongue, and he'd blurted it out before he realized it was the wrong thing to do. He climbed back down. "I have to call the police."

He took out his cell phone and tapped out 911. The nearest state police station would be five miles away, in Gloucester.

A woman's voice spoke. "Hello? Virginia State Police."

Parker said, "I need the police out at Burkett, Virginia. I think something might have happened to some people I allowed to stay here overnight."

"Sir? Burkett? What?"

"This is not a prank. I'm the new owner of Burkett, the property locals around here call Nowhere Land, and I think something happened to the paranormal investigators I had here last night. I didn't see any bodies, but their vehicles are still here. And," he paused, then soldiered on, "I found a finger in one of the shacks here." Parker continued by giving the dispatcher the GPS coordinates of the area since there wasn't an address.

The dispatcher said, "We've got a car headed your way. It should be there in about fifteen minutes."

***

Lisa stepped outside to hike back to Parker's car. The rain had stopped, but the cold remained. Before she touched the door handle, a crow called. Startled, she looked up and saw the biggest crow she'd ever seen. Or maybe it was a raven; she still couldn't differentiate between the two birds.

It sat on one of the lower branches of the loblolly pine that towered over the car. She blinked. For a second, the bird appeared to have red eyes. She closed her eyes and counted to ten, then reopened them. Nothing but a black beady gaze stared back at her. It shook its frame, stretched out its wings, and flew away in silence.

Unable to say why, her heart a beating drum within her chest, she dove inside and locked all the doors. Parker had the car keys on him. He could damn well open the car. She'd remain inside even when the police arrived. She'd stay until Parker took her home. She'd never come back here. It didn't matter if someone offered her a million dollars to do so.

In fact, she'd asked him to sell it the first time she'd stepped foot on the ground here.

Her brother had refused; he'd gone on about how it would make a great historical attraction like Colonial Williamsburg and other museums, places like that. That it was their family legacy.

Just like Grandpa. Yada yada, history, and crap, she thought. *Give me the money. Let someone else handle the headache of this creepy spot.* With the money, she could convince her husband to move back to California. Her ancestors may have lived in Virginia, but she preferred where she had grown up.

All those stories about this land; Grandpa always going on about how his ancestors and the other colonists mysteriously vanished in 1730 and how the natives in the area avoided it. Parker's and Lisa's ancestor, Lucius Burkett, had been the only survivor of those who had settled here. He had been found wandering on the farm of the James family a few miles away in Gloucester on November 19, 1730. They ended up taking the little boy in and raising him as one of their own, even though they never legally adopted him. Whatever happened here, the James family could never get anything out of him. Instead, it appeared he had a memory block of his short time living there. They gave up trying to get anything out of him. Lucius later married the youngest James daughter, who inherited the farm. Supposedly, he remembered it all after he came upon the place while hunting, putting it all in his diary.

Lisa tapped a finger against her chin, realizing that the crow had been the first bird she'd seen since Parker and she first came here. For all the times she'd been to the area, she had never seen any animal or bird, even insects, along with the lack of noise from any of them.

The crow's caw reminded her of laughter.

That scared the bejesus out of her.

***

Black silhouettes of trees stood to the right of Neri Phelan, hulking shadows of shacks rising from the ground at her other side. Nowhere to run and nowhere to hide. Except in the woods or inside one of the buildings. Her psychic sense told her something terrible waited for her no matter what she chose. No safety for her anywhere. Worse, no moon or stars graced the night sky, so she had no light to guide her way out.

She was screwed. If this was real. This must be a nightmare. She remembered going to bed around nine, so she had to be asleep in her lovely, warm bed. The problem with it, it felt real. Damn, scarily real.

Whatever set off her psychic Spidey senses, it knew she treaded here. Damned if she did and damned if she didn't, but she needed to get out of plain sight, dream or not. She ran to the nearest building and placed her hands on the hewn wood, touching her way around to an open doorway. The darkness beyond threatened her. She ignored her screaming senses and slipped a hand inside, jerking it back out with a cry. Whimpering, she cradled the frost-bitten appendage against her breasts.

As if a separate entity, her intuition screamed at her: *Didn't we warn you about going inside*?

She talked to herself. "Sorry, but what else can I do? Remain outside, build a campfire, and invite whatever is here to come toast marshmallows with me?"

Taking a deep breath, she plunged all of herself inside. Right into the....

Neri gasped, awakened from the terrifying nightmares that she'd been having for the past six months. Every inch of her body drenched in sweat, gluing her pajamas to her. She tossed aside the soaked covers and stared with bleary eyes at the glowing LED of the alarm clock on the table beside her side of the bed.

It's only 3 a.m.?

Witching hour.

Neri wiggled off the mattress and stumbled to the bathroom, to take another of the prescription pills the doctor had prescribed to help her sleep. The second pill rode down the back of her throat, the bottle taunting her from its spot next to the sink faucet.

Damn, I'd really hoped to get off these pills. I hadn't had a nightmare for a week.

Until tonight.

"Guess I'm stuck with the damn medication." She stared at her reflection in the mirror and made a sour face.

Nasty. Besides possibly being addictive, the pills tasted awful. Like black licorice. Neri never liked that candy and never understood how anyone did.

Kelly loved it. The whisper pushed into her mind.

She ignored it. It wasn't one of her spirit guides, and she would be damned before she let her depression overtake her. The running water shut off and her sweat-sticky pajamas discarded in the dirty clothes bin, she padded out of the bathroom and headed back to bed. Too tired to care about digging out another pair of pajamas from her dresser drawer, she crawled into bed to sleep naked.

Except she didn't fall asleep, but she laid there and frowned, staring up at the ceiling. The room felt empty and quiet. She thanked God under her breath, as not one spirit had bothered her this night. They liked to come to her; she was a medium, so she heard and saw them. Usually, she said a prayer before bedtime to keep them at bay, to continue her sleep uninterrupted, but she'd forgotten this time. She mentally recited a quick one in her head.

Like she could help them. Or that they even wanted it. Sure, there were those few lost souls not sure they had died. To those, she pointed the way to the other side of the veil.

Most ghosts didn't want assistance. No, they just wanted to talk to someone. Unless they had a digital recorder or a Frank's box or an Ovilus, like paranormal investigators used, most of the living did not hear them or, even more likely, ignored them if the spirits did manage to get through to them.

After all, did anyone need to hear Aunt Millie gossip as she had in life? Back when the gossipy old lady lived, her relatives avoided her by not answering the phone, or just didn't visit her, except maybe during the holidays. When Aunt Millie died, trying to get away from her became difficult. She grew angry, and this time, she displayed it, by throwing stuff or pulling hair. Yanking bedclothes off her sleeping family members. That's how Neri used to make money, by convincing the dead Aunt Millies to leave their relatives alone.

It worked ninety-five percent of the time; for the five percent that it didn't, she suggested contacting their priest or minister for a house blessing or an exorcism. Although she doubted that would work. Stubborn people in life didn't change their personalities when they passed on. They became stubborn phantoms in the Afterlife.

Finally, Neri dropped off, and slept until seven o'clock in the morning.

***

Eating a bagel slice painted with light cream cheese and drinking coffee laced with peppermint non-dairy creamer, Neri watched the early news. Chimes of a familiar Star Trek theme filled the air. Ben Neilson's cell phone number lit up the screen of her cell phone.

Ben? *This early in the morning*?

She laid the bagel remains on a plate next to her on the couch, wiped her hands with a napkin, and snatched up the phone.

"Ben, what has gotten you out of bed this early to give me a call? That's a first."

The man held a night job as a security guard. He would have never survived a standard nine-to-five job; he hated getting up earlier than noon. That made him a great paranormal investigator. He'd formed a team three years ago, Seekers of Paranormal World, SPW for short. She'd been a member of it until a year ago.

"Ha-ha, funny, girlfriend. Neri, we might have a chance to investigate one of the places that I've always wanted to."

She didn't breathe. Didn't say anything, just closed her eyes as her stomach cramped. The nightmare came back—although it was not the only reason she felt ill at what Ben had just uttered. The air began to suffocate her, and a headache formed behind her eyes.

Oh God, oh God, Oh God!

"Neri? Neri? Neri, are you listening?" He shouted that last sentence.

Neri gripped her cell tighter, the acid in her stomach bubbling like a pot of soup. She fought the need to throw up. Her headache went into overdrive, raging. Taking a deep breath, she spoke.

"Ben, I don't do paranormal investigations anymore. You know that, especially after what happened at the last one that I did a year ago. Hell, all I do these days is give readings at psychic fairs held at the Alchemists and the Aquarian Bookstore, plus a few out of my home to supplement my income. Nothing else. Hear me? N. O. T. H. I. N. G. Else!"

God, Neri felt she should have gotten herself a cup of herbal tea instead of coffee. Caffeine brought on jittery nerves. She needed her prescription pills, but she didn't get up, just remained on the couch.

Ben's voice softened. "Look, I'm sorry that Kelly died last year. I know that—"

"Know what?" Gripping her phone tight until her palm hurt, she shouted, "That my little sister wanted to tag along with me on some investigation in some ragtag cemetery on a night when a storm rolled in? That lightning struck her? That she died? That I didn't even get a warning psychic-wise about her death, so that maybe then I could have made her stay home?"

Silence.

Guess he still doesn't know how to answer that one. Neri grew ashamed for even thinking that. For insinuating his fault in her sister's accidental death.

He spoke again, though she could hear the hitch in his voice. "Neri, there's nothing I can do about that. I don't have a time machine to go back and save her. There are times I wished I did and I'm sorry that she has never communicated with you afterward, like the other spirits. I don't know why. Maybe she's happy in the Afterlife. But I think you can help with this investigation."

Neri's headache worsened. It wasn't thoughts and memories about her sister that caused it, but something worse. "All right spit it out."

"John Peters and the Virginia Ghost Trappers..."

"What about John?" Her heart squeezed as if an in invisible hand had fingers wrapped around it. Her headache pulverized.

She and John had been engaged until she found out that the jerk had formed a paranormal group and told her that she couldn't be a part of it because they used science and not paranormal "woo-woo". That's when she'd finally understood the truth about how he felt about her abilities. Neri had broken it off with him. Kelly told her that she had been too good for the man and that she would find the right guy someday. Someone that would accept her abilities along with herself. Neri rejoined Ben's team after that.

Ben's voice broke in her thoughts. "—he and his members disappeared two weeks ago, during an investigation. Well, not all—"

Her breath caught her lungs, and she almost smothered, gulping in air, she asked, "What do you mean, not all?"

"A small amount of blood and a finger with a ring was found in one of the historic buildings. The police identified the blood and finger as John's. Plus, their equipment was still there, outside, but not a sign of any inside the places. The police haven't been able to find the rest of him or the other team members. Not above ground anyway."

She straightened, and her breath hissed out of her. "What! How?"

"No one is sure."

"No human element involved?" She gripped her phone until her hand hurt.

"You mean like murder? The police went over the grounds with a fine-tooth comb. Nothing. They still spout off that it must be murder, due to the evidence. Thinking that maybe it could even have been a member of the group that did it. Or some unknown person is the other theory. They're still searching the land though." She heard a sound like Ben stopping to take a breath and blow it out. "But the police couldn't find evidence of anyone, other than the group themselves in the ghost village or the surrounding woods. No other DNA than members of the group, of course. Also, the owner's and his sister's, but otherwise, the next stuff came from three months and older—mainly from crews Burkett hired to do work on the land and the ghost village."

"Who found this?"

"The owner, Parker Burkett. He and his sister arrived to find the team missing. They're the ones who came across the blood and finger, too. And before you suggest that the investigators might have gone home, their vehicles were still parked there."

Her headache went out of control and visions from the nightmare taunted her. Her stomach whirled like a clothes dryer. She managed to keep it together and not spew, "Wait a moment. Ghost village? There's no ghost town in Virginia; the urban legend of that lost city near the Richmond Airport notwithstanding."

"There is, it's just not well known. It's a village where the settlers who built it vanished one night, never to be seen again. Except for one little boy, who happens to be the ancestor of the current owner and his sister. You know the spot. It's not far from Gloucester; nicknamed 'Nowhere Land,' in legend, with old buildings from the 1700s falling apart on it. You grew up near it. Remember, you told me about it."

Her nerve endings tightened, and the acid in her tummy spiraled into overtime. She curled into herself on the couch. "Oh, God. That place."

"The legends about the cursed land have nothing to do with Him, I've heard."

"You know what I meant. I never felt so glad as when my parents moved away from that area to Chesterfield County." She rolled to sit up. "John and I may have ended our relationship on a bad note, but I would never wish anything like that happening to anyone, not even him."

"Neri, I'm calling back the old crew for this. Please, will you join us? Though there's a small catch; I still need to contact the owner and get him to allow us to do it. I gather he's refusing all paranormal groups to do any more investigations after what happened."

"I don't blame him. Ben, you're nuts. He'll say no, and your pipe dream will be just that, a pipe dream."

She stared at her living room, not seeing it, but in her mind's eye, that land again from her childhood memories. Remembered the god-awful silence. The fear it brought to her. How it almost had gotten her older brother. The evil....

Luckily, her parents had moved away when she'd turned six and Mike, twelve, after Kelly's birth, to Richmond. She had never been back near it since.

Except for the nightmares. I've been revisiting Nowhere Land for six months not knowing, except for the terror.

Did she even want to do it if Ben got the owner to give them the okay to investigate? She still saw Kelly dying in her head. The dreams after her sister's death haunted her for a few months. The flicker of lightning came alive again in her head, and she saw it arrow down and strike her sister in the face. Not the body, but the face. Her sister never even screamed, just danced like a marionette without strings and fell on top of a tombstone. Kelly's face black as ash, lifeless, except for one arm swinging back and forth.

The torment about Kelly faded, until these new ones took over. She always awoke to no memory of what they'd been about.

Nowhere Land. What the legends always called it. Not by its legal name of Burkett.

"Neri? I need to know."

"Ben, I don't know. Anyway, you won't get permission, and I wouldn't blame the man if he slams the phone down on your ear."

Her heart beating hard, she clicked off their connection. Then she pressed the button until the phone shut off completely. She got off the couch and ran to the house phone to unplug it.

There. Now the only way he could contact her would be to drive up to her house. That's if he had the guts to do that. She doubted he would, though. He'd never ever pressured her, but let her make the decision. Always.

No way could she do it. Not because of Kelly's death, nor because she never got along with John Peters. She felt she owed it to John, to solve what happened. To verify his death and prove what happened to him. She chided her conscious poking at her before she ignored it.

With a fresh cup of coffee laced with creamer, she sat back down on the couch and used the TV remote to click the television off. Taking a gulp to get the caffeine in her to rid herself of the pain in her head, she thought back to last night's nightmare.

It held the facet of unreality that something dark waited for her.

At first, not remembering why the dreams terrorized her, she'd taken to sleeping at night with a nightlight on, something she'd never done, not even as a child, even with all the ghosts coming to her. A couple of months in, she'd gone to her doctor and got prescription pills to help her sleep.

It seemed strange that last night had stayed with her.

Especially with Ben calling her this morning about doing a ghost hunt on the land.

Something wants you to remember. Maybe.

She put down the cup and reclined on the couch, closing her eyes. Drifted off to sleep.

The nightmare returned.

Ten minutes later she awoke and sat up with a gasp, her heart like a frantic bird battling against her chest, trying to escape.

Unlike the past six months of the nightmares, she saw what waited for her this time in vivid detail. The woods. The trees loomed large and scary, their branches reaching out for her. The cold. It seeped beneath her skin, taking up residence inside the marrow of her bones.

Unlike last night's dream, she'd wandered down the path until she saw the dim outlines of several buildings. They reminded her of hulking, threatening shadows. Ones she didn't want to go near. Worse, something waited for her. Out of the corner of her eye, she caught sight of a figure. Tall, thin. Dark, too, though the head appeared milky pale. It stood there, not far from the shadowy buildings.

She'd wanted to run away, but she couldn't, as her feet had rooted to the spot. Like television static, the figure approached, closer and closer. It made no sound, just like everything else around her.

Frantic, she'd fought to escape. She couldn't face it; have it loom over her. Didn't want to see its eyes. If it even had eyes. She would've slipped her feet out of her shoes; except she was barefoot. Though, she doubted she could have moved her feet. Giving up, she looked up, and her breath caught, unable to scream. It stood only a few feet away, a dark silhouette against the night. But before it drew close enough for her to see the details of what it was, or more likely before it snatched her, she woke up.

The cold in her bones didn't leave her for hours afterward. Nothing drove it away, either. Not her blankets nor cups of hot tea or coffee, not even hot soup, or oatmeal. After a while, the cold left on its own. The real chill anyway, but not the icy terror in her heart.

She finished the cold dregs of what remained of the coffee in the cup. She needed to get out of the house. Into the bright sunlight, among crowds of people, maybe at a nearby shopping center.

No pills. They made her sleepy, and this time they might not keep the nightmare away.

Or keep the tall figure from seizing her.

CHAPTER THREE

Ben set his phone on the table and—oblivious to his surroundings—stared off into space. The paranormal investigator knew Neri's sister's death had affected her, but he'd assumed she'd gotten over it by now. It'd been a year, and Ben thought she would have been anxious to get back into paranormal investigating. Some people would call him selfish, but he knew her and what might snap her out of her doom and gloom. Hell, they'd been good friends since high school.

She'd always been psychic, and he had always been interested in the paranormal. That's what had brought them together. They met when they'd both joined their high school's occult club. Well, the club didn't use the occult tag—the school wouldn't have sanctioned that— those outside of the club knew it by Matoaca High School Horror Club. School faculty and classmates not in the know thought members read horror fiction or watched scary movies. They met to discuss the paranormal in all of its guises.

After graduation, members went on to college or got jobs and dropped away from anything paranormal, except watching shows on the television or talking about it. Ben and Neri formed an actual paranormal investigation group. Got others to join. They checked out all the haunted spots until Neri met John. Until John wooed her away from the group.

Away from Ben.

Except, Neri had never been Ben's in that sense to woo away. From her side, there'd been love, but the love of a sister for a brother, nothing more. From his....Ben closed his right hand into a fist and focused back to Kelly and her death.

I should have seen how much Kelly's death had hurt Neri. Been to see her more often than the few times I did. I'm such a jerk.

Being her friend meant being near her. Helping her in her time of need. Even when being near her meant pretending he felt happy for her whenever she dated. Then they both attended a paranormal conference where one of the speakers was John Peters. She fell for the bastard. To poorly phrase it: hook, line, and sinker.

If Neri hadn't been careful about saving herself for marriage and, instead, had given herself to the creep, Ben doubted John would have stayed around. But Neri resisted and to Ben's shock, John proposed at his New Year's Eve party held at his apartment two years later. The engagement only lasted six months before Neri understood what John thought about her being a medium and threw her engagement ring in the jerk's face.

Of course, Ben was there to pick up the pieces. Like always. But picking up the pieces didn't mean she saw the light; that the man who stayed by her side through thick and thin should be the one to hold the key to her heart. When the lightning killed her sister, she broke off contact with Ben. With the others in the paranormal group, too. This phone call had been the first communication between them in a long while.

Ben went to the refrigerator and fished out a can of soda. The cold liquid felt good going down his throat. Not as good as a beer might be, but he was out, and he couldn't stomach going out anywhere to get some.

Forget about her for now. Get back on track.

After he drained the can, he crushed it in his hand and tossed it at the garbage can in the kitchen. It bounced off the edge and fell to the linoleum. Not even stopping to pick it up and shove it in the trash, he stomped out of the kitchen and headed to his home office. He thumped into the chair at his desk and turned on his laptop.   Once online, Ben googled 'Nowhere Land,' and endless links to various sites, all about Burkett and its grisly myths, appeared in the search.

The latest news of what happened at the village jostled for top space, sending the myths farther down the screen. There were many theories by so-called experts. Only the police kept closed-mouthed about any of the details and findings, other than what they already released about what happened to the paranormal team. Paranormal enthusiasts posted their own explanations on blogs, forums, and websites—from angry Native American spirits to UFOs to even Bigfoot. Hell, even the Devil got blamed.

Ben didn't find anything concrete for the why and what-for. Of course, a lot of the stories went back to the Burketts and their ancestor being the only survivor of a mass disappearance of the settlers who built the village after settling the land, which appeared to be not unlike what happened to the colonists on Roanoke Island off the coast of North Carolina. The Lost Colony's disappearance transpired in the late sixteenth century, while what happened to the Burkett villagers occurred in the early eighteenth century. This being the twenty-first century, with police investigations armed with technological advances, inevitably, John and his group would be found.

No matter how much of a jerk he is, John would not pull such a stupid stunt. His group wouldn't go for it, not even for publicity. Faking their disappearances is a crime. And if someone killed them, sooner or later their bodies would be uncovered. Right?

It bothered him, the fact if they had been killed, one person couldn't have murdered them all and not leave clues more than the finger and the bit of blood. He assumed that the cops didn't give out much on what they had found and Parker Burkett or his sister refused being interviewed by the media.

A few blogs and posts later, Ben got offline, and he sat, rubbing his fingers through his hair. Frustration ate at him. He wanted to go to the cursed land and inspect things for himself. Unlike those idiot paranormal groups who would try and sneak in at night, he decided to be honest and gain Burkett's permission. But in one after another of the posts he'd read, the man refused to let anyone back on the property. Only the police were allowed on it; a couple of uniformed cops in a squad car to park at the dead-end road to the land and two others outside the gate of the other entrance, to keep intruders and others from sneaking in. Though by accounts, the land's spooky reputation kept people away. No one wanted to check it out. According to the story passed around, even the police guarding it at night felt uneasy being there.

Ben slammed a fist on the desk. Papers scattered, and a ghost paperweight toppled to the floor with a dull thud. Flesh and blood people just didn't disappear like phantoms. He itched to find the truth. The place had always been off. He leaned toward one theory of the land having a vortex. No matter what the facts inferred, there was still a reason why.

He punched in Parker Burkett's cell number that another investigator had given him. The investigator had told him that he doubted that Parker Burkett would cave and let him do an investigation on Nowhere Land, besides Ben being crazy to even go near that place. After a few rings, a voice recording told him to leave a message. He left one with his number.

To get his mind off wondering when Burkett might call him back—if at all—Ben turned back to the screen and began a search on Google for various well-documented historical websites, to dig beneath the history and legends. Maybe he should start with the Powhatan Native Americans. Being the tribe that had lived in the area, they also had the oldest stories about the land.

CHAPTER FOUR

Neri strolled through Carytown. Her fear evaporated; she felt glad she'd decided to do this and not the mall. The shops and eateries along this street exuded cheerfulness and color, even on a cloudy day. The fresh air and exercise from walking were better than an enclosed mall full of bodies.

After lunch at the Galaxy Diner, she perused the World of Mirth and Shelf Life Books and made some purchases at both. She stopped in front of the Bygones window and checked out autumn leaves scattered around a dummy dressed in clothing from the Sixties. It wore a white mini skirt, a green turtleneck top, and white go-go boots. Halloween decorations had vanished right after October 31st. The promise of Thanksgiving and Christmas replaced witches and skeletons with a mixture of fall leaves, turkeys, and even early showings of Santa Claus in most of the shops in Carytown.

"You think they would have given her a coat or sweater, with the change in weather."

The hair at the back of her neck rose at the unknown deep male voice. Neri turned around. For a minute, the sun blinded her enough to see only the tall shadowy figure from her nightmare, and her breath hitched as she wondered why her psychic sense hadn't warned her.

"Are you all right?"

She blinked, and the sun shifted its beams, and she saw only a tall man looming over her, with short hair the color of a raven's wing and sparkling blue eyes. He was not slender, but had a more muscular build. He wore blue jeans and a black leather jacket over a T-shirt, part of a wolf's face revealed where the jacket was open. Afraid he might catch a glimpse of the momentary fear she'd felt, she didn't answer but returned her gaze to the window display.

How could she have believed him to be the tall, shadowy figure from her nightmare? She worked to compose herself and return to normal.

A sigh reached her ears. "I was just trying to be friendly."

She kept her eyes on the display. "Maybe. Or, more likely an attempt at a pickup line?"

A chuckle. "It could be. But it appears it's not working in my favor."

Neri turned to look at the man again.

For a second, he vanished, and the dark figure from her dreams rose over her again.

She gasped and stumbled back, her heart battering her chest like a frightened bird in a cage. Before falling against the window, a hand reached out and hooked her arm, stopping her and breaking the vision.

Concerned blue eyes stared down at hers.

Her heart still thumped like a frightened rabbit fleeing a predator as coldness enveloped her. Bone-chilling cold, a chill that did not come from the autumn air. She wanted to give in to the need to flee, even now, when she only saw the man and not that frightening visage.

"Look, I didn't mean to scare you." He tightened his grip as if he thought she might run away.

"Scare me?"

"Yeah, I've never seen the panic in someone's eyes like I just saw in yours. I felt your flesh shrinking from me. Like I'd become every monster from under the bed and in the closet wrapped into one."

She licked her dry lips and shuddered. "It's not you."

"I don't see anyone else here."

Neri took a few deep breaths, calmed down, and gave him a weak smile. "I'm fine. You can let go of my arm."

He blinked and stared down at his hand gripping her arm and let her go. Redness splashed across his cheeks. "God, I'm sorry. I didn't hurt you, did I?"

Neri slipped her arm out of her coat sleeve and scrunched up the long sleeve of her T-shirt, revealing her arm. No bruise or reddened handprint marred her skin. "See? No bruises or any other kind of marks. I'm all right." She rolled the sleeve back down and shoved her arm back into the coat sleeve before wrapping both arms around her and her bags. The chill still haunted her insides. *Smile at him. Otherwise, the poor man will think your still blaming him for grabbing your arm.* Neri flashed him a smile, hoping it didn't look fake.

"Let's start over. Hi, I'm Parker Burkett." He stuck his hand out. A lock of hair fell over his eyes, and she itched to push it back, but he brushed it back himself.

She frowned. *Wait a moment. Parker Burkett? The name's familiar.*

She searched her brain for why and then it hit her. Nowhere Land. Burkett, Virginia. John Peters and his group. *Oh, God!* She pressed back against the glass of the window as if she could meld with it and escape him.

That of all places, they ran into each other, here. Some would call it fate. Neri thought of it as a possible misfortune.

He narrowed his eyes. "What's wrong? You just became pale as a ghost."

Ghost. Not a good choice of words, especially coming from him.

She fought the laugh that threatened to slip from her mouth at the irony of his words. The icy feeling inside her bones deepened when the black humor left her. Fighting to get a hold of herself, she managed not to let him see her trembling.

When she thought she had a firm grip on herself, she asked, "Did you say, Parker Burkett?"

"Yes, but my name has never had a reaction from other women like you're showing me now."

Should I tell him? She blew out a breath. *Do it. Tell him why you're acting the way you are. Otherwise, he'll think you're some ditzy dame.*

"I know you own Burkett near Gloucester, and I know about the paranormal investigators that vanished while investigating it."

He tucked his hand back inside his jacket pocket and lines formed in his forehead. "You read about me and what happened in the *Richmond Times-Dispatch*?"

Startled, she shook her head. "Was it in the paper? Gosh no, I don't get the paper much, sometimes the Sunday one. To be truthful, I haven't gotten it for the past month. Or watched the news on TV either, well, not lately, anyway."

"Then where?" His voice roughened.

Oh, I don't like the way his voice changed.

"My friend. Ben Neilson."

His eyes grew hard, and his lips morphed to thin and angry lines; he pulled his hands from his pockets and tightened them into fists. "I see. Of all the people to run into, you're one of his paranormal idiots."

A flame of irritation replaced the embarrassment and the fear. "One, I'm not a part of Ben's team now, though I was a year ago. Two, I don't like being called an idiot."

He crossed his arms. "You just admitted to being part of his group a year ago. What did you do for him? Tech or something else?"

She stuck her chin out. "I am a professional psychic. Precisely, a medium."

He blinked, then bitter laughter burst from him. "Oh, God, you talk to ghosts!"

The irritation shifted to fury. Most of the time, she handled nonbelievers well, not letting it bother her. They were better than those Bible-thumping Baptists who called her evil and a demon's whore. But from this man, who had hired a paranormal team to come out and check his cursed land, it pricked beneath her skin.

"Look, I'm sorry that psychic abilities are not something most people believe in," she gritted her teeth, "but you brought in paranormal investigators to prove or disprove something about your property. The same 'something' that may or not have killed them. At the very least, it made them, or their bodies, vanish to who knows where. I knew John Peters, and I know everyone on his team to be scientific or gadget types—not a psychic among them. I do know that geeks though they might all have been, not one of them had been ill, so their deaths if their bodies are found, would be questionable. Right?"

"Maybe."

"Look, I know the police told you to keep quiet about it to the media, although it seems to been in the paper. My problem is my friend, Ben, wants to investigate that place. I grew up near that area, and I know there's something wrong with it. Please, tell me. I won't go blabbing to anyone. Not even Ben."

He shuffled his feet and stuck his hands back in his pants pockets.

"I'm not supposed to talk about any of this as per police orders. My sister was the one who told the newspaper, not me. But I will tell, just to you." He drew closer, boxing her in, the cold glass at her back, his body radiating heat at her front. "No bodies have been brought to light yet, so any deaths are debatable for now. I thought they might have just left when my sister and I got there the next morning, except we thought it strange that their vehicles were still parked not too far from the buildings. The police checked out their homes and places of business, and no one has seen them. It's like they just upped and vanished into thin air. The only sign of someone having been there happened to be the discovery of a single finger with a ring." The man's gaze found hers. "I just returned Mr. Neilson's call an hour ago and told him I'm not allowing anyone else on that property at night. Daytime, either." He quit looking at her and stared at the window display instead. "There goes the historic attraction I'd planned on doing with Burkett. I may not believe in psychics, but something's wrong with that place. Something happened to those people. I don't know what, but I believe it's just adding to the supernatural fodder about the land. People will still come if I do get the place ready as an attraction, just not for the history, but to look for ghosts or monsters."

He turned away. "I've got to go, Ms..." He walked away, not even waiting to get her name.

She called after him. "It's Neri Phelan."

She doubted he heard her. Time to go home anyway, so Neri walked to her parked car.

A half hour later, Neri unlocked and opened her front door and stepped inside. She tossed her purchases on the table by the door and dropped her purse and keys on it, too. Though she needed, no, wanted, a hot cup of tea, she headed to the bedroom first. Once inside, the medium crossed over to the dresser, removing and scattering her clothing across the floor. She snatched her flannel lounge pants and an oversized T-shirt from the top drawer and after she slipped them on, left the room.

When the microwave beeped fifty seconds later, she took out the steaming cup of tea and wandered into the living room. Curled up on the couch, she didn't turn on the television or pick up the novel she'd been reading. Instead, after her drink had cooled enough, she stared off into space and sipped the tea.

The drive home had given her time to cool down and to think about what Parker Burkett said. He made sense. Let another team into that place, and she knew deep down in her gut, they would be no more. Though she'd never been to the area since her parents moved to Chesterfield, there had been a couple of times when she had driven to Gloucester and passed by the dead-end street that led to the woods that sheltered the buildings. Two roads led to different parts of it, but it was always that second one that got to her. A feeling of dread had arose and clutched at her both times. The shudder slithered along her nerves. Worse, the voices screaming inside her head. Frightened, lost souls calling for help and begging her to save them. Neri ignored those voices as best she could and drove past. Although she was always ready to help spirits, Neri knew if she went to Nowhere Land, she might never leave it. Besides, she wondered if the voices came from the lost ones, or from something else trying to lure her in. Because what happened to all those people who vanished? Other mediums claimed they didn't get a sense of any spirit on the property. She never told anyone about what she heard from there. Not just from the fear of being laughed at, but because why did those spirits know to call her name?

Now if she drove past that street, would she recognize John Peter's among the others? He'd been an ass, but no one deserved being stranded in that cursed place forever. When Parker Burkett mentioned a finger with a ring on it, she knew it had to be John's. That it must be the one she'd given him two weeks after he'd asked her to marry him. John had not kept many of the presents she'd given him, only that ring. It had been a signet ring with his initials.

No one deserved to become lost in hellish limbo forever.

The tea cooled, and no longer wanting to drink it, she got off the couch and walked to the kitchen. A headache thundered behind her eyes as she poured the remains of the tea down the drain. She ended up taking a couple of prescription pills and laying down on top of the covers of her bed. She drifted off and dreamed again; this time no shadowy figure haunted her, just John's wraith calling her name from some strange city built of blood-red crystal.

CHAPTER FIVE

Parker stepped into his house. Though upset, he took his time and hung his keys on a hook in the wall by the door. But when the shaky man draped his jacket on a hanger in the hall closet, it slipped off and fell to the floor. He didn't care and shut the door. He dug out the Scotch from the kitchen cabinet he kept it in and gulped the contents straight from the bottle. The burn rushed down his throat; his eyes watered. Still feeling the need, he took another slug. After that, he grabbed a glass and poured some into it, before he put the bottle back in the cabinet and wandered back to the living room. He switched on the television, but after channel surfing and finding nothing he cared to watch, he turned it off. Finally, he downed the glass of alcohol. The glass clinked as its bottom touched the wood of the coffee table. A slight headache from the combination of the stress he'd been under for the past couple of weeks and the drinking pick-axed in his head. With the pain came the memories of ghosts, symbolic and actual. Thank God, they weren't haunting him...yet. Unless those people at Burkett hadn't died, but he doubted that to be true.

Maybe he needed to get more drunk? No, he might have found a bit of solace in the liquor, but it didn't keep the nightmares at bay. Or stop him from seeing the spirits he'd seen since childhood. He almost itched to go to his doctor and demand some prescription pills to help him sleep at night, but he never followed through. No way did he want to explain why he needed them and maybe end up seeing a shrink.

Hey, Dr. Thompson, I keep having these nightmares, where this tall, thin, dark figure is always there. A voice still calls my name, too. Worse, that group of people that vanished on that property I own? I now see shadowy gray somethings, begging me to set them free. One of those voices sounds exactly like the voice of the head investigator. And you know what's worse, Doctor, I've seen phantoms since I was a child. You know, the kind that haunts graveyards, houses, and spots like that. The first time it happened when I was six. My parents thought I had an imaginary friend. How many kids have a Confederate soldier from the Civil War for a playmate?

Right.

Doctor Thompson would look funny at him, before writing a referral for a reputable psychiatrist. Parker doubted any shrink would rid him of ghosts—or the fear-driven dreams with the scary figure who haunted his nights since he was ten. His parents had died in a violent accident while the family had been on a visit to his grandfather, not far from that cursed land. Due to luck—or maybe not, it depended on the viewpoint—his grandfather had convinced his daughter and her husband to let him, and his sister, stay with him while they went out to eat, otherwise Lisa and he would have died, too.

The figure stalked his dreams since that first night. For the first year, his dead parents starred in his nightmares, too. Their voices called to him, and he would see two shadowy figures, barely discernable in a city of bloody crystal. Always, it ended when the taller, thinner shadow came and swiped them up, taking their wraiths to some place in that scary city. His dream self's scream joined theirs and he'd always awake, still shouting.

He kicked off his boots and stretched his legs on the couch. Funny thing about the nightmares; his sister, Lisa, never had them. Guess that just showed who handled tragedy better. Of course, she never saw his imaginary Confederate soldier, either, or any other ghost. None that she ever admitted to, anyway. He propped his head on the arm of the couch and didn't fight the sleep overtaking him.

***

He stood on the street, at the edge of the woods. No way would he enter them. His breath escaped in a hiss as lights from a vehicle lit up the road and the woods. He stepped back into the shadows.

An SUV parked alongside the curb, and the engine died. Being dark, he couldn't tell if he recognized the vehicle or not. A slim figure stepped out from the driver's side. The person held a flashlight that shot out a thin beam of light. Pointing the light toward the ground, he/she made their way up the path through the woods, dead leaves crunching beneath their shoes. When whoever passed right by him, not even acknowledging him, enough light revealed the individual to be his sister, Lisa.

Oh God, Lisa, don't go on the cursed land! Forget that fucking village. Get back in your vehicle and go home.

Lisa paused and looked back over her shoulder as if his thoughts had taken voice. Frowning, she continued walking the path until she passed between two massive oaks that stood like sentinels. Her light faded and she disappeared from his sight.

Parker sweated, and his heart protested its fear; he debated going after her like he would if awake. Nothing would happen to her. Just a dream, nothing more. He never saw the future. If he had, he could have saved his parents from dying.

The struggle for and against tore at him. "For" won.

He entered the woods. Not questioning how he didn't use a flashlight, but he could see the path clear as day. Silence ruled the night as he stepped past those massive oaks. It unnerved him, but he kept on going.

The buildings loomed as formidable shadows. He swallowed the knot of fear clogging his throat. Nothing would stop him; he came here for Lisa. Shack by shack, he searched for her but didn't find a living soul.

"Let me go!" A voice boomed in the unnerving quiet.

Parker ran past one of the structures, calling out. "Lisa!"

A high-pitched scream rent the night, but he couldn't tell where it originated. To his right? Left? In front or behind? Inside one of the dilapidated buildings?

That's when he saw her. Lisa lay in the arms of the tall, thin, dark stranger of his nightmares. He couldn't tell if she was dead or only unconscious.

"Let go of my sister!"

Dark laughter filled the air. It glided up Parker's spine, cold as ice. His vision blurred, and he fought to move toward the figure. He tripped over something, but never landed on the ground, spiraling instead down and down into darkness. A male Alice who'd fallen into the rabbit hole.

Parker awoke and sat up, gasping. "Fuck." The terrible headache from the drinking had worsened, and he felt ill. He bolted to the bathroom and kneeled before the toilet, vomiting the contents from his stomach.

Shudders rippled through him, and he stumbled to his unsteady feet. A bitter taste spoiled the inside of his mouth, and he poured himself a glass of water and downed the contents. It didn't take away the taste completely, but still, he felt better. He staggered back to the living room, dropped back on the couch, and, snatching his cell phone, dialed Lisa.

It rang and rang, until after the tenth ring, when Lisa's cheerful voice came on to tell him to leave a message. Something had to be wrong. No matter what distracted her, she always answered by the fifth ring. *WTF?*

His stomach cramped, and not from his earlier binge. Ignoring the voice inside him about the possibility of him being drunk, he snatched his jacket off the floor of the hall closet and his keys from the hook, and he stalked out the door. Twenty minutes later, after stopping for a large cup of coffee at the Wawa's down the road, his truck roared down I-64.

He just hoped Lisa had forgotten her cell heading out to work. In his head, he heard the dark laughter again, and his body grew icier than he already felt.

CHAPTER SIX

Neri met Ben for dinner at his favorite Mexican restaurant on Midlothian Turnpike. She found him seated in the back, biting into a tortilla chip covered in salsa. What remained of the chip, he waved it at the seat across from him.

"Sit."

She slipped off her coat and slung it over on the chair to her right, setting her purse on the seat. Perched on her chair, she grabbed a chip from the bowl and after dipping it in the salsa, took a bite.

Ben waited as her teeth crunched through the tortilla chip.

"Why have you decided to do the investigation, Neri?"

She waited until after the waiter took her order before she answered. "I met Parker Burkett."

Ben's eyes widened, and he rose halfway out of his seat. "What? Where? How?"

She nibbled at another chip. "Today, in Carytown." She used another chip to point at him. "Except I know that he hasn't given you permission to investigate."

"Yeah, there's that. But now you're onboard; I am going to call Burkett tonight and renew my efforts at getting his consent."

She shook her head. "He may not allow you because of me. He knows I was a part of your group once. And that I'm a psychic, which I am pretty sure isn't an endearing quality in his eyes."

"Well, give me a chance. I'll still call him tonight and see what I can do."

The waiter appeared, carrying two steaming plates of food. He set each order down before the person who ordered it. Neri and Ben tucked into their food and didn't say anything more about the investigation, only conversing on more mundane subjects.

Ben walked Neri to her car. Just before she drove away, he tapped on the glass of the driver's window, and she rolled it down.

"I'll call you tomorrow morning and let you know what's what, one way or another."

"'Night, Ben," said Neri, and she rolled the window back up.

She drove away and could see his receding figure beneath one of the parking lot lights in her rear-view mirror. It didn't take her long to get back home. Locking the front door behind her, she stared at the lit living room. Despite what she'd told Ben, and she doubted Parker Burkett would let them on the cursed land, especially her, her psychic senses told her the opposite. She looked down and realized she'd been twisting her purse strap. She had never been this intense before. The damn place had gotten to her.

"It's just land. Historical, but land. Land haunted by ghosts."

Ghosts don't frighten people to death. Or make people disappear.

No, they didn't. Only people with weak hearts or medical problems could be affected by a haunting. At her last physical, the doctor proclaimed her in good health. As for people vanishing, that only occurred in fairy tales, or if someone kidnapped the person, killed, and buried the body. Unless it had been a gang with weapons, no way a group of people could be overcome and taken away.

Demonic entities can hurt the living, even just one.

That's what she feared the trouble with Nowhere Land was, that it was something along that nature. If Ben received an okay, maybe she should suggest a demonologist accompany them on the investigation. Someone who can perform an exorcism.

Like he would. He thinks you would be able to take care of any spirits or demons. Thinks of you as a super medium, able to exorcize with a snap of your fingers.

Ben had too much faith in her and her abilities. She still wanted that demonologist. Maybe she should get in touch with one and get him or her to drop by after they were there the first night. Nothing Ben could do if the person arrived out of the blue.

She dropped her purse on a table and after slipping off her boots, padded to the bedroom, where she undressed and slipped on her fuzzy blue robe. After getting a glass of her favorite chardonnay wine, she sat on the couch, her legs tucked beneath her and turned on the TV to the news. She didn't want to go to bed yet. If she slept, the nightmare might come.

Her eyelids drooped until she lay on the couch and her empty wine glass slipped from her fingers to the rug.

She stood at the edge of the woods and saw the path, lit only from the moon above. It was a lovely night, the moon almost full and stars spread across the dark sky, like glitter sprinkled everywhere. Tension drew her nerves too tight for her to notice or care, but for a second. The atmosphere felt thick with something she couldn't put her psychic finger on, except that it frightened her. It made all the hair at the back of her neck and on her arms, rise. If she followed that path to its end, she knew she would discover the reason for her fear.

The problem was, she didn't want to find out what that might be.

Fighting the call to take the first step, she woke up with a gasp. The house had gone all dark. The TV was off, too. Had the power died? She jumped off the couch and ran through the house, switching on all the lights. Not the power. Her clairvoyance tuning fork inside her gave off a warning, and she headed to the kitchen. Nothing attacked her. No shadows moved. Her clanging bell quieted as she grabbed her container of coffee grounds.

After she made a pot of coffee, she turned on the television and channel surfed until she found a romantic comedy from the 1940s. A cup of steaming coffee laced with cream in hand, she settled down to watch it. She needed her sleep, but she could not, no—dare not—go to bed.

Something waited for her in her nightmares. The same something that turned off the lights in her house. And she was afraid to find out what that something was.

CHAPTER SEVEN

A chubby boy with longish black hair snatched his friend's arm, stopping him. "Wait a minute, Jake. Doesn't this lead to that haunted spot? The one all the kids at school talk about?"

The other boy twisted his greyhound-thin body around, his African American features letting the other know his disdain, as he shook off the other kid's hand.

"Hey, Bubba? You believe that crap?"

Bubba shoved his hands in his jeans pockets and kicked at a rock on the ground, which only moved a few inches. "You think I'm dumb or something?"

Jake sneered. "Something, all right."

Two other boys, Saul, and Scary Terry, caught up to them. Both jeered at their comrade. "Bubba's a big wimp afraid of ghosts!"

"Wimp, wimp, wimp!" All three boys chanted and pranced around Bubba. "Afraid of ghosts. Ghosts ain't nothing, but dead people. A bunch of moldy bones stuck in the ground."

Jake stopped and poked Bubba in the chest. "I dare you to go with us to the ghost village. Help us bring something back from there to show the other kids that we were there tonight."

Bubba shook his head. "Maybe there ain't no ghosts, but what about all those legends about people going there and disappearing? What about those ghost hunters vanishing from there a couple of weeks ago? My daddy said it might be a gang or something."

Scary Terry wobbled his arms up and down like a monkey and made a goofy face. "Bubba does believe in ghosts. Believes in monsters. Monster's gonna get you, 'cause you're the fattest of us and more meat to eat."

Bubba shoved the other kid. "Shut up!"

Jake whispered into Bubba's ear. "Dare you to go with us."

"No...."

"Double-dare you."

The double dare did it. Bubba drew in a shaky breath and nodded, stepped on to the dirt path that led into the woods. "Okay, I'm going. Don't wanna, but I'll do it."

Crazy Terry and Saul whooped as they scuttled past him down the path, dust rising behind them like a spirit itself. Particles of the dust found its way into his nostrils, and he coughed. He wiped at his dirty face. Jake slipped an arm around his back, forcing him to walk faster, and both boys caught up with the other two.

Dead leaves crushed beneath the boys' footsteps, crackled loud in the night air. The only other sound came from a deer who'd been nibbling at the grass, and it lifted its head and crashed through the brush to escape the humans. That was the last noise the boys heard; slipping between two large, gnarly oak trees, they entered the muteness of a dead man's tomb.

Nothing, no wind or breeze, shook the leaves dangling on the trees. A sliver of the moon had arisen, but its moonbeams couldn't force their way in, except as a sickly pale light that couldn't wash away the pitch blackness. It did manage to reveal the dim outlines of buildings.

Saul switched on his flashlight. The beam of light fought to banish enough of the dark so that they could see their way. It lost as it flickered once, twice, then died. The others hadn't thought to steal flashlights from their home, but Bubba had taken his father's cigarette lighter, and he thumbed a tiny flame to life.

It lit the few inches in front of their faces, nothing else. Disoriented by the darkness, the boys stumbled through tall grass and avoided trees and bushes to approach the silhouettes.

Bubba pressed the palm of his hand against the wood of the first shack they'd arrived at. "Ouch!" He withdrew his hand, and under the lighter's fire, he saw the splinter embedded in the flesh. He jerked it out, and a small patch of blood trickled out.

Scary Terry giggled. "Did Bubba get an ouchie?"

"Oh, shut up, Terry. That hurt. Let me stick a splinter in your hand."

The other boy shrugged his shoulder. "It's nothing that hasn't happen to me before. It's not liked the building bit you."

Bubba brought the flame closer to the wood. "You know, that did kind of feel like a bite. You know, like when a dog has bitten you?"

The wood siding caught fire from the flame. Bubba put it out, but not before it left a burn mark. Bubba was taken aback, as for a moment, he thought the wood rippled like skin beneath his touch.

That's not possible. It's just an old shack.

His stomach cramped, and his heart pounded. He did not want the others to see his fear, so he tamped it down inside him. The flame blew out, and though Bubba flicked the lighter several times, it didn't catch. "Dang, the lighter quit working."

Saul shrugged a shoulder. "So? Maybe it's out of lighter fluid."

"It's brand new."

Bubba stuck the lighter back in his jeans pocket. He didn't dare lose it; otherwise, his father would figure out he'd stolen it and take it out on him. His father was a mean drunk and ninety percent of the time he drank, so that meant he was mean most of the time, too.

Saul went around him to the front of the building. "Hey, you guys! There's an open doorway over here."

Jake slipped past him. "Let's go inside and check it out." He entered before anyone else replied.

Saul said, "Come on before Jake finds any good stuff."

Scary Terry stopped beside his friend and snorted. "You act like there's a hidden treasure inside."

"Who's to say there isn't?" Saul melted into the darkness.

Terry followed, leaving Bubba outside alone. Bubba hated the lack of sound.

Shouldn't there be some noise? Like an owl hooting or flying bats squeaking? Bet if I had a pin on me and I dropped it, it'd be like that stupid quote about not being able to hear a pin drop.

Thump, thump. Thump, thump.

Oh, God, noise finally!

His skin crawled, and his breathing hitched as he pressed himself against the building, until he realized the thumping came from his heart beating. The beats echoed loud in the still night. Then even that sound muted and though his heart still acted erratic, he couldn't hear it.

The silence. Dead as a graveyard.

Why would I think that?

The boy called out. "Terry? Saul? Jake?" They didn't answer. Could they be playing with him? Freak out the scaredy-cat? "Hey guys, come on. Let's go."

Still nothing. Maybe Bubba needed to go inside.

Right. The others probably waited for him to do that very thing and when Bubba walked in, all of them would jump out at him in the dark. Make him pee in his pants. Laugh at him and call him wimp or boob-faced Bubba. Some insult like that.

Go on, step inside. Nothing in there, but the idiots that you hang out with. You can handle that, long as they agree to go home.

His feet stayed cemented to the dirt. He blew out a whistle that didn't dent the air. It made a white fog though, a phantom from the chilly air.

"Guys! Quit playing with me." The words echoed back in a low whisper, even though he yelled.

A chill enveloped him, from the inside out. It matched the cold air that grew more bitter as it wrapped itself around him.

"I'm going! Serves you right, me leaving your butts in this cold dark place. You're assholes anyway." The words vanished as soon as they left his mouth, as if the cursed land sucked them up with a vacuum.

He blundered away from the ghost village and a hush settled over the land. No night sounds. Only a damper of nothingness. Not even his footsteps made noise.

Do I want to hear something? Anything. I don't care what, just...a noise.

He stood at the edge of the clearing, tree branches making scarecrow shadows over his head, listening. No crashes, tinkles, jangles, clanks, just zilch.

He stumbled onwards. His footsteps should have made thuds, but they didn't. Could he even be on the path? Not able to see where he was going or detect where the track led caused him to sweat, even though he swore the night had grown unkinder. Forget the path; he couldn't find any trees. Dark. Frigging black as ink. His belly convolved, and his sweating grew terrible enough to soak the sweatshirt he wore beneath his jacket, sticking it to him like a second skin.

The cold air dug its icy fingers beneath his sweatshirt and jeans and stroke his flesh into goosebumps. Bubba's heart twisted, the cold seeping into the pores of his meat. He stumbled, tripped, and fell hard on some small stones. His hands felt wet afterward. He felt pretty sure he'd torn the skin, and the wetness was blood. No doubt he'd ripped his jeans and scraped his knees, as they hurt, but he didn't stop to check but scrambled to his feet.

The back of one leg from his buttocks to the knee screamed in protest. He almost fell again but managed to keep to his feet and hobbled, thrusting his hands out to guide him.

Tears welled up in his eyes, and the blurriness made the darkness worse. *I wanna go home. It's no longer fun. Please, God, let me find a way out.*

His fingers pressed into the wood, the splinters from it poking at the skin. *A tree*? Further investigation told him what it was. One of the buildings.

What...?

What happened? How'd he gotten back? Had he gone in a circle?

You can check in, but you can't check out.

A sort of warped giggling reached his ears, and Bubba realized it came from behind him. His heart beat his chest like a tom-tom and his breath whooshed out of him; he whirled around. He saw nothing, but then, it was dark. Fumbling in his pocket for that lighter, he found nothing. He tried the other pocket. Same thing. Had it fallen out? He crouched down and swept his hands around, searching. Nothing. If he lost it somewhere, he wouldn't find it in the dark. *Oh, oh. Dad's gonna kill me for even taking it in the first place, then losing it.*

Another thought, sounding like another voice, broke in. *I wouldn't worry about Daddy, boy. You might die here.*

He stood, trembling. Stories filled his mind. Why they called this place Nowhere Land. People going into this place at night and vanishing. Maybe some vortex took them. Maybe monsters. Maybe the ghosts that haunted the area. So many tales and theories. He'd even heard tales of the bogeyman. The last disappearance wasn't a legend, as a group of paranormal investigators had disappeared after staying here overnight. That story had been in the *Richmond Times Dispatch* his father bought before coming home from his job in Richmond.

Something else about those ghost hunters. He thought harder. He grew colder than he already felt when he remembered the news report.

Not all of those people had vanished. There'd been a thumb found. He wondered if something ate the people.

He called out again. "Jake. Saul. Terry. Guys, please tell me you're pulling a joke on me. I'll call 'uncle.' I want to go home."

The others did not reply.

Bubba kept going, mirroring his fingers on the outside wall like his legs walking. The wood vanished and his fingers wiggled in the air. The toe of his tennis shoes hit something. The air meant an open doorway. He wondered what his shoe struck. Bubba bent and found not one object, but two. He picked both up. One felt squishy. The other, a flashlight and when he thumbed it, a sickly light lit up in his face. Saul's? He turned that light on the other object in his other hand.

He screamed, his mouth open, but nothing came out. Unable to help it, he wet the front of his pants. The urine ran down his right leg.

An eyeball lay on the palm of his hand. He squealed and dropped it. The light flickered. Once. Twice. Out. Then nothing but darkness.

And him. Alone.

Breathing. No, not his. He wasn't alone. The warmth from someone's breath tickled the hairs at the back of his neck. Those hairs rose. He turned around and slapped the flashlight against his hand, hoping, no, praying that its light would come on one more time. The light flickered, a shade of its former brilliance. He pointed it up with a shaking hand. Lukewarm though it might be, it was enough to see what stood in front of him.

Something grabbed him by his face and he choked on a silent scream. It lifted him up and up, his piss raining down as his bladder loosened for a second time.

***

Parker parallel parked at the curb and shut off the engine. He didn't move to get out of his vehicle but stared through the passenger window at the trees that barely were outlined due to the night. The sky held no moon or stars, just a stygian blanket of storm clouds that had arrived within the past ten minutes. He began to wonder if he'd been hasty in coming here. Maybe he should have called the cops.

I called my sister, and she never answered the phone, officer. I think she came here.

How do you know she would, Mr. Burkell?

A dream I had....

They'd lock up his ass for calling them out for no good reason. All because of a nightmare. Still—He flipped the interior light on and snatched his phone from the passenger seat. His thumb swept over the numbered buttons, but he didn't press any.

What would he say? Something in his nightmare took her and upon waking and calling her on the phone, no one at her house answered? They'd tell him that didn't mean anything. Besides, once they discovered she was over eighteen, they'd say to call her friends and see if she was with them, or if they knew where she might be. She might even be with her husband. Anyway, it took about twenty-four or seventy-two hours before the police could do anything.

She'd kick your ass for embarrassing her, too, and say she's a big girl. That she didn't need to report her movements to him every minute of her life. Declare that he needed to get a life.

She would be right. Sitting in the car, the interior light on, all due to a dream, it did seem Parker's actions were foolish.

He had just shut off the light and laid his phone back down when something small crashed out of the woods and fell in front of his car. His headlights still on, the glare revealed a white face and the stark, black eyes of a boy.

He dashed out of his car and went around the front of the vehicle to the child. As he gathered up the boy, the child went limp, his mouth opening and closing like a fish out of water. His skin felt freezing to the touch. On closer inspection, Parker saw not a little kid, but closer to preteen.

"What happened?" demanded Parker.

The boy didn't answer, just looked dazed. Parker stood and carried him around to the passenger side of his car and after opening the door, placed him on the seat. A quick 911 call assured him the local police would be there in ten minutes. As he crouched down by the kid and tried to get a response, the hairs on the back of his neck stood. Turning his head and upper torso only, he looked back at the dark woods. Nothing moved, not even shadows.

He swore though that something watched him.

The police car rolled to a stop behind his vehicle.

The boy still hadn't come to his senses.

Parker rose from the crouch as two officers left the police car and walked up. Their headlights lit up Parker's car, Parker, and them. The woods remained dark. One held a flashlight and used it to light up the boy's face.

"I don't know what's wrong with the boy," Parker said and pointed at the woods, "but he came crashing from out of there."

One of the officers looked at the woods, and for a second, Parker thought his face went white, but he thought that maybe he had been mistaken as the man ducked into the car and leaned over the boy. The kid's face appeared normal. The other cop remained standing with Parker, keeping his flashlight on the boy.

The officer with the kid shook his shoulder. "Hello, son? Can you tell me your name?"

The boy opened his eyes and stared at the cop with a blank face, not moving or saying anything. The officer tried again, and this time, he waved a hand in front of the boy's eyes.

"Hello? Where did you come from?"

The boy blinked, then looked up at the policeman. His expression no longer looked empty, it appeared to change. Become cagy.

"Where do you think I came from?" His voice hinted of oiliness. Sneakiness.

"Are you all right now?"

The boy sat up. Began to laugh. A chill ran up Parker's spine and he thought the laugh held a hint of wrongness. Too adult in manner for a kid of possible middle-school grade.

"I've never been righter." The boy got to his feet. "Hear that?"

The officer stood and waved Parker and his partner back a few steps. "Hear what?" He flashed Parker and his partner a puzzled look, before returning his gaze to the boy.

The boy giggled and got out of the car. "That's just it! I hear all sorts of noises. I even hear myself talking. Unlike where I came from, where sometimes there is no sound at all. And then again, there would be terrifying noises." The boy whirled around. "I got away. Can't stop me from making noise. Can't, can't, can't."

He halted and looked towards the woods. His eyes grew rounder, blacker, and he thrust his hands out, all ten fingers splayed.

"No, I don't want to go back. I don't want to join my friends." The boy swept his gaze back at Parker and the officers. "Please, don't let it take me back. I want to go home."

Parker asked in a gentle voice. "Where is your home?"

Tears welled up in the boy's eyes. "I used to be Terry. The other kids called me Scary Terry. But you know what? There is something even scarier than I ever pretended to be. The tall, thin shadow man says I can never go home. Never, ever." Though he cried, Terry giggled. "I blew it. My friends blew it."

The other officer spoke. "How did you blow it, Terry?"

The boy snorted through his nose and his giggles grew louder. "By letting the shadow take me. It got Bubba in the end, but I snagged his skin so that I could escape. Except it caught up." He looked at the trees and cried out. "Please. I don't wanna go back. I wanna go home. I want my mother. No, oh, please, no!"

His voice rose into an ear-splitting scream as his whole body shuddered. The boy turned his gaze back to theirs. Parker saw desperate fear in his eyes.

Terry shrieked. "Tag, I'm dead!"

The boy slumped to the ground.

One of the cops dropped to his knees beside the boy, and he placed his fingers against the pulse at the boy's neck. He raised his eyes to meet Parker's and the other policeman's. There was confusion in them.

"Dear God, I can't find any pulse. And his skin is cold as a corpse's."

Parker thought of Lisa at that moment and jammed his fist to his mouth to stop the cry threatening to escape. As he stumbled toward the trees, his smartphone on his leather belt rang. He raised it, and he saw his sister's cell number on the glowing screen.

He pressed it and put it to his ear. "Lisa?"

"Parker, where are you? I called your home phone and only got your answering machine."

"Lisa, I called your place earlier, but you didn't answer."

"I had my phone turned off, and my home phone never rang."

"But I left a message on your cell. Off or on, that should be there."

"There's no message from you on my phone. Parker..."

"What's the matter?"

"I had a nightmare. In it, someone died, but I couldn't remember who it was upon awakening. I just thought of you and called to make sure you were okay."

Parker told her about the boy, as he watched one of the officers calld for an ambulance. After he promised to call her when he got back home, he clicked off. He waited with the police and the body until the ambulance arrived, never looking at the woods; instead, he kept stealing looks at the corpse.

The boy that claimed he was already dead and that he'd stolen another boy's body to run away from whatever chased him. The only way he could by taking someone else's body would be if he was a, a...ghost.

That last word pressed heavy on his mind as his gaze found the boy's face again. Maybe it might be smart to have another investigation in Burkett. Find out what the hell haunted his property, but his psychic intuition reminded him that might be dangerous.

He ignored it. *Yeah, that might be a good idea, I'll call that paranormal guy that's been bugging me and get another investigation here.* He climbed behind the wheel of his vehicle and started the car, about to drive away

His vision blurred, and he jammed on the brakes, then shut off the engine. Breathing heavy, beads of sweat forming on his forehead, he fought the temptation to lay his head against the steering wheel.

"God, why am I thinking of doing that? The last ghost hunt failed, and people went missing."

He heard rustling from the passenger seat, and he turned his head. The dead boy sat there; an evil grin splayed across his lips.

"Want to play? Tag, you're it."

A tall, thin shadow replaced him, so large it passed through the roof and Parker's eyes rolled back in his head before he blacked out.

CHAPTER EIGHT

Neri was on her second cup of coffee and reading the current *Richmond Times-Dispatch* tossed in her driveway earlier that morning, when several raps at her front door interrupted her. Right after, her cell rang and recognizing Ben's cell number, she answered.

"Neri, it's me at your front door," said Ben's voice coming from her phone.

"The door's unlocked. I'm in the kitchen."

A minute later, after grabbing a cup of coffee, Ben plopped down in a chair at the table. A big grin shone on his face.

"Guess what?" he said, after taking a sip of the hot liquid.

Exasperated, she asked, "What?"

"I got the investigation."

The cup jiggled in her shaking hand in mid-air, and it almost tipped over when she set it down. She righted it before it spilled any of the coffee. "Really?" *Oh God, not that place. And why is he telling me? You know why...*

His grin widened and he got up to snatch a doughnut from a box on the kitchen counter and sat back down, biting into it. "Yum. I love Krispy Kreme doughnuts." He stopped when he saw her folding her arms. "Really. Parker Burkett called me at seven o'clock this morning to give me the okay."

She sighed. "You want me to do this."

"Please. I can't do this without you."

The beginning of a headache formed behind her eyes. "I don't know. I need to think about it. It's not something I can do on a whim."

She heard the desperation in his begging voice. "Neri, you have to. You can sense things, things the rest of the team and I can't."

She didn't look at him, but stared down at her cup, no longer wanting the coffee. "You can get any psychic to investigate with you."

"Maybe so. But I've worked with you, and in my opinion, you're the best."

Yeah, I'll sense things, all right. I'll see what happened to John and his team. He might be haunting that place, besides whatever else has control there.

She looked at Ben. "Ben, give me twenty-four hours to think about it—"

He nodded. "All right. I'll call you at this time tomorrow."

After downing his coffee and finishing the donut, Ben got up and left the house.

No longer able to finish the newspaper, Neri tossed it in the trash, dumped her now-cool coffee, and turned off the coffeemaker, before leaving the kitchen.

A day spent trying to watch television and even reading a library book due in two days didn't chase away the headache, and she went to bed early. She took a twelve-hour painkiller so that she could get some actual sleep.

She had a dream about her brother who'd died in Afghanistan back in January 2021. He was saying something to her, but no words came out of his mouth. It felt like something was between them, making it hard for him to talk to her.

The official report from the U.S. Army said it had been a bombing from the terrorists that destroyed the village he and his team had been searching at the time, killing them and the villagers. But her spirit guide had told her the truth about the ten-year-old boy possessed by the demonic jinn, how it had killed all the villagers and then awakened the dead to attack the soldiers, tearing them apart. The bomb by Al-Qaeda insurgents had just struck at that moment, destroying the buildings and all else. Hiding the real truth of what had happened.

A thought crossed her mind and she wondered if that jinn had gotten Mike's soul. She hoped not. Though he never contacted her as the other spirits did, she prayed he'd crossed over and was with their parents, that he had been there to guide their sister over when the lightning killed her.

Except now he was in her dream. Spirits sometimes used dreams to communicate with the living. Why was he doing this now, instead—

A ringing interrupted the dream, and she awoke with bleary eyes. Although the headache no longer tortured her head, she felt drained, as if she'd been running a mile. The ringing penetrated her brain. After a moment, she realized that it was real and not some aftermath of her dream. She picked up her cell phone and saw the number on the screen. It was Ben's.

"Why is he calling me now and not tomorrow?" she asked herself, grumbling.

He wanted an answer she still couldn't give. She hadn't given any thought to it at all during the daytime, although she felt pretty sure it'd haunted that last dream.

"Neri." His voice sounded odd, hoarse. "The investigation begins tomorrow! I need you to join us—"

She cut him off in mid-sentence. "What the...? You asked me to join already. Told me I had a day to think about it."

A loud screech blasted her ears. She pressed the red emblem to shut the cell off. Unnerved, she got up and went into the living room to yank the house phone connection from the wall plug. Times like this, she wished she'd gotten rid of the house phone since she used the cell more often. But she'd kept it for calls from customers for her psychic business.

After double-checking that the house was locked up, she ran back to her bedroom and crawled into bed, shivering.

Her stomach curdled like sour milk, her heart pounding loud in her ears, she fought from closing her eyes. If she closed them, she worried it would follow her into her dreams. Unable to help herself, she fell asleep.

She woke again, gasping. With her heart beating as if she'd just run a marathon and still feeling as if she hadn't gotten any sleep, she sat up. Her fingernails dug into the mattress, and she crawled out of bed and headed to the window. The bright sunbeams passed through the glass like phantoms to caress her face.

Had she dreamed the second time she slept? She felt pretty sure she must have, but the thought filled her with a bad taste. She remembered Ben stopping by and telling her that Parker Burkett was permitting his team to investigate his property.

The phone call in the night came back to her.

She grabbed her phone and turned it back on. The only number from Ben was from yesterday morning. Her cell fell from loosened fingers the short distance onto the bed.

A dream, then? No, she doubted it. Doubted it was Ben last night, either. And that one dream she remembered—her brother. Why had he tried to contact her? Unless it hadn't been him.

God, it must be whatever haunts that land.

Turning back to stare through the window, she knew it wanted her to go there. An open invitation. After all, why would Parker Burkett agree to the investigation, when he had denied anyone who asked him after what happened to the first investigation?

Something terrible must have happened that he felt he needed another ghost hunt. Whatever haunted the property had forced his hand to make the call.

Maybe she needed to call on her spirit guide, Aggie. Just as she always had in the past, Aggie would let her know the truth.

Aggie had become her spirit guide when she'd turned six. In life, Aggie had been a plump mother of seven strapping lads, and she'd lived in Williamsburg in the 1700s. She had been shot by a British redcoat when he caught her assisting her rebel eldest son's escape during the Revolutionary War. Motherly in death as much as in life, she had understood when Neri refused to do paranormal investigations after her sister's death. She had kept the other ghosts at bay until Neri felt able to communicate with the dead again. But when the nightmares about the haunted land started, Neri hadn't heard from Aggie, not even when she'd sought her help about them. That puzzled and worried her. She just hoped Aggie would answer her call now.

She down sat in a chair she kept in her bedroom. "Aggie? Aggie, I need you."

Nothing.

"Aggie, please. I need some answers I am hoping you can give to questions I have."

"You want to know about Nowhere Land." The soft, feminine voice held a hint of British accent.

Neri whipped around and saw a shadow in the corner of her bedroom. It pressed against the wall, but it drifted away from the area after a minute and inched closer to her. The entity became the dim outline of a short, plump woman dressed in a pale blue hooped gown with sleeves ending in lace ruffles. She wore a white cap that covered the back of her head, like a hood over greying brown ringlets, and surrounded her face with a fringe of lace.

Neri smiled. "Aggie."

The ghost stopped a few inches away and nodded.

"What do you need, Neri?" A sad smile flittered on the spirit's pale lips. "Though I can guess."

"First, where have you been for the past few months while I've been having nightmares about Nowhere Land?"

Aggie shifted, dissipated, reappeared right next to Neri. "I've been afraid to contact you."

"Afraid? Why?"

A cold spot enveloped Neri.

Aggie's voice filled her head.

"I was terrified I would attract its attention."

Neri wrapped her arms around herself for warmth. It didn't help. "Whose attention?"

Aggie floated around until she stood in front of Neri. Her eyes became dark pools. "Join us, Nerissa Phelan. Your soul will be a welcome addition to the power." The voice deepened, and Neri couldn't tell if it was male or female. It pulled at her psychic abilities as if to possess her.

Neri leaped up, and the chair toppled on its side. She staggered backward and almost hit the end of her bed. "You're not Aggie! What have you done with her? What are you?"

Aggie's visage morphed into a tall, thin shadow that touched the ceiling. It gave a dark, cruel laugh. "Your Aggie is no more. I caught her and tasted her essence and found it pleasing. I made her a part of us. Added the power needed." The shadow bent down until she stared up into a face of swirling shadows. Neri bit back the scream that threatened to release. Tentacles of shadows shot out and touched her with a chill that reached into her soul.

Neri lurched away from it until her back slammed into the closed bedroom door. She seized the doorknob with a trembling hand. "Leave me alone. Let Aggie go free."

Wailing erupted. Neri closed her eyes.

"No, no, no. Cannot do that. Soon, I will have your soul. Many more souls are needed."

"Why do you need the souls?"

"You will learn soon enough. Come, let us take your soul now. I will be as gentle as I can. Later, I cannot promise, for I love the taste of terror and pain. The same terror I enjoyed when I killed your brother and the other soldiers."

Neri screamed, "Leave! Me! Alone!"

More dark laughter filled the room and blackness rained down the walls like blood. The light from the sun pouring through her windows failed as the darkness crawled over the glass. Filthy darkness that carried a fetid odor. She fought from gagging and closed her eyes, jiggling the doorknob that refused to turn so she could open the door.

Neri kept repeating the mantra, "Go, go, go," praying it would. Suddenly, the noise stopped, and when she opened her eyes, she found the walls unsullied, the windows clean, and the shadow was gone. The air felt fresh.

Her cell phone rang, and she jolted. Quivering, she snatched it from the bed and swiped across the green phone receiver emblem.

Ben's voice spilled from it. "Neri?"

Her racing heart slowing, she said, "Ben?"

"Are you in or not?"

"Ben, did you call me in the middle of the night?"

"Neri," his voice sounded incredulous as he broke in. "I never called you last night. This call is the first time today since we talked twenty-four hours ago."

God, did whatever that thing was, make that call? Or did I dream it?

What had just happened now wasn't a dream.

She gripped the phone tight, feeling it dig into her palm. Her shaky legs were no longer able to support her, so she thumped on the edge of the bed and brought the phone back to her ear as Ben's yelling voice broke her out of her thoughts.

"Sorry, Ben."

"What the hell is going on?"

"It visited me. At least, I think it did."

"It? Oh God, you mean, whatever is the cause of that cursed land?"

"I'm pretty sure. It pretended to be my spirit guide, Aggie, at first. But it didn't keep up the pretense long." She began to cry. "It said it took her and added her to it." She scrubbed at the tears rolling down her cheeks. "I should have wondered why she'd never come to me when I had the nightmares for the past few months. I should have sensed it."

"I'm so sorry about the loss of your spirit guide, Neri. Maybe you're right. Maybe I should get another medium."

Neri shook her head, but stopped when she realized he couldn't see the movement. "No, I need to do this."

"Neri, I am dropping you from this investigation. If it's haunting you—"

"Remember my brother?"

"Mike?"

"Yeah, Mike. Like you know that many Michaels."

"I have three as Facebook friends."

"You knew who I meant."

"Yeah, I do. I don't understand where you're going with this. Mike died in Afghanistan in 2021."

"Ben, there is something I never told you. No one knew, not even John." She took a deep breath and told him about Mike and Nowhere Land.

"God. Now, I know I don't want you near that spot. I knew you guys grew up near it, but not that you land Mike had ever been there. Whatever haunts that spot remembers you from that time. It may be even holding a grudge against you. That could be the reason it zeroed in on you and took your spirit guide. After all, Aggie warned you about the place and saved Mike."

"Ben, you can't keep me away. I want to put a stop to whatever made this place the nasty legend it is. Make it nothing more than a possible historical attraction for Parker Burkett to open up to the public." She paused and took a breath before she forged onward. "I never told you that Aggie had told me that a jinn had killed Mike and his men and not the bomb as the Army reported. Worse, that thing told me it had killed Mike and his company. If it did, it finally got Mike."

"Sorry, but you will not be going," said Ben in a stern voice. "It appears to know how Mike died overseas and that is not good."

She shouted. "No! It wants me, and I lost my spirit guide to it way before you ever wanted to investigate that damn Nowhere Land. It's been filling my nights full of nightmares, and I hadn't thought about that place in years. And it did harm to Mike! I will not let the damned thing scare me off anymore. It needs to be stopped!"

"All right." She heard the defeat in his tone. "You're part of the team. But this goes against my better judgment."

"Okay. When do I need to be there?"

"Not until seven days from now. Friday, November 14th. We get to be there until the following Tuesday morning. I will pick you up at two o'clock in the afternoon. I want to get there while it's still daylight. With the time change, it gets dark by six. I'd like to get the team settled in and set up for a daytime sweep before the nighttime fun begins."

"I'll be ready. Goodbye." When Ben clicked off, Neri put the phone on the bedstead.

A heaviness weighed her down ; she would be going where she never wanted to. She flopped onto the mattress, and memories of her childhood and the last time she had gotten close to the land assaulted her. As an adult, she had driven past the two streets that led to it, always keeping her eyes from straying that way, thinking that if she looked, it might lure her to it.

From her birth until she turned six, her parents had owned a house a block away from Burkett. Mom and Dad had lived in an apartment with her older brother, Mike, in Hampton, but with her birth, they'd needed a bigger place, and a house sounded perfect to them. This was a few years before her sister had been born.

The neighborhood children warned each other about Nowhere Land and to stay away from it. The kids, of course, still taunted the others to dare to venture on to it, to get a prize from one of the buildings to prove they'd been there. A rite of passage so to speak, to show they had stepped into the mouth of the dragon and survived. Most never did it, preferring to be called a scaredy-cat, but the few that did would disappear.

Police investigated, but never found them, and their faces would end up on milk cartons. After that, parents kept an eye on their kids.

Only two hadn't vanished. One ended up in a place for crazy people. That's what her brother said he'd heard. The other child? Her parents had taken her and moved away. No one ever saw the girl again, happening years before her family lived there and over time, people forgot, and children were allowed once again to wander from their yards.

Mike had been dared by some older boys in school, to go there at night and meet up with them. She'd found out and said she wanted to go with him.

"No." Mike had said, "You'll get scared by the ghosts, and no one needs a crybaby."

Neri had stomped her foot. "I am not a crybaby."

"Yes, you are. But that's okay. You're my little sister."

She'd grabbed his hand. "Don't go, Mike. Stay here with me, and we'll make popcorn and watch some cartoons."

He had looked sad. "I wish I could, Neri. But if I don't meet the guys and go with them to bring some proof we've been to Nowhere Land, I'll be branded a scaredy-cat at school."

"I don't think you're a scaredy-cat."

He had loosened his hand from hers and headed for the open window in his bedroom. "Thanks. But that won't mean much to the other kids."

He'd slipped a leg over the edge and, grabbing hold of the branch of the large oak outside, climbed out and shimmied down the trunk to the ground. Neri had run to the window and watched him bolt across the yard and down the street. A cool breeze had blown in and, feeling cold, she'd shut the window.

Go after Mike, Neri. Feminine, the gentle voice of a woman inside her head had urged. *He goes there, and he will never come home. The place will keep him.* She had been hearing this woman in her head a lot lately. But everything she'd told Neri had come true.

She had jogged over to her parents' bedroom, but hadn't knocked on their door to awaken them. Instead, she'd sneaked downstairs and grabbed a flashlight from the kitchen drawer. Before leaving, she'd thrown on her coat. She clicked on the flashlight and followed the beam of light. It drew her like a will-o'-the-wisp, dancing over the pavement until it lit the trees at the end of the dead-end street. She saw the dirt path, the one that her brother probably used.

"Mike." The word came from her mouth like a frosty phantom, merging with the chilly night air.

Sickness cramped her tummy, and fear rooted her at the beginning of the path. The light from her flashlight began to fade.

"No." Her little voice shook.

Go on, Neri, the disembodied voice prodded. *He needs you.*

The light grew stronger again, and she walked, determined to find her brother and bring him home.

Because if she didn't do it, he would be lost forever, as her imaginary playmate had told her. And whenever her imaginary playmate told her something, it always was proven to come true.

He stood at the end of the path, about to head into the village. Neri's light flittered over him.

She yelled, "Mike—stop!"

He turned, his brow furrowed, and his mouth a thin slash.

"Neri? What are you doing here?"

"You need to come back home with me. There's nothing here but bad things. You go there, and you'll never come back home."

He looked back at the shadow-darkened buildings where the voices of the other boys waited. "Yes, I will. It's nothing but a bunch of broken down shacks."

She had never told her brother or their parents about her imaginary playmate, but she knew circumstances demanded it. "My friend came to me and told me to get you because if you step past those trees, you will never come home again."

"What friend? You went and told someone about me doing this?"

She blurted, "Aggie is my imaginary playmate. At least, I think she is imaginary. Whenever she tells me something, it always comes true."

"So, I have to listen to you because your fake friend doesn't want me to go there?" said Mike with a sneer. "I promised to help three other guys. If I don't join them, I don't dare show my face at school tomorrow."

"Please, Mike. A bad thing will get you."

He looked at her, then swung his gaze back at the buildings. He didn't move. Gathering courage, Neri trotted over to her brother and took his hand. She jerked on it as she turned back to the path. He held fast. Finally, he let her lead him away.

Had he believed her finally, otherwise why did he leave with her to go back home? She never knew for sure, as he had never told her. The only thing that mattered to her was that he survived that night.

He did die, but years later and in Afghanistan. Now, she wondered if whatever controlled Nowhere Land, if it hadn't taken his soul in that war-torn country like it told her. Hands together, she always prayed that he found his way to the other side, for though she tried to use her abilities, she dead-ended at where he was on the other side of the Veil. She couldn't stand the thought of where he really might be.

The next morning, the news on the television reported that three boys had vanished, and a big search was being organized to find them, the same three boys who had dared Mike to go to Burkett with them. A month later, they still hadn't been found, not even as bodies rotting in shallow graves. There were speculations about child molesters and murderers, but Neri knew better. Something evil stalked the place where she'd found Mike. Neither Mike nor she told their parents. Her parents had moved the family to Chesterfield when their mother found herself pregnant with Kasey, buying a house there.

Kasey, who died when a lightning bolt struck her. Neri wondered if there had been a price to pay for her to get Mike away from Nowhere Land. That maybe Kasey had been the price. She hoped that her sister was in Heaven, and not wherever that thing came from. At least one family member was safe.

Neri broke off the memories, snatched her smartphone, and headed to the kitchen to get herself a glass of water. She sat down at the kitchen table and stared down at her phone. It took her a few seconds, but Neri brought up her phone list and hit Ben's number. She waited while it rang a few times. Just as she figured that maybe she might have to leave him a message, he picked up.

She stood and crossed over to the window to stare at her backyard. The backyard blurred and the village from that night years ago replaced it in her mind's eye. She spoke into her phone.

"Call Burkett and pushed the investigation out a week. I want us to learn all we can about what has happened there, discover when the first story was told, and most of all, figure out what makes it tick. Because when we go there, it will be more than a paranormal investigation. We're going to exorcize that area once and for all."

CHAPTER NINE

When Parker regained consciousness in his car a block away from where he had been, the paramedics finally arrived after the call from the police. Although shaken, he got out of his car and walked back to where they and the police were. The revolving lights made the trees appear bloody. Even with the lights, the forest seemed more shadow than alive. Not real at all. Once pronounced dead, the paramedics lifted the boy's body onto the stretcher and settled it into the back of the ambulance.

All this while the police asked him questions, why he had driven off and why he was back plus why he had been there at all. He made up some story that he parked there to go check out his property at the end of the path. That afterward, he returned and got in his vehicle, the boy rushed out of the woods and collapsed on the street in front of his car. No, he didn't know where the kid originated. That he'd never seen the kid before (which was the truth).

He decided it wouldn't be smart to mention his nightmares about a sister that came here, but that she hadn't. They might think him loony, or worse, that he might have something to do with the boy and his death.

After the police had finished questioning him, Parker didn't think twice before climbing in his car and restarting the engine. He fought not to squeal the car's tires as he drove away. Within fifteen minutes, he took the offramp back onto I-64 west, heading back to Richmond. Not to his apartment, but to his sister's. To make sure she had never gone to Burkett, that what happened in his nightmare wasn't real. Maybe something he should have done in the first place, instead of running off half-cocked after the nightmare.

He shut off the engine in front of her house. It belonged not only to her but to his brother-in-law, Chris. Chris had quit his job back in California and sold their home there, moving with Lisa to Henrico County. Lucky for the guy, he got a job with the county, when many others during this economy couldn't find any job.

Lisa had been excited about it. His sister seemed always to have the misfortune to get together with creeps. Or maybe she was just lousy at picking men, starting with her first in college, where he worked as a janitor, and after an all-night drinking binge, they woke up the next morning in a motel, married. The man had quit his job and never worked a day after that while Lisa had left college to work at an office, supporting them both. Nothing Parker said made a difference. Not until Lisa had caught Buddy in bed with another woman. It appeared this had been the latest in a long line of women for the man. The only difference with this particular floozy? She had a good job and money. Good old Buddy agreed to a divorce from Lisa and a week after that went through, married his latest meal ticket. Parker felt sorry for the foolish woman, but better her than have his sister still stuck with the asshole.

Lisa met Chris Polivka a year later. This guy had a job, working for a computer company at the time. Now he worked in the payroll department for Henrico County, typing in the all the employees' days they worked and took out taxes and deductions from the County paychecks. Parker thanked the stars she had gotten smart and found herself a good guy this time.

Until he almost ran into Chris at the Short Pump Shopping Center. He had noticed the guy outside TGI Fridays, kissing a woman whom he thought was his sister. Except as he drew closer, he noticed she had long, darker brown hair than Lisa's blonde-streaked light brown short cut. He ducked into a store and peered around to watch Chris with his arm around the woman's shoulder as they sauntered by.

So much for a good man for Lisa. She would never believe Parker; she hadn't with the past jerk. So, he kept his mouth shut.

He strolled up the walkway to the front door. The house was dark. No doubt after her call to him, she went to bed. Parker saw both vehicles parked in the driveway. Which meant that Chris wasn't out with his 'honey.' He raised a finger to push the bell, but paused mid-way and dropped the hand.

He could always drop by tomorrow after Chris had left for work. He sneaked back to his car and slipped inside. After starting the engine, he guided the wheels away from the curb and drove home.

A half hour later, Parker stepped through his doorway and tossed his car and house keys into a brown woven basket on the small table he kept by the entrance. He toed off his boots and padded in stocking feet to the kitchen, where he grabbed a bottle of Scotch he kept stored in a cabinet by the fridge. Several fingers later, his head buzzing, he stripped and climbed into his shower. A stream of hot water rained down on his skin as steam rose in the bathroom. It almost alleviated the slight drunkenness, but not by much.

Good. Parker needed to keep the feeling of being smashed, and he might go back to finish the rest of the bottle. He needed to be out when he fell into bed, hoping that would keep the nightmares at bay. He needed to keep the dead boy from talking to him, keep the dead on that land out of his head and his bed.

Hell, keep all the dead from trying to converse with him. Ghosts used to chatter at him since he was a kid, but by trial and error, he'd learned to block them out.

It had taken a Navajo shaman friend to show him how. Since moving here and inheriting Burkett, it appeared that he might be losing the control to do that.

The water shut off and as he dried off, he doubted that all the alcohol in the world would be able to shut the phantoms up. Drinking might blur some visions for a while, but the real nasty ones? The dimness faded away after a short time, and the nightmares bounced back with a vengeance, in Technicolor and widescreen.

Parker didn't head back to the kitchen. He went straight to bed. Not stopping to put on pajamas, he crawled into bed naked.

Seconds later he drifted off and slept the through night without a single nightmare. At least, not any he remembered.

***

Parker awoke to the discomfort of a full bladder and a morning stiffy, but a quick trip to the bathroom helped him there. It didn't alleviate the hangover from the Scotch, a headache behind his eyes, just lessened. He took a quick shower.

Afterward, he dressed and barely made it made a few inches down his hallway when his smartphone rang. It revealed a number he didn't recognize. *It must be a wrong number or one of those scam calls.*

Parker swiped the green answer button. "Hello?"

"Parker Burkett?"

The soft brush of a woman's voice caressed his ear and went straight to his groin. Forcing himself to think of something on the level of a cold shower, he spoke when he felt able to.

"Yes, this is he."

"This is Nerissa Phelan. I got your number from my friend, Ben Neilson."

He sat down on the couch. In his mind's eye, he saw the tall blond he ran into in Carytown. The electric feeling to his groin returned. The feeling deflated when he remembered their conversation at that run in and her claim about being a medium, plus his calling her a paranormal idiot. Having psychic abilities himself, he always felt others were frauds when they made a business of it.   "Ah, Miss Phelan. From Carytown."

A minute went by before she said anything. "You remembered."

"How can I forget? What do you need, Miss Phelan?"

"I'd like to know if you have any information about Burkett, Virginia. Especially, with any connection with your family."

He scooted to the edge of his couch and replied with a cautious tone. "I might. Why do you need to know?"

"I'd like to get it from you to read. For research. Notes for the upcoming investigation."

"I don't see how anything about my family and ancestors can help with your ghost hunt. I don't think whatever is the cause behind what happens there has to do with my family."

"Look, your ancestor was the only survivor of a whole village disappearing back in 1750. Everyone else vanished, per the legend, including your ancestor's parents and his siblings. Like Croatoan legend."

What the hell is Croatoan?

"Like...what?" His voice came out like a croak.

"There was this English settlement on an island in North Carolina. Around 1585-1590. When the English returned on a ship in 1590, they found all the colonists gone. Only the words, "Croatoan, carved on a tree. Croatoan was an Indigenous word."

"You're saying that Burkett and this island in North Carolina are the same?

"Could be. Then again, maybe not. There was never any mention of a curse attached to that other colony.

That's why I'm researching before the team goes there in a week. Then again, I might find there's not a curse concerning your land either. Now, can I get the information I need?"

Parker gripped the smartphone tighter, digging its edges into his skin. "Yes. Can you stop by my house to pick it up? Between three and four o'clock? I'll have it ready for you then."

"Sure. What's your address?"

He gave it to her.

Just as he was about to shut off his phone to go looking in his attic, she asked another question. "Do you know what people might have called the land before your ancestor named it Burkett after your family name?"

"I don't. Though maybe it's in Lucius Burkett's diary."

He heard the excitement in her voice. "He had a diary?"

"My family never let it out of our hands, not even when the Virginia Historical Society wanted it for their collection some years ago. My grandfather told them no. I plan to make the village a museum when I open it as a historical attraction and place the diary under glass for visitors to view when they visit." He took a breath. "I was told that Lucius didn't write in it until he became an adult and married my ancestress, Constance James. I never read it, and I gathered none of my family had, though I suspected that Grandpa might have. It's yours with everything else, and I hope it will help with the investigation."

"Thank you. I'll take extra care with the diary. I promise to wear plastic gloves so not to get fingerprints on it when I read it. See you at three, Mr. Burkett."

"Parker."

"What?"

He felt his cheeks grow warm. "It's silly after we already met, especially since I tried to pick you up. I'm Parker."

"I'm Neri...to my friends. I hope I'll be able to count you as one after this." Her voice softened.

"I'm always willing and able to become friends with smart women."

She chuckled. The connection clicked off.

He grinned, sliding his phone onto the clip on his belt before he headed upstairs to the attic. Before he twisted the key in the attic door, it hit him.

He would join the investigation.

Why not? It's his property. If these people wanted to investigate it, they would have to accept his stipulation that he be involved, too.

He couldn't stop the shiver that chilled him to the bone as he walked through the doorway into the attic.

CHAPTER TEN

Neri's buttocks had grown numb after hours sitting in the hard chair at the Library of Virginia. She read and read page after page in book after book. Snapped pictures with her smartphone of some passages that referenced Nowhere Land, Powhatan myths, and even other local legends and some true hauntings in homes and land near Burkett, as they might have a connection to the cursed land. Anything could help with the upcoming investigation.

A glance at her phone showed her it was fifteen after two. She returned all the books to their proper shelves, stuffed everything else into her book bag, and rushed to take the elevator down to her car parked in the library's garage. It was around 3:40 p.m. when she pulled alongside the curb in front of the address Parker had given her.

Minutes later, she stood before a red door and rang the doorbell. The door opened, and she saw Parker.

"Right on time," he said. "Come in."

She strolled past him and found herself in an entryway with a coat rack. Parker took her jacket and purse and hung them up on it. She noticed that he wore a T-shirt and jeans, but was barefoot.

He led her to the living room.

"Sit on the couch," he said. "Like something to drink? I have iced tea, soda, and milk. And there is water, of course."

"No, thanks. Just the diary and papers you said I could borrow."

"I'll get them. It's all in a box in my bedroom." He left her alone and climbed the stairs near the front door.

The living room looked nice.

Neri sat on a couch of black leather, with a matching chair nearby. A coffee table of cherry wood with a couple of coffee table books and a television remote control nestled in front of the couch. A flat-screen TV hung on the wall; below it rested a shelf with a Blu Ray player. A large wall unit stuffed with Blu Rays and DVDs stood against the wall. Books vied for space on a bookcase on the opposite side of the room. The golden wall-to-wall rug looked vacuumed and clean. It seemed that Parker kept everything in order. There were no messes anywhere.

Of course, she hadn't been upstairs. Maybe Parker only kept the downstairs clean. She doubted it. Something told her this man liked his life in well-kept order. What had happened on the land he and his sister inherited must be driving him nuts, no matter how he pretended otherwise. That time in Carytown when she ran into him and now had her psychic senses tingling about some secret that he held close to him. But she couldn't get a handle on him then nor now and decided to leave it be for the moment. She would leave it to him to tell her, as she never could read the living as well as she could the dead. When people died, they were all anxious to talk to her about everything and would never stop if she didn't block the blasted spirits most of the time.

She got up and crossed over to the bookcase to check out his reading taste. Everything in alphabetical order, by the author's last name. Just like a library. She saw a few novels by Stephen King, Jim Butcher, and other bestselling writers of science fiction and fantasy. That surprised her, as she never expected his taste would run to these. Most of the nonfiction books did show his taste for history, particularly Colonial

Virginia and the Civil War. Or maybe he had these to help him set up his future historical attraction?

A noise at the top of the stairs had her going back to the couch. No need for Parker to catch her sniffing out his reading matter.

Parker stepped off the last step, lugging a jam-packed trunk. It appeared to be light enough for him to carry it. "Here's all of it." He set it on the coffee table in front of her.

Stacks of papers and photographs caught her eye, especially the small book with the fraying brown cover laying on top, covered in plastic. What she could see peeking from between the front and back covers revealed yellowing pages.

Parker said, "I think my grandfather did that. Put a polyester sleeve over it to protect the diary from dust, fingerprints, and other things. Reminds me of collectors of comic books."

Neri took a pair of plastic gloves from her purse and slipped them on. She lifted the book with care, withdrew it from the plastic and opened it. The first page had Diary of Lucius Burkett written in precise printing, though the ink had faded.

Images slammed into her. She saw an old man with wispy white hair wearing wire-framed glasses perched on the end of his nose, dressed in khaki pants and a buttoned-up plaid shirt sitting at a kitchen table, a frown on his lined face as he slid the plastic sleeve over the diary. He stopped when he heard a thump from above him that made him look up with a fearful expression.

The old man dropped his fear and said, "It can't reach me here. It needs the right spots to use, and my house isn't one of those. Even though my home is on the other side of the land."

A weird sound, like a sudden wind roared in her vision, and Neri saw the old man clutch his chest, moaning in pain. He toppled out of his chair to the floor and died, his eyes wide open. The noise faded away. A glowing white shape rose out of his body. A gigantic shadow covered it, and both vanished. A cold chill filled her body.

Another vision replaced that one. A red-faced woman in a brown dress with the skirts falling to her black shoes ran through snow-filled woods; the diary pressed to her breasts. Her heavy breathing filled the vision, raspy and no doubt painful. Her hair had been caught up in a bun, but now had fallen into loose locks, wild and ratty. Over and over she screamed. Reaching the edge of the woods, she tripped over a branch, and the diary flew out of her hands to land at the feet of a pockmarked pre-teen boy. A wagon with two draft horses in its reins stood nearby. Both animals snorted and rolled their eyes, their flanks growing sweaty, though they remained in place.

"Pick it up," yelled the woman, "and run! You hear me, Thomas? Run like the devil is after you! Because it will be!"

"Mother, I need to help—"

"Forget me. Take the book and get yourself away from here and to safety, to where the Devil cannot catch you. No looking back either, you hear? Now, go!"

She rolled over, and her face went from red to white, her eyes bulging. "It's the Devil. Go, go, Thomas!"

He grabbed the book, and her screams followed the kid as he bolted, not looking back, as his mother had ordered. They cut off just as he jumped onto the wagon seat and snapped the reins. The horses snorted and whinneyed. Partially rearing, before they took off at a gallop.

Mist covered the fleeing wagon, and when it dispersed, Neri saw a unit of Confederate soldiers come upon the ghost village. This time, she felt as if she had merged with one of the soldiers and saw through his eyes.

An officer turned to her.

"Corporal Burkett, is this a safe place to camp?"

Dear God, she saw through the eyes of a Burkett. Was it Thomas? She searched the mind and found that was indeed who she inhabited. Except she controlled his body, as she had stuck a frightened Thomas in the corner of his mind. It had to be her doing that, and she hoped not something else.

She saluted, figuring that's what Thomas would do. The officer's name, plus what Thomas knew, came to mind and she said, "Yes, Captain Totten. This land has been in my family since my many great-grandfather. His father bought it from another, although they all died, from what I gathered from the family legends I grew up hearing."

"You don't know, Corporal?"

She flexed a sheepish shrug of Thomas's right shoulder. "Sorry, sir, but I don't have the foggiest idea. There was Grandpappy's diary, but I never learned to read. My mother tossed it to me and told me to run when I was about twelve, that the Devil was after her. I brought back help, but we never found a lick of her."

Captain Totten eyed the area. "Well, I don't believe in the Devil. I've gone to church and the preacher talked about devils and angels, but I always felt the real monsters came from mankind."

"Like those damn Yankees," said another soldier with a snicker.

A few Rebel yells filled the air. Captain Totten ordered them to hush.

"Enough of that! Check out the buildings. We might all be able to use them." He turned to a man at his side. "Sergeant Gilfen, build us a fire to cook on and keep any wildlife away."

Sergeant Gilfen looked around, looking unsure. "Yes, Captain, will do. Though I hadn't heard any sound from wildlife or seen anything since we stepped foot on this ground." He walked away, spitting out a wad of tobacco and picking up sticks, before dropping to a crouch to build a fire.

She left Thomas's body and entered the captain's next.

Captain Totten's uneasiness filled her; he agreed with his sergeant. The place had been quiet as a mouse. Being summer, animals should be about and birds should be chirping. Instead, he heard nothing. Not even the buzz of insects filled the hot, humid air.

The vision faded and returned.

Now it was night, with gunfire sharp in the air. Still inside Totten's body, she fired bullet after bullet at nothing. Yes, at nothing. But she knew he saw something, just like the other men. But Neri herself couldn't. That scared her. The men began dropping to the ground, dead. White mist rose out of their bodies: their spirits! One by one, they dissipated. Only Totten and Thomas remained.

Thomas flashed a shark-tooth grin at the captain. "You should never have come here." His voice was deep and cold, not sounding human at all.

Neri felt Totten's heart beating fast and erratic, such that she believed he might be having a heart attack.

Thomas raised his pistol. Then snickered and said, "That's all right. Needed more souls."

A boom, then flash and smoke. Pain. Riveting pain. The splatter of blood filling her sight. The bullet had hit Totten's nose.

The vision cut off, and Neri fell from the couch to her knees, nearly hitting the edge of the coffee table, shaking and sweating. "Oh, God." She touched her face. "My nose is still here. It felt so real and hurt so bad. Terrifyingly realistic." She pushed the coffee table away, fell onto her side, and rolled over onto her back.

Parker rushed over to her and helped her back onto the couch. "My God, what happened?"

She could barely say anything; it was as if bile jammed down inside her throat. The sweat on her skin cooled, and she shivered. Nothing supernatural, just the reaction she always went through whenever these visions struck her. They made her feel like she had stepped outdoors into a hurricane. Although, this one put all the others she'd ever had to shame.

A gasp escaped her. She rolled over onto her hands and knees and coughed up the bile onto the rug.

She said, "I'm so sorry about your rug."

"That's all right. It can be cleaned up. What the hell happened?"

"I had vision after vision and saw the past. The first one had an old man putting the diary into plastic. Her gaze met his, "I assumed that was your grandfather. I'm sorry, but I saw him die at that moment. The second one had a woman dressed in a long brown dress that looked like something from the 1800s running from someone or something. She passed the diary to a boy she called Thomas and told him to run for his life from the Devil. The third vision concerned the same Thomas, all grown up, and passing through the land dressed in Confederate gray. He was with his unit. They all died. At least I assumed they did. Do you know how Thomas Burkett died?"

Parker blinked. "I'm not sure. I thought he died in the Civil War. That's what's written in the family Bible. He left a widow and two sons. They never lived on the property, but lived in Suffolk. The son of the eldest son came to take over the property when his father and uncle passed away. Shane Burkett built the house my grandfather lived in."

Neri straightened. "Can you find out about Thomas though? I'd like to know." She frowned. "I'd like to find out how those who lived in the house died, too. If their deaths were normal or caused by something else."

Parker stood. "Let me search through that trunk I brought out. The Bible is in it, along with any death and birth certificates, and other Burkett family business. Sadly, my grandfather never kept it all in a fire safety box like I always urged him to. I'm glad the house never caught on fire after he died."

He joined her on the other side of the box of papers and began rifling through them. After ten minutes, excited, he withdrew another book with a black cover and the words, *HOLY BIBLE*, scrawled in red across the front. He dug a yellowing envelope from within it.

"Found it. A letter to his wife from General Lee." He took the letter out and unfolded it to peer at the writing, faded and small, but precise. "From what I read here, his whole unit had vanished, with no bodies found. Lee thought that Union soldiers killed them, and their bodies tossed in some mass grave, or the whole unit had deserted." He placed the paper back in the box. "It says the last place they stopped and camped would have been Burkett." He looked at her. "Lee sent a detachment to check out the land, but those men too disappeared without a trace. Lee didn't send anymore soldiers after that."

Neri nodded. "In my vision, I entered Thomas's and then his captain's body, and could feel and do whatever they did. Thomas shot me—I mean his captain. I don't know what happened to Thomas. That's why I asked."

Parker went through the box again, pulling out papers. His forehead wrinkled, and he flashed Neri a perplexed look.

"There's no death certificate for Thomas Burkett in that box. And I'm sure I got every one of the family members."

"Maybe you missed his?"

He dropped all the papers back into the box. "Could be. But I know I have them all. There's a small trunk full of stuff in my bedroom. Give me through tonight and call me in the morning to see if I've found it."

Neri gathered up the box and stood. "I'll do that." She stuck out her hand. "Thanks for this. I'll make sure it's taken care of and get it back to you before the investigation."

He took her hand but didn't shake it. Instead, they both stared at each other. Neri broke eye contact first and shook his hand, then dropped it. She strolled to the front door. When he didn't join her there to see her out, she turned to find him looking down at his hand, bemused.

She cleared her throat. "I'm leaving now."

He looked at her. "Ah, right." He strolled over to her, his hands stuffed in his pants pockets. "Drive safe."

She laughed, stood on tiptoe and kissed his cheek. "Goodbye." She walked outside.

She heard the click of the door as it closed, but she had a psychic feeling that he watched from his window. A smile on her lips, she went to her car, unlocked it, set the box on the back seat, and climbed in. She knew he watched as she drove away.

There might be some perks to returning to investigating the paranormal, after all. Sad that Kelly wasn't alive to meet Parker Burkett. She would say no one on any of the ghost hunting reality television shows ever looked as sexy good as he did.

Too hot to be haunted.

***

Parker called Ben and made a change to the arrangement of the investigation. "I want to join your team for that investigation of Burkett."

"Well, I don't usually allow that with civilians..."

"I own the place, and I'm allowing you guys to investigate it, so I think my request to be with you isn't that much."

Ben didn't answer him; Parker only received silence from the other end for a couple of seconds.

Then Ben said, "All right. It goes against my rules and better judgment. But you must follow the rules I have set, and you must do as I say. Is that all right with you, Mr. Burkett?"

"No problem, and please call me Parker. When do I need to be there?"

"We plan to be there while it's still daylight for a walk-through and to set up camp. Any time before it grows dark—by five o'clock at the latest?"

"I'll be there by five. Do I need to bring my tent? Plus, any food you like me to bring—as a contribution?"

"We got it—tents, food, and drinks. How about four pizzas of different kinds from some pizza place for the first night? That way we don't have to cook anything. We'll have soda, coffee, tea, and even hot chocolate, to go with it."

"Fine. See you at five, then."

Parker clicked off the call with a smile.

CHAPTER ELEVEN

Lisa's migraine had been growing steadily at work during the day. A couple of headache pills she'd taken hadn't worked, and tears blurred her view of the computer screen. She had finished most of her work, except for this final, damn project. If she could get this last page done, maybe her boss would let her go home early. Wiping away the tears, she forced her fingers to tap the keys.

There, done. Lisa looked forward to lying down for an hour in her shuttered bedroom and getting over this throbbing before she had to make dinner.

She printed up that last page. It joined the other sheets of paper she placed in a folder that she carried to her supervisor.

"Mr. Pope, my work's done." She deposited it on his desk in front of him. "Can I leave? I've had this nasty headache all day, and it's making me sick to my stomach."

She peered at him with a frown as he looked up at her. His eyebrows reminded her of fuzzy caterpillars meeting over the bridge of his nose like they were kissing.

He said, "I hope you're not coming down with something catching."

"No, I think it's just a nasty migraine. I get one every so often."

"Well, if that's all it is, I'd rather you stayed. Maybe, you can assist a couple of others that are behind with their projects."

Her headache suddenly became a monster. She leaned over and gripped each side of the man's chair, her face inches from her boss's. The pain flared so intense that it made her see everything cast in a pale red.

Another voice—she couldn't tell if it was male or female—whispered in her head. *Damn, the bitch is right, his eyebrows are like caterpillars.*

"Look here, fat boy. I said I had this killer headache and I want to go home. I've seen your ass sneak out early or not come back from lunch many times. You work us all like some Southern plantation overseer, whip in hand. So, that's right, I can't work. How can anybody work with you standing over them like you do when you're here? You should see us all party when you do go home early. It's like an amusement park."

His caterpillars reared up in shock.

"Are you saying, I might be the cause of your headache, Mrs. Polivka?"

"You said it, not me, Mr. Pope."

The fuzzy caterpillars did a wild dance.

"Maybe you need to leave work, and that so-called headache might go away for good. You're—"

Lisa's headache dulled to a small ache as it hit her, she might have said things she shouldn't have. What, she wasn't sure, and that scared her.

Oh, God, what did I say? She was losing it. Lose this job, and Chris would do things to her that will hurt worse than a headache.

"Mr. Pope, I'm sorry. I don't know what came over me."

Pope's piggish nose wrinkled. He stared at her as if she had grown two heads.

She pressed on.

"This headache has gotten to me. You're right; I need to go. Just let me off early, and I'll get some rest, maybe even go see a doctor. I promise tomorrow morning I'll be back, bright and chipper as normal."

"Humph. I don't know..."

"Please?" Tears leaked from her eyes, blurring Mr. Pope's face. She swiped at them with a finger.

"All right. I'll forgive you. But this will be the last time. Go on home before I change my mind." He pursed his lips as lines grooved into his forehead.

"Thank you, sir. Goodbye, Mr. Pope."

She stopped at her desk to shut off her computer, gathering up her purse and lunch bag, and forced herself to walk, not run, out the door. Outside the office, she turned around to face the door. The pain behind her eyes returned with a vengeance, and she blacked out.

***

Mr. Pope had seen her lips become a slash, and her eyes go dark in the glass of the door's window, as she snarled, "Next time, I'll ripped those fuzzy caterpillars off your face, fat boy." The door slammed behind her as she walked out.

***

Lisa awoke to find herself standing outside the office and staring at the door, her head no longer throbbing. *Odd. Why am I standing here?*

Afraid to think about it, she traversed across the parking lot to her car, unlocked the driver's door, and climbed in, driving home minutes later.

Once she got home, she went to the bedroom to set down her purse on the dresser and replace her work clothes for a pair of pants and a sweatshirt, slipping her feet into bedroom slippers. She took a couple of painkillers.

Her husband would be home in a couple of hours, and he expected his dinner to be hot and waiting on the table. Lisa grabbed three defrosted chicken breasts from the fridge and seared them in a pan on the stove, before adding them with potatoes to a baking dish she stuck in the oven. She poured wine in a glass and sat down on the couch and relaxed.

Why are you cooking for that jerk? You know he might not even be home from work at six. Lately, he seems to be working late. A lot.

WTF. Did that come from inside her head?

You bet your sweet tatas, it did.

She nearly spilled her wine, but she caught herself in time and put the glass down on the coffee table with a shaking hand. All right, she must be going crazy.

Crazy? You should have been crazy like a fox and known why he always works late.

Freaked, she picked up the wine glass and downed the wine. She bolted to the kitchen, stuck it on the counter and grabbed the dinner from the oven, remembering at the last minute to use potholders. Keeping busy, she scooped the hot food onto plates she placed on the kitchen table, along with glasses and utensils. She took a bowl of green bean salad she'd made before she left for work this morning out of the fridge, adding a cup of it to each plate. Then she poured more wine in her glass and sat down at one side of the table to wait.

And wait.

Usually, Chris arrived home at six, but now it was going on seven. On her third glass of wine, Lisa mulled over things. Like how he seemed to be getting home late, more and more. How he always had excuses about working beyond his regular hours, and she believed it—but now? She'd questioned it one time, and Chris had punched her in the chest.

He always made sure if he hit her, it was never where anyone could see it, especially her brother. Parker would have knocked Chris out and taken her away, forcing her to file for divorce.

This past Saturday, when Chris said he had to go into work all day, she'd called his boss at his home to find out why.

"I didn't tell him to work today; Henrico County doesn't allow OT," he said. "If he told you that..."

He didn't finish the sentence, but she understood what he implied. She pleaded with him not to say anything to Chris, and he promised, though she heard the reluctance to do so in the man's voice.

She drained the last drops of wine from her glass and debated about pouring another glassful when the glow of headlights lit up the front of the house. *Oh God, Chris is home.* She darted to the kitchen sink and washed out the glass, drying it and placing it by her plate before she ran back to the living room.

The front door swung open, and Chris stomped in.

She smiled as she met him but dropped the smile when she saw his stone face. Though he promised not to, she wondered if Chris's boss had mentioned her call to him. Either that or whatever he did on all those times he 'worked' late hadn't panned out; he made it home only an hour late today. She just hoped it didn't mean more bruises or worse, a broken bone, for her.

"Hello, Chris," she said, then she kissed him on the lips.

She hoped her breath didn't stink of wine. Chris hated lushes, and she'd forgotten to wash out her mouth.

He grunted and stalked past her, dropping his lunch container on the floor at her feet. She frowned after him.

"What's for dinner?" he asked. He paused at the entryway into the kitchen. "That's dinner that I smell, right?"

She giggled as her cheeks heated. Oh hell, her husband might suspect her of something with that silly girl giggle and the telltale evidence of redness that no doubt colored her face. He might grow angry, enough to shake her or even deliver a burning slap.

She didn't move, but said, "I made chicken and potatoes, plus green bean salad."

"You know I can't stand green bean salad. Aw, hell, let's get to eating," Chris said, sounding aggrieved.

"I need to dump what's on the plates. The food has gotten cold since you didn't get home at six. There's more I kept warm in the oven."

He turned and glared at her. "So, the cold food is my fault?"

"No, no. I just need to get you warm food. I doubt you want cold chicken and potatoes."

"Hurry. I'm damn hungry."

She slipped past him, wincing for a second when he shifted his body. When she understood he wasn't going to strike her, she continued to the kitchen.

She scraped the cold food off Chris's plate into the trash and set the plate into the sink. After she'd got a new one for Chris, she layered it with hot food from the oven. Since he didn't want the green bean salad, she went ahead and scooped some of that from the bowl she'd gotten out of the fridge plus what was left of the warm potatoes to her plate with her cold breast. She fought the sigh threatening to release from her at the sight of his wasted food in the trash.

Her mother's voice chastened her in her head. *How can you waste food when so many go hungry in the world, Lisa?*

It saddened her that she would have added his chicken breast to her other one, but in the past, she'd done that, and Chris had thrown her plate of food to the floor and punched her in the mouth.

Food on their plates and wine in their glasses, they sat down at the table. Chris ignored her and began to shovel everything into his mouth. Too shaken to eat because of his attitude. Lisa drank her wine, adding more of it when she emptied the glass.

Chris acted like he didn't notice. But then, now she thought about it, he never saw much about her, unless he grew angry at her. Lisa pretended to her brother that things at home were great, but they weren't. The lies she told.

You knew about the bitch he's been seeing. His boss only verified it. Look how he's treating you. In bed and out of it.

Yeah, she knew the truth, knew about the other woman, long before the voice warned her. Like the lipstick on his shirt collar. The strange name and phone number she didn't know in his cell phone contacts when she sneaked a peek at one night while he slept. The plastic bag with a box of condoms on the floor of the back seat of his car that he must have forgotten to hide. The next time she looked in the back seat, the bag had vanished. He didn't need condoms with her, as she was on the pill.

She'd kept quiet about seeing them.

Look. A vision appeared like a movie in Lisa's mind. Chris and another woman going at it like naked bunnies. His face planted against the brown curls between her thighs. The woman squealed like a stuck pig as his mouth and tongue worked on her. His hand skimmed up her body to snatch a breast.

Just like he used to do to you, Lisa. That was one of the things you liked about him.

His magic tongue. Now that tongue is working its sorcery on that other woman. Bet he doesn't smack her around.

The vision dissipated. A woman with brown hair like hers, huh? He told her he thought brown hair dull. Well, it showed him touching someone with hair her color, fucking her, hell, doing plenty with the slut.

A calm settled over her as the voice continued to whisper in her head. A strange smile plastered her face, and she downed the last dregs of the wine in her glass.

Look, it's working. Told you lacing the jerk's food with that poison would do the job.

Lisa broke out of her musings. She saw Chris choking, struggling to rise from his chair. His hand gripping the chair to support him, his legs wobbled as his face blushed pink. His hand slipped, and the chair overturned, crashing to the floor. His face went from pink to red. He toppled to the floor like a felled tree, his head striking the chair. Blood gurgled from his mouth and his face mottled. His mouth opened and closed like a fish out of water.

Lisa got up and walked around the table. She kneeled beside him.

His eyes looked up at her—beseeching—reaching a hand out to her. Blood dribbled down his chin and neck. The front of his shirt darkened with the growing bloodstain.

Lisa said, "I know about your slut, dear Chris. Someone told me. Showed me."

Confusion flickered in his eyes. It mingled with the pain.

"That someone told me what to do about you. I am so tired of the men in my life who can't be loyal to me. Tired of you slapping me around. Tired of lying to my brother about our marriage. I am not planning to go through a divorce. Again. It's too messy. Troublesome." She saw his frantic hands trying to snatch at her, and she knee walked back a few inches out of his reach. "Death is messy, too. But my new friend says he'll help me clean up. We reached an agreement beneficial to us both."

"No fuss, no muss." A voice spoke again, this time outside of her head. A foul odor filled the air.

Chris looked past her shoulder, and his eyes widened in horror. He tried to scream, but more blood sloshed out. The man struggled, wheezing. His hands clawed at the floor.

Lisa rose to her feet and proceeded over to stand by the stove. Although she'd promised her friend not to look, she turned her head in the hope she might see the owner of the voice. Instead, her gaze filled with Chris. He wasn't paying attention to her anymore. His eyeballs bulged toward the entryway between the kitchen and the living room.

She looked beyond him to behold the owner of the voice for the first time. For a split second, she understood why it told her not to observe. It proved too much for her mind to handle, so it shattered. Like her husband, she whimpered like a frightened baby. But as their gazes met, she quieted and stole pass Chris and the visitor, marching into the living room to make for the front door. Oblivious to the screaming she thought came from Chris at first, but it couldn't have because he'd died, she understood the sound came from his soul as something ripped it from his body. Nor did she acknowledge when the front door slammed shut behind her. Or when she sat on in the wicker chair on her front porch and a long, dark shadow flowed through the door, carrying a shrieking, glowing orb as the entity rose into the sky that darkened with thunderclouds.

Only when the rain began to fall in torrents did she rise to her feet and climb down her porch steps to her front lawn. The rain soaked her to the skin as she threw back her head and laughed. Her laughter started low, growing and growing to compete with the thunder booming.

The laughter of the broken and insane.

CHAPTER TWELVE

Parker rushed to the hospital after he'd received the call that woke him in the night. The police told him the paramedics had taken his sister to Chippenham Hospital and that his brother-in-law had been found dead. Their next-door neighbors heard her laughing and saw her dancing on her front lawn in the rainstorm. They also discovered her dead husband in the house, lying on the kitchen floor. They'd dialed 911.

Getting the hospital's number from dialing 411, he called and got a nurse's brisk, no-nonsense voice telling him that they'd checked his sister into a room on the second floor. Frantic, with pounding heart and upset stomach, he knew he had to see Lisa. He didn't stop to think that they might not let him.

A policeman stood on guard outside Lisa's room.

"I'm Parker Burkett, Lisa Polivka's brother."

"ID," said the officer, stopping him.

Parker whipped out his driver's license and the policeman scanned it, before handing it back.

"Hello," said the cop. "I'm Officer Talley. My partner, Officer Salisbury, and I were the ones who came when Mrs. Polivka's neighbors called. The dead body is still at the house with a couple of detectives."

Parker slipped the license back in his wallet and shoved the wallet in his back pocket. "What happened?"

"Honestly, I can't say much. Just that Mr. Polivka is dead, or we assume the body at the house is your sister's husband. There will be an investigation into that. I know that our coroner is on his way to join the detectives. The little bit more I will say, your sister was discovered by her neighbors, dancing and laughing on her front lawn in the rain. There hadn't been any blood on her, but the rain could have washed it off. The hospital staff checked her in after I brought her here." He stepped aside. "Go in, but only for five minutes." He added, "She's handcuffed to the bed."

Parker stared past the policeman into the room. Chris dead and Lisa arrested and in the hospital.

Had she murdered him?

Not that he hadn't wanted to strangle the bastard himself when he saw him with that woman that day. Still, how did she find out? Or was he making a mountain out of a molehill and something else happened to Chris? Maybe he had a stroke or something. Though why did the cop mention about her not having any blood on her and why would Lisa be dancing in the rain, he didn't know.

You know why. The time Parker found her with a sprained arm, Lisa told him she'd had an accident, fell down some stairs. Not at home, but elsewhere. He hadn't believe her, but he hadn't contradicted her and let it go. His conscience pricked him as he wished he had done *something*. No matter what he told himself, Chris hadn't perished from any reasonable means.

He drew closer to the bed and found Lisa asleep. Her hair still felt damp from her rain dance when he touched a strand, but she was otherwise dry and looking innocent of any wrongdoing...such as the murder of a cheating husband.

Her eyes popped open. A chill settled inside Parker at the look she flashed. Cold, cruel, and calculating. Not even human. A shark grin formed on her pale, cracked lips.

"One soul is now part of the equation. Soon, there will be others. Until the day of reckoning comes and worlds merge, then the screaming will begin for all."

Her voice was not her own; it came out abyssal and cold.

"What the hell are you talking about, Lisa?" demanded Parker.

Like a slate wiped clean, her face lost the strange evil look, and she blinked up at him, baffled. Her fingers clutched at the sheet in nervous movement.

"Parker? Where am I?" She struggled to sit up and stare around the hospital room. Halfway up, she collapsed. "Why am I here?" Her gaze found his. "Where's Chris? Oh God, he'll be upset with me. He'll be at home, without dinner." The words spilled out of her mouth, jumbling together. "I shouldn't be here."

Parker stared at her: this seemed more like his sister. Maybe she was going over the deep end? Schizophrenia?

He patted her hand. "It's all right, Lisa. Chris won't be upset."

He'll never be upset ever again. Parker didn't know if he should tell her or leave that up to her doctor. Telling her without consulting the doctor might bring her back over the edge. Bring back that awful version of her when she first woke up.

After finding Chris with another woman, he wanted the man to leave his sister. But not this way. Not in death. Had she figured out the man was cheating on her and killed him?

"Parker, what is it? You have this strange look on your face. Is it Chris?"

Oh, God. What should he do?

The doctor entered the room and saved him from deciding. The dark-skinned man wore a white coat and silver touched the hair above his ears. He stuck out his hand at Parker who accepted it, and they shook hands.

"I'm Lisa Polivka's doctor, Doctor Pershing. You must be..."

"Parker Burkett, Lisa's brother."

"Ah, yes." The doctor walked over Lisa and smiled down at her. "I see my patient is awake. Doctor Pershing, Mrs. Polivka."

She blinked up at him. "Where is my husband?"

"Husband?"

"Yes, Chris Polivka. My brother is here, but I don't see my husband in the room."

Doctor Pershing flashed Parker a lifted brow. "Ah, yes, Mr. Polivka. Well..."

She frowned. "Well, what?"

"He's..." The doctor's voice trailed off, as he looked down at the clipboard he held as if it might offer him the right answer to tell her.

Her eyes took glittered, and Parker realized they were tears. Her fingers twisted at the sheet.

Oh, hell, she'd figured it out.

"He's dead, isn't he?" Her voice came out tiny.

Parker took her hands in his. "Lisa—"

She screeched with that horrible voice she used earlier. "Don't bullshit me, asshole. The man is dead. Carrion for the buzzards."

Parker dropped Lisa's hands and staggered away. He couldn't believe what she just said to him. One thing he knew, his sister never cussed. Maybe *darn* on occasion, but nothing stronger than that.

Doctor Pershing said, "No need for that language, Mrs...."

She twisted her head around to glare at the other man. "Oh, fuck off. If you think I would let some dickwad like you place your hands on me? I'll rip that poor excuse for a penis you have in your pants off and stuff it in your mouth."

"Lisa," broke in Parker, "I don't know what's wrong with you, but he's your doctor."

She snickered. "Really? This man is better working on horses than people. I bet he likes to work on his pretty teenage stepdaughter, Annie." She winked at the shocked doctor. "Don't you? His wife always gone on trips for her job, and he and Annie crawl into his bed and—"

The doctor bolted out of the room. Not more than a minute or two later, he rushed back in, carrying a needle. He tackled Lisa and jabbed it in her arm. Pressed it and injected her, while his other hand hovered over her face as if he wanted to press it down on her mouth. Pershing jerked away as she tried to leap out of bed, but she couldn't due to being handcuffed. She growled.

Lisa narrowed her eyes at him. "That hurts this body, jerkwad. I'm going to make you sorry."

She closed her mouth before she said anything else, collapsing back onto the mattress.

Parker stared at a white-faced doctor; the empty needle still clutched in his hand. The man's chest raised and lowered at a rapid pace as sweat beaded his forehead. He turned wild eyes at Parker, who wondered how much of what Lisa had said was correct about the man. Worse, he now worried about his sister.

Had that been Lisa? Or someone, something else? His thoughts reminisced about the boy who said he was Terry using the body of the boy who indeed owned it. Parker reached over to help the knocked-out woman lay more comfortably on the bed. *Her skin's freezing. Like a corpse's.*

He let go of her and fell back as she jerked up and her eyes snapped open, solid ink black. His heart slammed against his chest as he saw another image ghosting over her. Thin and dark. Terrifyingly like unending night. The darkness drained out of her eyes until her eyes once more returned to the familiar brown irises against white that he knew. Whatever took its leave of her, it dashed past the frozen form of the doctor and out the door. The needle dropped from the doctor's hand, hitting the floor with a ping.

"Did you see that?" he asked Pershing. "The shadow?"

The doctor blinked. "See what? I didn't see anything, except your sister losing it."

A nurse that entered at that moment and snatched up the empty needle. "I need to destroy this tip." She walked back out the door and left them alone again.

Maybe the doctor thought he fooled Parker, but he had seen it, too. Terror colored his eyes when the shadow flowed past him.

Who—no, what had taken over Lisa's body?

CHAPTER THIRTEEN

The entity slipped down the hospital corridor, incorporeal, it paused to peek in each room. There were those who had the Sight and could see it and called out in fear, while others did not. It loomed tall and thin, reaching the ceiling at the nurses' station on that floor. It leaned over to listen to the conversation two nurses were having. Neither could see it.

"The woman the Chesterfield police just brought in killed her husband. I overheard the police talking."

"Sheila, you're not supposed to be listening in like some gossipy old woman."

Sheila snorted and crossed her arms. "Sorry, but I like to know if I'm helping some murderer to the bathroom or not."

The other nurse, a plump, pleasant-faced woman with dyed red hair shook her head. "You'll never change."

"You know me, always looking for the drama."

"If you wanted excitement, you should have become an emergency department nurse."

"No, thank you, too much of that even for me. Death and more."

Rachel picked up a clipboard. "Speaking of death, how is the patient in 2-D? The one with brain cancer they couldn't operate on."

Sheila shrugged. "Doctor Samuel just came by when you were gone fifteen minutes ago on break to tell me he made a turn for the worse. Want me to call his family?"

"Yeah, go ahead."

"Those vultures can't wait for him to die so they can get their inheritance."

A shocked look crossed Rachel's face. "Sheila!"

Sheila picked up the phone to call. "It's true. I overheard them talking the last time they came."

"It doesn't matter what you believe about the family, be kind and considerate when you give them the news."

"I will, even if they are vultures."

Rachel let out a sigh and returned to what she was working on before their conversation.

The being left them and continued down the hallway, this time to room 2-D. It passed by a woman in a wheelchair pushed by a male nurse.

The woman shuddered. She clutched the arms of the wheelchair. "Did you feel that? It felt like death passing us by."

The nurse looked disinterested as he kept pushing. "No, I didn't feel a thing, Mrs. Seton. Just a cold breeze. No doubt from an opened door, even an elevator opening. Nothing more. Come on; it's time for your PT."

It stopped and stared after the woman in the wheelchair. She had sensed it. That meant she was psychic. Maybe it should visit her next, after 2-D.

Souls. It was fulfilling its purpose. A few more souls and it could return to its realm with them.

So many souls in a hospital. A place of death, as well as life. Who would miss two or ten?

It sifted through room 2-D's door and stood still. The fresh odor of impending death perfumed the room. It shuddered in ecstasy. A nurse left the figure in the bed and headed for the doorway. It melted down into the floor. The nurse's shoes shuffled through its head. She paused, her hand pressed against the wall, shivering. She bent over to rub the ankles of both feet.

"Wow, that spot was freezing." She straightened, shrugged, and proceeded out the door.

The being rose from the floor and flowed over to the bed. It stared down at the man on the mattress before it leaned over and took a long sniff at his neck.

At that moment, the man's eyes fluttered open. "Nurse, why have you come back?" His voice cracked, weak.

He managed to pivot his head to look up, and terror filled his eyes when he saw the figure.

Death has enabled him to see me, for he cannot have the ability to do so otherwise. It drew closer.

The man struggled to escape, but the entity shoved a hand into him and hooked his soul like an expert fisherman, and yanked. It withdrew the screaming spirit from his body. The man's mortal flesh expired.

It opened its mouth, jaws unhinged, and the opening enlarged enough so it could shove the struggling soul inside. It clamped its mouth shut.

Then it rose upwards to pass through the ceiling to the next floor.

More souls awaited. Like that woman in the wheelchair.

***

Parker sat in his car in the hospital parking lot and stared through the windshield at the building, not seeing it. He had too much on his mind. The way Lisa had acted and her potty mouth. She'd never spoken like that before, and she always chewed him out for any cuss word that left his mouth

She'd cracked. That must be it, just as her doctor said during their ten-minute talk in his office. He'd told Parker to come back tomorrow, so he could sign some submission papers to place her in an institution, where she might be able to get the help she needed.

"Better that place than the prison where the police would lock her up. Until the trial, anyway," said Dr. Pershing. "If her lawyer can prove she has some mental instability, this might get her a plea of not guilty because of insanity."

Parker stared down at the car key in his hand. Sunlight filtered through the windshield and glinted off the metal. That kind of plea would be the best thing in a murder trial. Better for his sister in the long run. Of course, he had to find her a good lawyer first.

He rubbed a hand over his face, hoping to wipe away the tiredness that overcame him. Taking a deep breath, he let it out to slow his pulse and clear away the fear haze from his mind. It didn't work.

It's that damn land. Ever since we inherited it and moved to Virginia, things have been going to hell.

"Right," he spat in disgust. "The Burkett curse. No such thing."

What about those missing investigators? Your grandfather? The story of your ancestor? Your sister flipping out? If not a curse, what then?

He didn't like the way his thoughts tried to convince him. Maybe this new paranormal investigation might prove once, and for all, there was no curse on the land. That nothing haunted it. Just weird coincidences. He planned to be with the team. Help them discover the truth and settle everything, once and for all.

He stuck the key in the ignition and started the engine. He had much to do before that investigation began. Get his sister committed for now and find her a good lawyer, get his brother-in-law buried since the man didn't have any other family, and maybe check out the library at the Virginia Museum of History and Culture to see what they had on Burkett, if anything. Call Neri and see what she had learned from his ancestor's journal. If she were done with it, he would get it back and read it himself.

Knowledge was power, and in this case, it may save his life. Or even his sanity.

CHAPTER FOURTEEN

Neri bolted upright in bed, her heart banging against her chest as if it wanted to escape the terror. *Oh, God*! She floated in a sea of sweat. She touched her stomach and found her pajamas soaked along with the blanket, sheets, and pillowcase, too.

The dreams had grown more intense and frightening. Whatever controlled Burkett regulated her memories. She felt exposed, her soul and body undefended; no doubt something the haunter wanted. No, not wanted, relished. A hint of memory revealed that.

"Fiend." Her voice came out in a harsh whisper.

Silly, but she sensed that whoever, whatever took control of her slumber, was not with her now. She glanced at her smartphone on the bedstead and saw it was only 6 a.m. An hour before the alarm was supposed to go off.

Unable to stand her sweat-slicked body, Neri tossed her dirty jammies, along with all the sheets and blanket, into a clothes basket to wash later, and went to take a shower. The warm water sluiced over her, cleansing her of more than sweat. It rid her of the remnants of the all-night dream fest that refused to give up its secrets to her. If she couldn't get at the truth, at least maybe her exhaustion could be washed away.

By the time she'd dried and dressed, her alarm went off. Shutting it off, she hustled to the kitchen and made herself some coffee and oatmeal. As she ate breakfast, she went over the notes she'd been researching about the property.

Old Native American stories had proven sketchy in the written word, so she'd driven to the tribal land nearest the area, which was the Chickahominy tribe in Charles City. One old man claimed to be a shaman and she learned he was psychic, too. He told her all he knew about the tales about the land, but it wasn't much more than what she'd already collected. The man did confide that he tried to always avoid the area, as he sensed evil connected to it. That sometimes he felt the souls of those who had vanished from there, including many Powhatans, screaming for his attention and help. But he would just speed up his truck and drive away.

She asked, "Why not help those poor souls? Perform a ritual to cleanse the land? I know it can be done, as a Native American shaman did it for the Tuckahoe Plantation house when they filmed the movie, *The Broken Chain,* there."

His skin paled as he gave her a direct look. "Because I want to live more than save anything that calls from that land."

After she returned home from that visit, she discovered that the book written by a historian she'd ordered from Amazon had arrived. Inside, she read a few pages about those who settled and built the buildings on the property.

Jacob Burkett had bought the land in 1730 from Layton Stratton, a friend of Jacob's father-in-law, Percy Randolph. Layton's grandfather, George Stratton, had received the property in a land grant from King Charles. George Stratton had left his wife and two children in Jamestown and went to see the land himself, maybe to build a small house on it that his family could live in until he developed a manor house, but he never returned home. They thought that maybe he had fallen to hostile Indians. George's son,

Charles, inherited it, but neither he nor his son, Layton, ever visited it. Layton sold it to Jacob at a low price.

Neri straightened, her hands pressing at the small of her back to work an ache that had developed there. She wondered if Layton knew the truth about the area and the legends surrounding it. After all, he could have sold the land for a better price, but instead, he'd sold it—how did the letter from a friend of Jacobs put it? — for the price of a herd of cattle and a slave. Cows may have been valuable in those times, even slaves were, but not as costly as a piece of land.

She grimaced. "Layton, you cagy bastard. You knew the truth about that land, and that it was cursed. I bet somehow you knew that your grandfather had died there or disappeared in the same manner as my ex-fiancée and his team had. You just passed it onto some fool, anything to rid your hands of it."

Jacob, his wife, Abigail Randolph Burkett, their four children, plus four other men and their families, had headed out in horse-and oxen-drawn wagons from Williamsburg to the property Jacob named Burkett. All those settlers disappeared, except for the young five-year-old boy found wandering in a daze on farmland owned by Royce James. Since the child didn't speak and they had to call him something, James named him Christopher. He had hoped to give that name to a son of his own, but his wife had only birthed three girl children, and they never had any more after that.

The boy didn't speak for the first two years. Then one day, he spoke, nothing about where he had come from, what happened to his father, mother, siblings and the other colonists, or his real name, or what caused him to be mute the past two years.

He grew up with the James daughters, and married the eldest, who inherited the farm. It appeared to be a love match for both. One day, he went hunting and chased a deer until he came upon the land. He saw what remained of the village and the memories returned with a vengeance. He remembered his birth name. Lucius Burkett. He went back home and told his wife some things, but not everything. He did tell her his real name. That he owned the land, but that he refused to reclaim it. Instead, he left it in his will to his eldest son, and that he was not to touch Burkett but to stay away from it. He left his son a diary, as a warning of why no one should ever go there.

Neri put aside the book she'd bought and withdrawn the small cowhide-bound book, wrapped in plastic, from beneath a mess of papers. A strange feeling began in her fingers, spiraling up her nerves to her head. Like a spider skittering. She dropped the book, scooted her chair back, and stumbled to her feet. Frozen, she stared down at it, revulsion twisting inside her.

Neri blew out a hiss of air. "It's nothing but a book. A diary. Nothing evil about it."

No, books weren't evil, only the people who did nasty things. That's not to say that evil from that person or fiend didn't rub off onto inanimate objects. How else to explain curses and even spirits attached to objects? That described why people became haunted after buying an antique or something from eBay. Like the *dybbuk* box.

Picking up a pair of rubber gloves, she slipped them on and, after sitting back in the chair, shuffled it back up to the table. She picked up the book. It held the atmosphere of age, and it crackled when she opened it. Making sure not to rip it, she took care flipping the first page. Faded, tiny, precise handwritten words lined in neat rows covered the yellowed page from top to bottom. She snatched her magnifying glass from the table and used it to help her read. As her eyes followed the first sentence, a vision struck her, and she froze, her grip tight on both the book and the magnifying glass.

As if someone or something wanted her to see the visual in cinematic splendor, rather than just the intimacy of reading about it from Lucius' written words, she saw it all through another's eyes, those of Lucius Burkett's mother, Abigail.

****

270 years in the past
Dead silence. When the group of settlers in their wagons had left the trail that led through the flatlands and entered the thick woods around high noon, Abigail Burkett noticed the quiet. No sound from bird, animal, or—even stranger—not even the buzz of insects. Maybe she could excuse the lack of bugs, as winter was not far behind autumn, but no matter what kind of season, there should have been some noise from bird or animal life. Even the slight breeze that had played with the loose strands of her hair and whistled in her ears while they traveled hadn't crossed over into these woods.

Earlier, laughter from her children and the other young ones in the five wagons had filled the air. But as soon as they stepped into the woods, she hadn't heard a peep from them. Even the adults hadn't uttered much. The animals the settlers had brought stayed silent; the only sounds came from hooves and wagon wheels.

Now that she thought of it, the warmth seemed to be seeping from the air, too. She hadn't needed it earlier, but promptly she snatched her shawl from behind her inside the covered wagon, and saw her pre-teenage daughter, Beth, and her ten-year-old son, Sean, huddling under an old quilt. Shivering, she enfolded herself and five-year-old Lucius in her lap with the wrap. Lucius whimpered in his sleep and snuggled tighter against her. Something had disturbed his dreams.

"Do you not feel the cold, John?" she asked her eldest son, who held the reins and guided their oxen plodding through the forest. They had bellowed earlier, but as soon as their hooves touch the ground here, they remained silent. That unnerved her.

John kept his eyes ahead, but he nodded. "Yes, Mother, I have."

"Jacob." She turned to her husband, who rode his large black stallion, Trojan, beside their wagon. "Tis grown colder."

His horse spooked for a minute, not neighing, but rolling its eyes as it jerked its head, and he tightened the reins. "None of that, you old devil," he said in a chiding tone. Though its eyes still contradicted the truth, the animal calmed down enough for Jacob to look at his wife. "I expect tis nothing more than the cover of these trees."

"I don't know, husband, but I've been feeling nervous since we entered this land you bought."

"Abigail, you are ridiculous with these silly fears."

"But you told me that the Powhatans mentioned something about this area..."

"Are you saying I should have all of us turn around and head back to Williamsburg like whipped curs with tails between their legs? All due to some bogey tales of savages and your hair standing up at the back of your neck just because it is turning cooler?"

"But..."

"Nay! We paid for this land, and we are going to build a village and a way of life for us all." He snorted. "At least we won't have to fear about any savages setting out to kill us in our sleep at night since they have a fear of this land." He clucked to his horse, and his mount broke into a trot. He rode back to the wagon behind theirs and joined his friend, Charles Pickering, whose own steed had been acting fidgety.

Abigail blew out her breath. She knew being with his friend on this venture was a way of proving to her

Randolph relatives he was just as good as them. Many of the Randolphs had built large manor homes and were involved with Williamsburg and Richmond society and politics. Her father, Percy Randolph, thought she had lowered her standards in marrying Jacob. Not that Percy had been any better. The truth be told, being the black sheep of the family and on the lowest rung of the family ladder, he owned nothing more than a small house that his Randolph relatives had bestowed on him. If they hadn't, her father might have ended up in the streets. He would have denied her marrying Jacob, but Jacob gave him a bag of gold coins and Father had reconsidered.

Jacob wanted her the first time he saw her. That was what he told her, and he knew that would sweeten the pot to get her to marry him when he asked for her hand after gaining permission from her father. They'd lived in a small house in Williamsburg while Jacob worked on a plantation as an overseer. He told her it wouldn't be forever, that one day he would buy their own land.

Fifteen years later, Jacob sold Percy's house, which Abigail had inherited when her father died the year before, and he purchased the ground they now traveled on. Pooling his money with Charles and five other men, they bought the wagons, livestock, seeds for planting, and what else would be needed. He also kept a small amount of the inheritance money and bought Trojan. The horse bothered Abigail, as he seemed high-strung, but Jacob told her that not only was the stallion a good riding beast, but would be good for pulling the plow, and with such good blood, the animal would be perfect for breeding, too.

Her glance caught Trojan fighting the bit as Jacob worked to keep the horse in line. The stallion bucked and squealed, but Jacob mastered him into the clearing.

"Lots of forested land," she remembered Jacob saying to Charles the night before they all left, "and in years, a bustling village standing where the few buildings we will build will be."

Land the Powhatan called cursed. That it had swallowed tribes that had passed it or ignored the signs and settled there. The living may enter the area, but they were said not to be there the next day.

The chill grew worse, and her shawl didn't keep out the cold. She snatched a folded quilt from inside the wagon and wrapped around herself and Lucius. She handed John his woolen cloak. He slung it over his shoulders while she held the reins.

The oxen- and horse-drawn wagons and the men on horseback drew to a halt. Jacob reined in Trojan next to their buckboard. It didn't matter about the uneasiness Abigail felt, as the beauty of the land struck the colonists dumb. They stared at what would be their new home.

The saddle on his mount creaked, the first noise other than their voices she had heard since stepping foot on Burkett, and Jacob flashed a big grin at her. "Did I not say that this place is worth the sacrifice we made?"

Ignoring the feeling that clawed inside her, Abigail agreed. "That you did, Jacob."

John looped the reins tight and stepped down from the wagon, walking around to assist his mother to the ground. Lucius had awoken. When John swung him down, he didn't leave his mother's side but clutched her skirts, the thumb from his other hand in his mouth.

That piqued Abigail, as the boy hadn't sucked his thumb since he turned two, and was usually brave and adventurous, liking to wander off—which was why she always kept an eye on him. Screams and laughter reached her ears. Beth and Sean had jumped down from the wagon and chased each other in a game of tag. They darted inside the shadow-ridden copse of trees nearest the wagons.

Worried about what might be in the woods, Abigail called after them. "Beth, Sean, come here."

They ran to her. Both no longer acted playful. Instead, they quivered like nervous fawns that sensed a predator lurking nearby. After Abigail plucked a wildflower from the dirt, its color like blood, she and her children walked among their friends who had also dismounted or gotten down from their wagons. Beth and Sean went to stand with the other children, all of whom had grown subdued, too. The oxen and horses shifted, though they stayed in place. The colonists had brought other animals, dogs and a couple of cats, but none of them left their spots inside the wagons. The milk cows mooed and shifted. The pigs and sheep huddled together as if a wolf stalked them. The mare that had belonged to her father that Jacob hadn't sold off, tied to the back of the wagon by a rope, pranced in nervousness and rolled her eyes.

Abigail's nerves strained like violin strings tightening, as her stomach churned and made her ill.

One man, Thomas Painter, asked with a frown, "What about savages?"

Jacob shook his head. "No tribes in the area. When I came here a year ago with Layton Stratton to see this place, I learned from others in a nearby tavern that the local tribes won't come near this area. I never found out why." He laughed. "Most likely it's due to some heathen stupidity."

Charles spread his arms wide. "Then this land has to be God-given. Nothing or anyone can harm us here. Listen, do you hear it?"

"No, I don't," replied Thomas. "Nothing at all."

Charles grinned. "That is the quiet of God's country."

They were right. Abigail noticed that what noise filled the air came from them only. Otherwise, dead silence.

Her heart pounded. *That's what it is: the silence of the tomb.*

Later, after everyone settled in and set up camp, the men began chopping down some of the trees and had a couple of oxen drag the logs to what they decided would be the village green, to build the first cabin. They wanted to take advantage of that, get right to work on making basic cabins to live in before they tackled building their permanent homes. Tonight, and maybe even for the next couple of nights, everyone would sleep in their wagons. Dinner would be around the campfire they had started.

Jacob took a shovel and struck the spot where they had decided the first cabin would be. The blade cut into the dirt and Jacob stomped on it with his booted foot. He fought the shovel, forcing its blade in.

Thomas's wife, Anne, pointed a shaking finger. "Look. Is that water coming up? Why is it red?"

Jacob dropped to one knee and touched the wetness bubbling up around the spade. He sniffed it. Tasted. His nose wrinkled as he spat. "It tastes like blood, but that's impossible."

The people crowding around didn't say a word. They moved away and headed to their wagons. Anne had left, too, leaving only Thomas to converse with Jacob in a shaky, lowered voice.

Abigail shivered; it had grown even colder, maybe from even the weirdness of the strange liquid. *Jacob said it tasted like blood.* The chills were growing worse; she cocooned herself in her shawl and walked back to their wagon and climbed in. She drew her youngest son, who she discovered had hidden in there, into her arms and they huddled together under the quilt she'd used earlier, trying to get warm and for safety.

Lucius looked up at her with his big blue eyes. "Mama, I heard whispers. Someone is whispering to me."

"No, no, darling. No one was by our wagon."

His forehead deepened with frown lines. "The tall, thin man says you're lying, 'cause he is here, talking to me."

Abigail began to pray. She only hoped that prayer would be enough, for she doubted this land was God-given. No, it was more like something the Devil would claim ownership.

Stop that, woman. You think that is going to work? This spot is my place. A place where I need souls. Souls. More souls.

She stopped praying and looked at the back of the wagon. A long, thin shadow stood there. Impossible, as the wagon cover only went up five feet in height. This shadow appeared taller. The shadow flickered like a candle flame before it dissipated.

Her heart was galloping like a horse's hooves, and she turned to her son. "Get out of the wagon and run to Papa!" she told him, and when he remained frozen, she screamed, "Now!" The little boy scrambled into the front seat and climbed down to the ground, racing to his father.

Abigail crawled on her hands and knees to the back of the wagon, and slipped through the opening. Only to find herself blocked by a figure that rose almost to the top of the trees. It bent over until she and it were face-to-face. She widened her eyes, and her mouth opened. As if lightning has struck her, her nerves burned, and her vision wavered. The pressure veered to her head, and with a screech, she fainted.

***

Neri awoke from her revelation. Her mouth dry, a headache throbbing behind her eyes, she cast her gaze down at the book. The words blurred. Blinking, she stared at the writing again. No more visions assaulted her. She only saw faded ink.

"What do you want me to know, Abigail, and why did you stop?"

Her fingers traced the faint words. The paper felt thin and old.

Frowning, she looked around. "Come on, finish it."

No mental pictures or even a voice. Whatever Abigail began, she couldn't finish. Or maybe, something else wouldn't let her.

CHAPTER FIFTEEN

Regan Dodson couldn't contain the excitement inside her. Not only was SPW going to investigate possibly one of the most haunted spots in Virginia, heck, even in the United States, but she would be spending it with Ben Neilson.

All right; she wouldn't be alone with him. The other team members would be there, too. But she had no worries of competition from the other woman and men for his affections.

Kendra Quinn was petite and cute, with her red, curly hair that she could never control in an orderly fashion, and blue eyes that filled her face. Men wanted to cuddle her, protect her. Except for Ben. She had worried when Kendra joined the team two years ago, but after a couple of investigations, she understood that Ben saw her as nothing more than a sister. Besides, it was Zack Jennings who gravitated in the young woman's orbit. He wanted to be the moon to her earth. He had taken her training on from the first ghost hunt and for her birthday a couple of months later, he'd even given her a new piece of equipment. Not a new digital recorder or something cheap, but a rem pod! Still, he hadn't asked her out yet. So, Regan felt safe that Kendra would never try to hook and reel Ben in.

As for their gay investigator, Silas Carter, all he cared about was his husband, Jason Petsky. Jason didn't do ghost hunts and thought they were silly, but he took them in stride for Silas's sake. Russell McDowall wasn't gay—the black man's only love outside of paranormal investigating was his computer and video gaming. And candy bars—in particular, Milky Way. He just didn't have any interest in the opposite—or same—sex. Well, not that she knew of.

Regan was broken out of her thoughts at the knock at her front door.

Who would be here this late in the evening?

She threw open the door. Ben stood outside, his booted feet on her welcome mat. Frozen, she stared at him.

His eyebrows became one.

"Well, aren't you going to invite me in?"

She broke out of her daydreaming. "Ah, yeah, come in. Why are you here? Oh, God, is the investigation off?"

He wandered past her, and she closed the door. Plopping down on her couch and stretching his legs out, he looked at her.

Elation filled her. Ben was here and sitting on her couch. Maybe not how she would like it to be, but still.... An inner squeal bounced around in her head.

He said, "No, the investigation is still on. I managed to call the others with the additional good news, but I couldn't get hold of you. I even texted you a message after the second try."

His voice sounded like he couldn't understand why she hadn't seen it yet and called him back, instead of making him come here. Warmth burned her cheeks, and she prayed that they hadn't grown red with embarrassment as she slipped her cell from her jeans pocket and saw the telltale text waiting on the screen.

"I'm sorry. I was out getting a few things done, and I don't know why the phone didn't ping like it usually does when I get a text. Not even sure why it didn't ring either."

He stood. "Well, no matter. I wanted to let you know that Neri Phelan will be joining us."

"The hoodoo lady?" Oh dear, she'd let that slipped out of her mouth.

His lips thinned. "Neri is a psychic medium, and does not do hoodoo, voodoo, or witchcraft."

God, he still cares about her. Of course, that meant Regan wouldn't have a chance with him on this investigation or afterward. Maybe never, if she wanted to be honest with herself.

She perched on the edge of the chair opposite the couch. "I'm sorry. You're right; we may need a medium at Nowhere Land." She licked dry lips, though it didn't seem to help moisten them much. "I wanted to let you know I dug up dirt on the cursed land. Well, as much as I could find. From the Powhatan myths to the paranormal team that vanished there a few weeks ago. Did you want to take it home with you to read?"

Ben stood. "No, I trust you delved into it and have it all memorized. Plus, Neri has been researching it. I think she may have also gotten quite a bit of information about it from the owner, Parker Burkett."

Of course. That woman would be smart enough to check with the owner of the property himself. She should have thought of that.

"I'll pick you up at one o'clock on Friday."

It startled her when she realized Ben stood by the front door. *How long had I been thinking about Neri Phelan and not even noticed that he had walked to the door*? "What did you say?"

He folded his arms in front of his chest. "Weren't you paying attention?"

Her cheeks were heated. "You got another sorry coming to you. I was planning in my head what I needed to read tonight for the investigation."

A long hiss of breath seeped from his lips. "Well, bring what you'd written down with you to the investigation. That way, I might as well check it over, too. Also, pack warm clothing plus a jacket or coat, as I checked up on the weather forecast for Friday through Tuesday, and it appears the temperature will drop. A preview of winter almost. More like an Alaskan than Virginian version."

She nodded. "Okay, I'll do that."

He grabbed the doorknob and twisted it, opening the door. Before he strolled out the door, he turned to Regan. "I'll be here at one in the afternoon on Friday, so be ready. You did hear me this time, right?"

"Yes, I did, and I'll be ready. One o'clock sharp. Bye."

But he had already left, the door resounding with a click as it closed. Regan got off the couch and went to make herself an early dinner before she tackled the books and papers she had collected.

Over a grilled peanut butter and banana sandwich and a plate of tater tots, she poured over the three books and typed what she needed on her laptop, saving it as a PDF. After rubbing her tired eyes, she printed out a paper copy of the information.

As her inkjet printer printed, she thought about what she'd read. The Indian myths always interpreted in different ways, it all depended on how each person explained them. The American indigenous tribes fascinated her the most over the rest of the world's cultures. Reading and watching reality TV shows about myths and legends all her life had led her into paranormal investigation. Many ghost hunters (how she hated that term thanks to that TV show whose limelight made it the word the mundane public thought immediately of) never read nonfiction ghost books or read the legends and myths. Her opinion, most of what could be understood about haunted places might be figured out by trying to scratch beneath the surface of them.

One Powhatan tale about the 'land of the tall, thin monster' told how one brave warrior had gone to fight the fiend and win back the land for the Powhatans. But the monster ripped his spirit from him and flung it to the world where the monster lived. The warrior's stinking, rotting body dropped from the sky into the middle of his tribe's village three suns later. It had frightened the villagers, and they fled the area to settle elsewhere.

Regan sat back in her chair. "Maybe the Devil sent the warrior's soul to Hell? I hope a demon or demons aren't behind that damnable property. If so, I hope Neri has demon expelling in her medium repertoire."

A laugh came from above her, and she leaped from her chair, knocking over her plate of the tater tots. Books and papers fell to the floor and scattered everywhere.

"Come on, Regan," she told herself, bending to pick it all up, "your imagination outsourced that from the reading. No way is someone inside my apartment. I used my equipment here and got not one thing. It's free of the supernatural."

Loud laughter filled the room.

Regan whirled around, dropping what she held, and searched for the source. Her knees smacked the edge of the coffee table, and her feet tangled, and she tripped to fall face first to the floor. Pain registered immediately. Catching hold of the edge of the coffee table as leverage, she struggled to her feet, freezing on her knees and letting loose a gasp from her mouth as a voice curled inside her ear. Dark. Insidious. Male.

"Regan." The voice made her name sound disgusting.

"Oh, God, God, God!" she screeched as she scrambled all the way to her feet.

A hard push to her back and she found herself in the air, aiming for the other side of the room. Her skull thumped against the wall, and she slid down to the floor, dipping into blackness.

She regained consciousness the next morning. Her head hurting and no doubt, bruised, and with a touch of her hand finding a bump sprouting from her head, her memory of what happened that last hour plucked from her brain, she limped over to gather up the mess of papers, books, plate, and food scattered all over the floor. It took her about an hour to scrub the peanut butter and mashed bananas out of the rug. Once she got most of it out, she picked up the papers and two books. Lucky for her, none of the peanut butter and bananas ended up on them. The plate was cracked, and she tossed it in the trash. It puzzled her how it had gotten that way, unless she stepped on it?

She thought there had been more books than the two on her coffee table. The throbbing in her head escalated, and she forgot about any of the books, except getting to a doctor.

It took her a quick journey by car to the doc in the box. The doctor there told her to rest for two weeks, and he handed her a prescription for some stronger headache pills for the throbbing in her head. Regan agreed to come back in two weeks to make sure she was okay. Thrusting thirty dollars for her insurance co-payment, she almost ran out of the building.

She would pack her stuff, then take it easy until Friday by just reading. She called into her job that she needed to be off for a few more days than she had asked for the investigation. Her boss at the office hadn't sounded happy, but he gave it to her anyway, making it sick leave since the doctor gave her a note for that. She lied to her boss, telling him that she wouldn't be taking the vacation as she initially intended, but stay home and rest. The doctor would be having a fit if he knew about the camping and ghost hunting, neither considered 'taking it easy' as he'd ordered. There was no way she would leave Ben alone with Neri Phelan for those few days. Besides, what could happen to make her head worse? She was fine. Really.

Popping one of the prescription pills in her mouth and chasing it down with a glass of water, she crawled into bed to take a nap. Later, she would pack, including the printed PDF, and put away her books. The pain began to numb inside her head as she paused and thought about the books. Something felt wrong there... Something missing.... As she grew drowsy, she decided everything would be all right. With the last yawn, she laid her head on her pillow and dropped off into slumber.

And she forgot about the missing third book on the Powhatan myths.

***

Laughter filled the air as the tome was chunked into a scummy pond on Nowhere Land and sank to the bottom.

CHAPTER SIXTEEN

Neri rose from bed early that Friday and double-checked what she had packed, to be sure she had everything she needed for the few days at Burkett. There would be no power, other than the generator Ben was bringing for his DVR, camcorders, cameras needing to be hard lined, the small refrigerator, and anything else requiring electricity in his trailer. They would be cooking by campfire, but he would also have a coffee maker in the trailer for making coffee or hot water for tea and cocoa.

Ben had shot an email out to everyone about ideas for food and drink. Once he got what people liked to have, he sent a list of what they should bring for breakfast, lunch, dinner, and snacks. In a separate email to Neri, he told her to bring the coffee and four 24-packs of bottled water. Some would be for their drinking, the rest for the coffee, hot tea, cocoa, and for cooking, too. So, she didn't need to bring anything food-wise with her.

Once assured of what she packed, she headed to the bathroom for a last, hot shower. The only way of getting cleaned for the next few days would be by the two boxes of wet wipes stored in her mobile folding cart with lid. The water felt invigorating as it waterfalled over her. Even the headache she'd had for the past couple of days melted away. She nicknamed those headaches she always had whenever she was in the presence of the paranormal, "ghost" headaches. No spirits bothered her. No worries—for now anyway.

The tingling in her head warned her, putting her on high alert. Shutting off the water and drawing back the shower curtain, her headache returned full force, and she ignored her sodden hair dripping down her wet back. A quick snatch of the fluffy towel from the rack and she did a rapid drying of her body and hair, then wrapped it sarong style around her. The feeling overcame her. Like stinging flicks of electricity surging her 'inner eye.' The shower no longer felt comfortable, but more like the shower scene in "Psycho."

One foot at a time touched the linoleum. The floor felt like a sheet of ice. Damn it. Her breath formed clouds in the freezing air. Clamping her jaw tight to keep her teeth from clacking together, she took it slow and easy. She spied nothing within reach that she could use for a weapon. The biggest things in the bathroom were the bottle of shampoo and the toilet brush. What could she do with those anyway? Scrub the unseen like a toilet?

You can't smack something over the head that's already dead. Already a ghost. Something incorporeal and able to walk through walls.

She couldn't stop the gasp that shoved its way out of her mouth. The mirror had frosted over. Words formed across its surface, as if someone had taken their finger and wrote on the condensation. A text message from the dead?

I cannot wait for you to come to see me, Neri. Unlike the last time, I let you and your brother go. This time, you'll be staying as my guest. For good.

She turned her eyes away and shuddered, barely noticing the warmth returning. It didn't matter. Cold still iced over her insides. Once she let her gaze rest on the mirror again, she found the words gone. Most people would consider they'd imagined it all, but not her. What stalked Nowhere Land had left her that message as a warning. No, more like a promise.

Unable to breathe, Neri ran from there, down the hall, and into her bedroom. The wet towel thrown to the floor, she dressed in bra and panties, before snatching her jeans and sweatshirt off the bed and dressing in them. She shoved her feet inside the thick wool socks meant for winter. Still unable to stop shaking, she crawled beneath the covers on the bed and cowered.

It had been in her bathroom! How long? Had it watched her as she showered?

How can she go to its lair now?

Because, if you don't, it will always come back to your house. To watch you as you shower, eat, even as you sleep. Eventually, it will take you. Go there and give it an excellent psychic kick in its butt.

She sat up. Her pillow felt saturated from her wet hair. It didn't matter as her hair dryer could blow dry her hair. Which she did quickly, combing her hair out quickly. As for the damp pillowcase? She wouldn't be sleeping in her bed tonight. No, she would be camping at Burkett and show that fiend how it didn't frighten her. And let it know, she would find a way to revoke its invitation to her home. Of course, she needed to send it back to its dimension or spirit realm, or wherever it roamed, locking the door and throwing away the key. Just like she'd done to a couple of demonic entities in her past. She'd won those times, and she would win this round, too. After all, that's all it had to be, a demon or a nasty elemental. Nothing more.

After slipping her stocking feet into her black lightweight hiking boots, she walked down the hallway to the living room. Besides keeping her feet warm, when she'd bought the footwear, she'd made sure they were waterproof. Great for spending outdoors in the freezing weather, in haunted woods.

A last quick breakfast in her kitchen consisted of instant oatmeal and a cup of coffee. The bowl and cup washed, she stuck them in the rack to let them air dry and went to brush her teeth. Afterward, Neri sat down on the couch to catch the last fifteen minutes of the morning news. The weather person reported a drop in temperatures for the next few days.

Glad that she had packed nothing but sweatshirts beside jeans, thermal undershirts, and tights to wear underneath, her thickest jacket, some winter gloves (just in case), and a pair of sweatpants to sleep in.

A chill ran up her spine.

Was this a warning that the cold weather wouldn't be a good thing to experience besides the paranormal chill on this investigation? No way, that a spirit could change weather to suit it. The only two demons she ever exorcized had never done so.

What about elementals?

Unsettled by that thought, she clicked off the television and spent the new few hours until Ben came cleaning, taking time out to make a frozen dinner in the microwave for her lunch. After eating, she planned to bone up on elementals at a couple of good websites on her laptop and see if any could magick the weather.

She took the trash out after lunch. Just as she lifted the full bag into the trashcan she kept in her backyard; she jumped at a crow caw from behind her. The lid thumped on the can, and she whipped around to see a single crow on the grass. It cocked its head to one side and eyed her with a beady stare.

Though her psychic feelings tingled otherwise, she said, "Oh. You're only a crow."

Suddenly, another, larger bird landed beside the crow. A buzzard. It didn't attack the crow, and neither did the smaller bird fly away. The palms of her hands sweated, and the tingling soared through her body to her head, where a "ghost" headache thumped behind her eyes. Neither bird said anything but only looked at her.

The flapping of wings in the air alerted her to another bird. The hawk didn't land on the grass beside the other two but perched on the lowest branch of the maple tree near her. It stared at her, still as a statue. The whole scene reminded her of the Hitchcock movie, *The Birds*.

Prickles flashed everywhere in her nerves, and the pounding in her head worsened as the pressure of a thick atmosphere filled the backyard. It warned her to bolt back in the house. Instead, she took it slowly, one foot after the other, and climbed up the steps to her back porch. None of the birds moved.

Get. Inside. The. House. Now!

Her hand fumbled at the doorknob, and the birds took flight and flew at her. Heart pounding, mouth dry, and her psychic senses out of whack, she managed to twist the knob and turn it, but in her frantic haste, fought with the door as it refused to open. A couple of seconds later the door protested with a screech as it flung open. She got one foot indoors, but not before the buzzard slammed into her back with a force to knock her through the doorway and to the floor of her kitchen. Her hands and feet found purchase on the linoleum, and she scrambled to her feet to slam the door shut.

She turned around to see the buzzard in her house. It flapped its wings, hovering in the air, an evil look in its beady eyes. The crow and the hawk remained outdoors, perched on the railing of her back porch, silent and waiting.

She knew the other two birds were out there, but she still inched over toward the door. The buzzard flew in front of it as if daring her. Sweating and her heart squeezing in her chest, she looked around for something, anything, to use as a bat to swing at the bird. She didn't like to harm animals, but at this moment, she was willing to kill the damn thing. Her kitchen counter appeared too far away to snatch anything off it. Nothing on the table within fingertips and forget the refrigerator or stove, as, like the counter, both were too many feet away for her to reach before the bird got her.

"Rotten bird."

The buzzard didn't utter a call at her. The sound of its wings echoed in the room. More ominous than if the creature had squawked.

The stick of a mop caught her eye. Stuck inside a bucket full of water, it stood by the table and within reach of her hands. She had washed the floor earlier and hadn't dumped the water yet.

Neri whirled around and grabbed the mop, yanking it and droplets of water out of the bucket. Ignoring the water that spilled on the floor, she swung it at the buzzard as it flew at her, its sharp talons ready to slice her skin. The mop head hit the bird with a wet plop, and she rushed forward, pushing at the screaming buzzard to get it out the door that she managed to open at the same time. The other two birds rose in the air as they prepared to aid their fellow predator. But she thrust the mop and buzzard through the doorway and slammed the door shut.

The bang from the door rang in her ears, but she lunged to set the locks. Her ears quit ringing, and she stared through the small window in the door. No birds in sight and her mop lay halfway on the bottom of the stairs and on the grass. Forget the damn thing. No way in hell would she take any chances; the birds might come back if she went to fetch it. She would retrieve it when Ben arrived.

The endorphins in her body abated, and she felt the agony at her back. But she hefted up the bucket of water and dumped the dirty water down the kitchen sink, turning on the water to make sure none of the filth remained.

After putting the bucket away in her laundry room, she dragged her feet from the kitchen to her bedroom. She stood in front of the mirror hung on the door. Tearing off the shirt, she turned around to stare over her shoulder at the bloody scratches on her back in the mirror's reflection.

It damn well got her. Shedding the rest of her clothing, she took another, much quicker shower, dried, and did the best she could at applying salve to her back. No way could she put bandages over the scratches. Maybe a quick run to the doc in the box, but the birds may still be out there.

She glanced at her clock beside her bed. Only an hour before Ben came. That long? Had what happened cost her an hour extra? Neri grabbed some gauze from her medicine cabinet in the bathroom and wrapped as best she could. Then she donned a clean bra and sweatshirt, along with the jeans she'd been wearing; she tossed the bloody clothes in the washer.

Her stuff waited by the front door and after a quick check online about elementals, Neri sat on the couch as the washer ran and looked down at the diary in her hands. If whatever ruled Nowhere Land wanted her there, it had a funny way of showing it. Maybe it was afraid of her? After all, why possess the birds to attack her and not wait to do it then, when she stood in its territory? Then again, perhaps it had no rhyme or reason to what it did. Applying logic to a supernatural being never worked. It hadn't in the past.

She caught the sound of a car engine shutting off out front and Neri pushed aside the shade and peeked out the window. Ben's full-size truck with the large trailer was parked on the street in front of her house. She ran to the door and flung it open.

Ben walked up the stone walkway to her porch.

Anxious, Neri scanned the area for any birds, but other than a couple of sparrows on her lawn that flew away at the sight of Ben, nothing else marred the scene.

She pushed open the screen door as Ben clopped up. He strolled inside, and she let the screen go and shut the door quickly.

He looked at her with a frown. "What's wrong?"

She opened her mouth to tell him nothing, but sagged and said, "I had two incidents concerning Nowhere Land."

"What happened?"

"First, my bathroom grew Ice Age cold, and condensation covered my mirror, and there was a message written in it. That something couldn't wait for my arrival today."

"What about the other?"

She turned around and lifted the back of her shirt, revealing her gauze bandage. "I was attacked. By birds. Three of them: a crow, a hawk, and a buzzard. The buzzard slammed into my back just as I managed to open the back door to flee inside. The both of us ended up in my kitchen."

"Oh, God." Ben rushed over to her and lifted with a gentle hand a portion of the bandage to see one of the scratches. He lowered the back of her shirt down. "Did you kill it?"

"No. I managed to grab my mop and used it to shove the bird out the door, closing the door before the other two flew in. All three took off. At least I hope the feathered fiends did. Nothing attacked you anyway."

Ben went to the door and opened it, sneaking a peek. He closed it, and did the same at the back door, before stepping outside and coming back inside seconds later with her mop, placing it in her laundry room.

"I don't see anything. Maybe it got what it wanted. Scared you and tried to harm you. You haven't sensed anything or got a psychic message or something just before I got here?"

"No. Nothing since the attack."

He cupped her cheek, and she saw the concern in his eyes. "I think you shouldn't do this, Neri. You're hurt and—"

She jerked her face away. "No. I packed more gauze and salve. One of the girls on your team can help me change the bandages. Besides, it threatened me. That pisses me off. It's about time to stop this thing. I plan to be there when we banish it from Burkett for good."

Ben took off his baseball cap and drew fingers through his hair. "This goes

against what I feel we should do." A sigh escaped his lips. "All right. You're still in, but you follow all rules I'm setting up for this investigation. Like the rest of my team does."

"Like I do dumb things. You know me better than that, Ben."

"Yeah, I do."

"Besides, I've been feeling strange. That I'm not the only one it has gone after. Has any other member of the team said anything to you?"

His face tightened to stone. "No, but I plan to ask tonight."

"Have you heard from Parker?"

He stared at her with blinking eyes. "No. I assume he'll be there tonight, joining us."

She cast her eyes around the room, anywhere but back at him. He always knew the things she tried to keep to herself. Like her attraction to Parker Burkett.

More composed, she looked at him. "That's good. Not a great thing about it focusing on me, but it's good no one else has contacted you about anything happening to them."

Ben picked up the biggest of the totes. "Come on, let's get these in the truck and trailer."

She grabbed her backpack and two bags, following him out the door. Once they had stowed everything of hers in Ben's trailer, she did a last-minute check of her home to make sure all doors and windows were securely locked, and her security cameras worked, before she walked out the front door, closing it and setting all the locks on it. The mailman came by, and she got the envelope holding bills only, handing him the yellow card for holding her mail for a week, starting the next day. Her car was locked securely inside her garage.

She joined Ben who waited in his truck.

Ben drove down the street, and Neri started at three familiar birds. The crow sat on a tree branch while the hawk soared above. But the buzzard creeped her out. It stood on the edge of the curve and did a complete Linda Blair turn of its head to watch them drive past. It rose into the air, not to follow them, but to lower to the pavement of the street where a dead squirrel lay. A second later, her inner eye eased about the birds. But not about what lay ahead.

She placed a hand on Ben's flannel covered arm.

He looked at her, his eyebrows lowered over his eyes to hide what he thought from her.

"What, Neri?"

"The birds. We drove past them a second ago."

He stopped at the stop sign. "You want me to go back?"

She shook her head. "No. They're just normal birds again. The creature that controlled them is waiting for us. At Burkett."

Ben made a right. Ten minutes later, they drove straight through the toll plaza as he had an EZ Pass on his truck and continued down Pocahontas Parkway to 295.

Neri fisted her hands in her lap; there was a buzzard in the toll-plaza parking lot. If she mentioned it to Ben, he would say it had to be another buzzard. But she knew it was her buzzard. Impossible, as it had been pecking at a dead squirrel on her street and even by flight, she doubted it could have caught up with the truck. No, beat them to be waiting. The scary part? How could it even know that they would go this way?

No, better not to say anything to Ben. Not unless she saw the buzzard at Nowhere Land. Then she would say something.

CHAPTER SEVENTEEN

Excited, Regan ran out of her apartment as Ben's truck drew alongside the curb. *He's here*! She slowed down to a walk when she saw Neri sitting in the passenger seat.

He had mentioned that she would be a part of the investigation.

Regan grimaced. No chance in hell would she be alone with him on the drive to Nowhere Land. *Two's company but fucking three's a crowd*. Why couldn't Neri have told him no?

Maybe because she wants him, too. Regan stopped. She must have thought this, but the voice in her head sounded more...masculine?

Ben and Neri got out. Ben waved and walked around the front of his truck to her. Neri stood there, rubbing her hands against her jeans and looking apprehensive.

See? *The bitch knows he's yours and she is worried you'd guess it*. Regan narrowed her eyes at the other woman.

Ben said, "Hey, do you have everything you need and ready?"

She looked away from Neri and smiled at Ben. "Inside, by the front door."

Hands shoved into her jeans pockets, she led them up the cement path to her apartment and let them enter before she did. With their help, they loaded everything into the trailer. The front door locked, she climbed up to the truck. Neri already sat in the passenger side up front and grumbling under her breath, Regan crawled into the back seat behind the other woman.

Ben got behind the wheel and said with a cheerful voice, "Ready?"

Neri nodded as Regan said, "Let's go."

Her face pressed to the window glass, Regan didn't pay attention to the last sight of her apartment, but instead, listened to the voice in her head.

It whispered in a seductive tone. *See the back of Neri's head before you. Stab something sharp in it. One hard shove to pierce her flesh and the skull beneath. Or get rid of her by a car accident. I can lure Ben to...*

She spoke out, "No!"

Neri looked back over her seat. "Did you say something?"

Regan controlled the shudder that threatened to overcome her. "No, I just saw a deer by the side of the road. It looked like it was about to leap across the road in front of us. That's all."

Ben said, "Funny, I didn't see it."

The lie left her mouth. "Something must have spooked it at the last moment; it turned tail and bounded back into the woods."

Oh God. Something is telling her to murder. It would even cause the truck to crash, so Neri could die. She may be jealous of Neri's friendship with Ben, but no way would she kill, even for him. Besides, Ben would hate her, and she would end up in prison. As for the accident, Regan bet none of them would survive, including her. Unlike the movies, selling one's soul for gain never got the person anything. Just a one-way ticket to Hell or worse.

Oh, God, where did those last two sentences in her head originate? It couldn't be supernatural. The voice had to be her thoughts—she just made it sound male, that's all.

Such a smart girl—not. Think I need to purchase your soul to get it? I am waiting for you. For all of you. So many souls to add.

Silence. Whatever spoke to her in her head was gone.

Regan curled against the glass, but she didn't see the scenery they passed. Her shaking hands shoved between her thighs, she grew colder despite the heat blasting in the truck.

Neri's and Ben's voices reached her, and she looked at the backs of their heads. The tiny hairs on the back of her neck rose as if something stroked her hair. A lullaby sung in her ear and unable to help herself, she drifted off to sleep. The voice whispered into her ear, but she thought it was a part of a dream.

Don't worry. You'll forget all about me when you awake. All your souls are mine.

***

Ben peeked back over his shoulder into the back seat when they stopped at a red stoplight. "Looks like Regan fell asleep." The light turned green, and he drove through the intersection.

"Mmmmmm." Neri twisted around and saw for herself. The other investigator's brown hair had fallen over her face, partially obscuring it. Her breath caught as she sensed something. Tingles electrified through her nerves. Just as quickly as they had come, they dissipated.

She looked at Ben. "Ben. Something's here."

"What?" He glanced at her, but he looked back at the highway as a car almost sideswiped them. "Whoa." He hit the turn signal for right and pulled into the rest stop, rolling to a stop in a parking space.

The engine shut off, he settled a hand on the steering wheel and turned to Neri. "Did you say something paranormal was in my truck?"

"No, I meant a thing from another world. Yes, that's what I meant." She tucked a loose hair behind her ear. "I should have told you, but I saw one of those birds that attacked just before we left my neighborhood, back at the 895 toll plaza, watching us."

"Are you warning me not to go to Burkett?"

"No, I'm not. Even if we turned around and called off the investigation, whatever this is, it won't stop. It has an agenda. I think it has been taking all those missing people and maybe even animals for all those centuries, for a reason." She knotted her hands together and stared down at them in her lap. "You have a good idea there, and maybe you should call the others on your cell and stop them from going, until we can figure out what it is. It's not a ghost. It could be demonic—oh hell, I'm not even sure along those lines, that it's a demon."

"I would listen to you, but a demon, ghost, or the frigging Sasquatch, this is a big thing for Seekers of the Paranormal World. To solve this and make the land nothing more than...soil, trees, and plants. I could write an article about this."

"I know. I would be lying if I said I wasn't scared, but I am. This thing has had hold of this portion of land forever. As much as I dug up, it went as far back as the Powhatans living in the area. I believe it went back farther than that. That's why I don't believe it's a spirit. Not a human one anyway. There are inhuman entities. Those that our ancestors may have worshipped as deities. And I am not sure we're strong enough to take one of those on."

Ben reached over and laid his hand over her clasped ones. "Listen. Maybe, maybe not. But if we can prove something stalks those grounds, and we can rid of it for good, I..." He stopped and instead, he palmed the side of her head. Forced her to look straight into his eyes. "I believe if anyone can free Nowhere Land, it's you, Neri. I've seen you use your psychic powers since we first met and you're phenomenal." He smiled, and she couldn't help but smile back. "You would have given Edgar Cayce a run for his money."

She snorted before she laughed. "You make out like I'm some superhero."

He didn't say anything else, and for a minute they stared at each other. Neri never realized how dark blue his eyes were. How? She never felt a connection between them. Not until now. Like a fine live wire from him to her. But she didn't say anything.

The connection broke when Ben withdrew his hand and turned the key. The truck roared to life.

Regan snorted awake and blinked sleepy eyes.

"Are we there already?"

Ben said, "No, I stopped at the rest stop for a last-minute break."

"So, I didn't miss anything?"

Ben backed out of the space and headed for the on-ramp for I-64. "No, nothing happened." The truck merged with others on the highway. "Nothing ever will."

CHAPTER EIGHTEEN

Ben didn't make a right turn at the dead-end street that led to the woods that held the beginning of the trail to Burkett. Instead, he took the gravel-filled dirt road a block back. The truck and the trailer behind it rode over bumps, potholes, and rocks, dust rising behind it like some ominous cloud, until he jammed on the brakes and the truck screeched to a halt before a closed iron gate. The dust behind the vehicle and trailer blanketed the air before it settled back down on the road.

The gate belonged to a metal fence that went right and left. Going right, it ended at a field with an empty, dilapidated house on it. The opposite way, it stretched until it vanished into thick woods. That way led to what remained of the village.

Ben pointed to the house. "I gathered Parker Burkett's ancestors lived in that house from when they built it in 1910 until around 1935. He wouldn't tell me why they left it and settled in nearby Gloucester. But I can suspect it has to do with the hauntings and disappearances." He glanced at Neri. "Maybe, he'll tell us once he gets here, and I can interview him."

Neri rolled down the passenger window. Cool air drifted in. It still held the hint of the dust, but it also carried the scent of trees and other green things. Another odor underlined those, like the cusp of death. Not understanding why she was getting the hint of that, she opened the car door and stepped out. Her feet touched hard, packed dirt, small rocks mixed in it.

She walked around the front of the truck and toward the woods to her left.

Ben called out, "Hey, Neri, where are you going?"

Regan's voice joined his. "Hey, Neri, what the hell? Ben, what's going on with your psychic?"

Remaining silent, she kept going. Something inside her told her to do so. A spark that danced up her spine and across her fingers whenever she was within reach of the paranormal sprang to life. Dry foliage crunched, and twigs snapped beneath her boots. She stopped when she walked smack into an invisible wall.

The feeling burst into a hot flame. The palms of her hands grew sweaty, and she couldn't breathe. Though heat blasted her from inside, the air surrounding her grew icy. The wintry chill and her inner burning clashed with one another. The cold won, and a fog formed in front of her, building larger and pushing toward her until it enveloped her from head to toe.

She estimated that she couldn't be far from the dead-end street. Not far from where the path through the woods began. The beginning of Burkett.

Cold. I feel so cold. Uncontrolled shivering gripped her. She zipped up her jacket, but it didn't help. Every part of her became an icicle. From her skin down all the way inside to her bones, whatever haunted this property left its imprint. It wanted her to feel its power over this place.

She dropped to her knees into a pile of dead leaves. Slimy, wet mud underneath them pressed against the knees of her jeans, seeping into the fabric. Neri fought to drag in the cold air. When she did, it burned her sinus cavities and rolled down her throat to her lungs. It tasted foul.

She barely heard the running footsteps.

Ben stopped and grabbed her, saying, "God, Neri, what's wrong?" Anxiety colored his voice, but she kept gasping, trying to get air to her lungs.

He helped her to her feet. At first, she thought the shadow behind him was the spirit that had her, but as her vision cleared, she saw it was only Regan.

She joked with herself. *You silly psychic medium, can't tell the living from the dead.* The humor helped a little.

Ben looked over his shoulder at the other woman. "Regan, there's a roll of paper towels on the floor of the back seat of my truck. Go get them and bring them to me. A bottle of water, too. There are cases in the trailer." He handed over his keys. "The one to the trailer is the white one."

Neri barely heard the thud, thud of Regan's feet as she ran back to the truck. She was too busy fighting the paranormal sensations overcoming her. Her eyes rolled back. *God! It hurts!*

"Neri. Neri!"

With a gentle hand, Ben guided her to lean against him.

Regan's voice came to her.

"Here. What's going on?"

Ben pressed the mouth of a bottle to her lips and said in a gentle voice, "Drink, Neri."

She opened her lips and water sloshed into her mouth, flowing down her throat. She choked at first, but then she managed to swallow the water. Someone's hand with a bunch of paper towels wiped at her muddy knees. Calm overtook her as the warmth returned to her body. She could breathe again.

Reagan spoke again. "Tell me. What happened?"

Ben said, "Her psychic senses overloaded. Or something strained them on purpose. We'll have to wait until she's back with us before we learn the answer."

Neri felt herself being lifted into Ben's arms and he carried her back to the truck. Her sight cleared, and she looked up at his worried face and lifted a hand to it. "Don't worry, I'm fine...now."

He gave her a grim look. "We'll see. Let's get you back to the truck and settled inside."

Once he had her in the truck and handed her the water bottle, he made her drain it completely, before he tucked a threadbare blanket around her that he kept in the truck as part of emergency supplies. He dropped to a crouch beside the truck and looked up at her.

He said, "What happened?"

She drew in a shaky breath. "Something drew me to that portion of the woods. I understand that area isn't far from the dead-end street. The air became bone-chilling, and it wrapped me up in it and burrowed through my skin all the way to my bones. I tried fighting it, but I couldn't. It cut air from getting to my lungs, too."

He stood, his face tightened. "That's it. You're off this case. I'm taking you back home."

She tossed the blanket aside. "No, I'm not. We're here. Burkett is on the other side of that gate. There's no way you're taking me home now. Whatever happened, I understand now what just happened is not from the being that haunts the place. No, that's the psychic and paranormal residue that this place is saturated with, all due to the entity. Kind of like an alarm set to protect the spot." She slipped from the truck. "I'm not leaving now."

Regan toed the dirt. "I agree with her. Besides, in a few hours the investigation begins, and driving her back home and coming back will take a couple of hours. Hours we need to do a daytime sweep and set up camp."

Neri stared at the other woman. Though she never mentioned it to Ben or let on, from past investigations, she realized Regan had a thing for Ben. Something Ben hadn't picked up on. She'd felt the other woman's jealousy earlier. Now she was the one who agreed Neri shouldn't be taken back home. No matter what she personally wanted, the woman was a good investigator, and she'd never let her needs get in the way of a good ghost hunt. That was why Neri never said anything to her or Ben. It was up to Regan to tell, or for Ben to figure it out. Though, if Regan's jealousy did cause problems, that would be when Neri stepped in and told him.

Ben shook his head. "All right. Get back in your seat, Neri. Regan, back in, too."

Before he got in, he went up to the gate and unhitched the latch. The gate swung open without a sound. He walked around to the driver's side as Neri and Regan climbed in. Ben got behind the wheel, restarted the engine, and drove through the opening, stopping and putting the truck in park, then stepped out to shut the gate.

Psychic tingles sparked again inside Neri. Her heart pounded harder as the tingles spiraled from storm to hurricane. Something told her to roll down the window and look back at the gate, or even better, get out to see what might be waiting there. But she didn't. She curled into a tight ball and, closing her eyes, whispered a little prayer of protection for herself and the others.

She opened her eyes when a bump and the tires coming to a standstill told her they had arrived finally on Nowhere Land.

Her palms and face plastered against the glass; she stared at the old buildings in the clearing. Ben had parked here so he could unhook the trailer, before driving his truck back to the parking area. Rolling down the window, she listened but heard nothing.

Silent as the grave.

She shivered as cold air drifted inside the cab. It had not been this cold when Ben picked her up. Even the supernatural cold earlier that slammed into her hadn't been as bad as she'd thought. This was worse.

She turned to Regan. "What does the truck's temperature tell you?"

The other woman leaned over the back seat and peered at the dashboard. "Says its forty degrees."

"It was fifty-seven when Ben picked me up."

"Says thirty now."

"It's dropping that fast?"

"I agree. That's not normal."

"I wonder what the temperature is elsewhere. As cold, or warmer? I doubt it's colder though."

Regan said, "Now it says it is in the twenties." She climbed out of the truck and shut the door behind her. "Are you trying to say the cursed land is doing this? Really?"

Neri could hear the disbelief in the other woman's voice, but she saw her slip on her coat, shivering and pulling up the zipper.

Neri grabbed her backpack and got out, standing next to Regan. The other woman had slammed the door, but it hadn't made a noise. There should have been. Neri's insides iced over, not from the cold air, but from the knowledge of what this place could do. It could take away sound—what it wanted to, as she heard Ben asking her and Regan what the matter was. She had no doubt it could rob them of their voices, too.

Regan said, "Don't you feel it?"

Ben frowned. "What?"

"The heaviness of the silence. Call me crazy and I'm not psychic at all, but I think something is watching us."

Ben crossed his arms and scanned the area. "The silence?"

Neri nodded. "She's right. Something controls sound here, else why are we able to speak and yet, when the truck's door slams shut, it's mute? It watches us. Waiting to see what we do next."

Ben shifted his arms. "Well, it can only do that here. Probably does that for scary effect."

"Oh, I agree it does that to scare us," said Neri, shuffling around to the trailer to fetch her tent, so she could set it up. "I would say that it can't leave here, but I had an experience showing me it can." She turned and stared at Regan. "Have any odd things happened to you lately?"

Regan looked down and toed the dirt with the tip of her boot. "Why are you asking me that?"

Ben opened his mouth, but he shut it when Neri drew closer to the other woman. "You have," Neri accused.

Regan lifted her gaze. Defiant brown eyes glared at Neri.

"Nothing happened. Just because something did to you, doesn't mean it did to the rest of us." Sarcasm filled Regan's voice.

Ben grabbed her arm. "Regan..."

Regan tore her arm from Ben's grip and whirled around. "Nothing she does or says is wrong, is it, Ben? Maybe having her here means things will transpire. Bad things. Downright nasty things. But you have a thing for her and nothing she says is wrong."

She stomped over to the trailer and yanked out her tent and a backpack. Her back stiff, she headed to a spot in the middle of the village and threw them to the ground.

Ben flashed Neri an apologetic look. "I am sorry about her tirade. I know sometimes she has an attitude, but never like this."

Neri said, "It's all right. She always had a crush on you and any other woman you even said hello to would upset her."

Ben glanced at Regan, who was putting her tent together. "You're saying she likes me—in that way?"

Oh, the poor man. He never really saw Regan as anything more than a fellow investigator, but Neri realized the truth the first time she met Regan.

"Yes, she does. But you don't. I'm sorry."

It would be horrible staying the next few days at Nowhere Land. Now that Regan's lovesickness was out, there would be awkwardness, too. Worse, Neri always sensed Ben's affection for her was more than for a friend. She just couldn't find it in herself to think more of him, in that way. Though for a bit earlier, something had sparked between them. Then nothing. If only she could—damn fine man. Unlike John Peters, who showed his true colors fast in their relationship. She sighed as Regan clomped back up to them and the truck.

Neri snagged her tent in its pouch and then grabbed her backpack from her seat, slinging it over her right shoulder, and headed to the camping spot Regan picked. Better to let Ben diffuse the situation. If she said something to Regan, the other woman would tear into her. But keeping everyone's tents near each other would be the safest thing to do.

Just as she had gotten her tent up and her bag inside, ready to head back to the trailer for her sleeping bag and other equipment, another couple of vehicles—a Blazer and a station wagon—drew up to the gate. Ben jogged away from the two women to the gate and opened it for them. Both vehicles passed him and after a few feet, parked in the dirt parking lot.

After they were all done, Ben would unhitch the trailer, and drive the truck back outside of the fence, as his vehicle would be the one used to get more supplies if needed.

To get away from this place if we need to and the other vehicles suddenly don't work.

It hit her. Something watched them.

She didn't look around physically. Instead, she reached out with her psychic abilities, and right into an invisible wall.

Naughty girl. Using your inner eye. I am not ready for you to see the real me. But we can play.

Her palms grew sweaty, and she wiped them against her jean-clad thighs. Her heart pounding, the prickling growing as strong as a lightning storm, she inched her neck around, to her left. Nothing. Just a building. Dilapidated. Barely holding together.

Whoever, no whatever, spoke to her was inside that place. It waited for her to approach. Open the door. Come inside.

A step, followed by the next. Everything inside told her to stay still. Wait for the others. But she couldn't fight it, as something had taken over her feet and kept her moving.

"Hey, Neri, where are you going?"

She stopped as whatever had controlled her walking, left. Another of the investigators, Russell McDowall, stood in front of her, frowning and waving his hand back and forth in front of her eyes. She blinked.

He said, "Are you okay, girlfriend?" His shiny white teeth shone startling in his dark face as he teased her. "You act like you never saw a black paranormal investigator before."

A laugh escaped her. "Yeah, that's what the problem is. You got me there."

"Guess psychics don't watch those *Ghostbusters* movies then."

She smacked him on the chest with a gentle hand. "I have, too. Winston Zeddmore is one of my favorite characters in those movies." She whistled the tune, and he joined in.

They broke up laughing.

Ben walked up to them, shaking his head.

"Hey, Russ, get your tent. Did you think I'm going to grab it from your station wagon for you?"

Russ flashed Ben a pained look. "And here I thought I finally would get you to do some work with this group." He snickered and headed to his car.

Ben lay a hand on Neri's shoulder. "You okay?"

She found his gaze and noticed the probing. "Sure. I couldn't be better in one of the most haunted, dangerous places on the planet."

He gestured with his head at Regan, who talked to another woman. "Not sure how much is all right on my side, either. But she spoke to me. Well, for a tiny bit." He stared at her again. "Are you sure everything's fine?"

Neri stared at the building. She couldn't get a sense of whatever had waited for her. It didn't matter, as whatever had been there, was gone. "Yeah. For now."

CHAPTER NINETEEN

Neri stood at the edge of the village, a few inches from the loblolly, the only tree that appeared to dare grow close to the buildings. She reached out to touch the bark but then drew back when her hand touched some strange energy that sparked and hurt her fingers. Keeping the pain to herself, she dropped her hand down by her side. Another of SPW's investigators, Zack Jennings, slipped past her to attach a field camera to the tree. Lines furrowed his forehead as he leaned in closer to peer at the trunk.

He said, "It looks ill."

Neri looked at him, startled. "What?"

"I work for a landscaping company—my father owns it—and I learned to tell a healthy tree from a sickly one." He pointed at the strands of blackness in the brown wood. "See that black stuff? That's rot."

"Why would it be rotting?"

The young man shrugged. "There could be all sorts of reasons why. Though knowing about the paranormal as much as about landscaping, maybe this cursed land could be the problem. Seems to me as good a reason as any other. But again, could be something more organic than haunts."

"Can you figure out the underlying cause?"

"I can cut off some of the wood and have it sent to a lab to be analyzed, like the one my father uses."

"Now?"

"No, since we have to stay here for the next few days. But I will get a sample before we leave. It would be interesting to see if that correlates with the paranormal here."

Neri looked up and noticed clouds thickening in the sky. Returning her gaze to the area, she caught sight of mist beginning to form. Nothing spectral, just ordinary mist. It swirled around the buildings, almost like caressing them. The scene reminded her of a horror flick.

They only do those special effects to freak out those watching the movie. Mist is just a cloud of tiny water droplets suspended in the atmosphere at or near the earth's surface. The only thing it did was limit visibility to a lesser extent than fog.

Her senses told her that this village did hold something out of the normal. Whether spirits, demons, or a vortex to the other side, no one had been able to prove what lay beyond the legends that circulated about it. What most did agree, this was one of the most dangerous places in the world paranormal-wise concerning the disappearances over the centuries. People vanished. As if they'd stepped off the planet. Neri doubted that mist, fog, or will-o-wisp did that.

That frightened her. The danger it posed to her, Ben, and his team. All those stories she found that went back to the Powhatans, of people and animals vanishing and never seen again. Except for the occasional body part—like what remained of John Peters' team, the two kids that had come here some years ago, still here the next day, but changed, and that young ancestor of Parker Burkett who got away, but never revealed what had happened to his family and the other settlers.

What about that modern kid? Oh yeah, the boy that came out of the woods from here to where Parker parked on the dead-end street. She'd written that down in her notes when he'd called and told her. It hadn't happened long ago, only last week.

Died? The paramedics and later the doctor at the morgue claimed that he was already dead before he died. That maybe Parker and the two cops imagined the kid talking. A couple of hours dead. As for the other kids he said he had been with, where did they go?

Gripping her bag with one hand and balancing a case of more equipment with the other, ignoring the psychic warning bells going off in her head, she stepped closer to the buildings. Her gaze lighted on Ben exiting from the first building where he had just set up. She picked her way over to him. No birds were chirping, nor did she hear the cracking of tree branches due to the ice coating them, not even a sound from a large stone she just kicked that hit the outside of the building.

This place got to you.

Ben grinned. "Hey, since we have no electricity here, I went and set up battery operated cameras in all of the buildings. Now, I'm going to unhook the trailer, and I'm going to park the truck outside the gate."

Neri flashed him a smile that was lukewarm at best, but he didn't notice. He had already turned to head back to his truck. The sun burned away the mist to mere tatters of lace as Ben unhitched the trailer. Setting the items in her hands on the ground, Neri crossed over to help him. Anything to further ignore the unbearable silence. She'd never run into anything like this in any investigations and house cleansings she'd done. Minutes later, the trailer unhitched, Ben climbed into his truck and drove it outside the gate. The wheels rolled over gravel, thick clouds of dust rising and dirtying the mist, but still, no noise.

By eleven, they finished and stopped for lunch to eat the hamburgers Ben had driven to buy at the nearest fast-food joint. Trash stuffed in the plastic garbage bag, people broke off to do a daytime investigation of the land itself. They would do the buildings later in the afternoon.

Neri paired up with Regan, the young woman dressed in black sweatpants and a UVA sweatshirt two sizes too big for her. Since it had gotten warmer (the thermometer Ben brought had said fifty degrees), Neri stored her hooded jacket in Ben's trailer, hoping her Seekers of the Paranormal World sweatshirt, jeans, outdoor socks, and tennis shoes would keep her insulated enough.

Regan called out. "Neri."

Neri joined her at the base of one, old maple tree.

Regan's EMF meter flashed all its lights in continuous sequence. Beautiful as Christmas lights, but something about them put Neri off.

"The beast hiding behind the beauty," she muttered under her breath.

Regan turned and frowned at her. "What did you say?"

"Nothing, nothing. Let's find out if this is something paranormal or not."

Both women turned on their recorders and set them on one thick root that reared out of the dirt like the humps of a sea serpent in the sea. Regan stuck her meter next to them, too, more in the shadows, enabling them to see the lights better.

Neri curled her hands into her jeans pocket. "Hello? I'm Neri, and this is Regan. Is there anyone from the spirit world who wants to communicate with us?"

The meter quit flashing. Neri reached out and touched the tree, fighting the need to flinch. It held the same weird energy she'd encountered with the loblolly earlier. She struggled to keep her palm pressed against the bark and not turn away to throw up.

It feels like rotting, cancerous flesh.

She tried again. "Okay, if anyone is with Regan and me, can you bring on the second light on the meter?"

The second light flared. Right on its heels, came the third, fourth, and fifth. No flashing in sequence, just staying lit.

Regan chuckled. "See, it wants to prove to us that it's here."

Neri withdrew her hand, wiping it against the side of her jeans. "Or more than one entity." She pointed at the two recorders. "You can talk into those recorders. Answer us. Or talk out loud to us, or me, as I am a medium. Use my energy if you need help to manifest."

For the first time since she came to Burkett, she heard a crack. Not loud, barely a whisper. But the crack of a branch.

Regan shouted, 'Look out!" as she dove at Neri and shoved the both of them to the ground and out of the reach of the tree.

A large branch dropped to the ground, hitting where Neri had been standing seconds before. Shaken, Neri got to her feet with Regan's help. The shaking continued as she stared at the branch lying on the ground. Heavy enough to put her out of commission for this investigation.

It wanted to get rid of me, hurt me, or worse...kill me.

"It manifested a sound," Neri said, horror curling in her stomach. "It gave me an answer."

Regan's forehead furrowed as she went over to it and swiped up both recorders and her EMF meter. "The tree branch must have been ready to break free."

Neri made fists. "No, something did it. Didn't you hear the crack of the branch breaking? Haven't you noticed the lack of sound since we arrived?"

"No...wait, you're right. I hadn't heard anything."

"Not even when Ben drove his truck and the trailer. We should have heard the roar of the motor, the wheels crunching over the ground. It's still autumn, so there should be birds chirping, cold or not. I haven't seen anything with feathers fly in the sky over this property since we arrived. Listen to our talking; even that has lowered by decibels."

Regan whitened. "That is an odd phenomenon. What can control noise?"

Neri shook her head as they trudged back to the village. "I don't know. The phenomena must be more than ghosts. Even if a multitude of entities were haunting here, it would take an extraordinary amount of power to control noise. Like magic."

"There's no such thing as magic," said Regan.

"I think after spending the night here, even the rest of the week in this spot, that might change our perceptions if magic does or doesn't exist." The other woman handed Neri her recorder and she thumbed it off, sticking it in her jeans pocket. "I think we shouldn't have come here, and before the night is over, I feel you and the others will agree with me."

It's just a branch that broke free. Regan had trouble believing the other woman.

All right, it did make a sound, unlike what hadn't been happening since they arrived. She gave that to the medium. But there had to be a logical reason for that phenomenon. Maybe something about the area made people and animals deaf at times? Or perhaps something that caused this spot to stop sound and brought it back? There were no nearby military installations or anything else that could be the problem.

Ben should have kept the woman out of the loop. Regan glared at the trailer. When another team member strolled by, she lost the expression and headed to her tent.

Blowing through her nose, she plugged her recorder into her laptop and uploaded. Lack of sound or not, if anything paranormal hung around that tree, it must have left answers. After she listened, she would search on the Internet to see what could cause the lack of sound.

***

Neri uploaded the file of her recorder to Ben's PC he kept in the trailer for investigations. He had a small portable generator, and he had just filled it with gasoline and started it up. The computer came on, and she attached a cord to her recorder and inserted the other end to the slot. It uploaded with no problems, and she pocketed her recorder. Grabbing Ben's headphones, she put them on and plugged them into the same slot, turned on the recording, and listened.

Nothing, not even her asking questions, Regan's voice, or the sound of the branch breaking and crashing to the ground. Absolute silence.

Suddenly Regan's voice blared to life. "There's no such thing as magic." A deep voice said, "I'll give you magic. I'll give you hell, stupid woman."

Nothing else after that. At that moment, the power went out, and the computer died.

Ben busted inside. "Power went in here, too?"

"Yes. At least I got to hear what did record when Regan and I did our rounds." Neri gestured at the dead computer. "Of course, the evidence was uploaded to your PC and erased on my recorder. So, it may no longer be there when the power died, as I never got to save it."

He said, "I'm sorry about that, and we'll talk, but I need to see why the generator failed. It lasted through the last hurricane when we lost power. I'm not sure what's the problem. Stay in here."

The door banged shut behind him.

Neri slipped off the headphones, unplugged them, and set them aside. Standing, she walked over to the door. She cracked it open and peeked out and saw people scurrying, hardly hearing their voices as if choked down in cotton. No breeze or wind, but it had grown chillier, and it sneaked beneath her sweatshirt to place cold fingers against her flesh. Goosebumps popped up. She shut the door and stepped away. It began growing colder inside, but she suspected the supernatural was the cause rather than the weather. Maybe half an hour from now, the weather would be the cause, but for now, her inner senses told her different.

The door creaked, and Ben reentered, followed by Russell close behind.

Russell was speaking. "I cannot find any regular reason, Ben."

Ben replied, "It's paranormal related? You sure?"

"Yes, I am. Can't you feel the drop in the temperature? There is a nip of Arctic in the air in this trailer, and it's not due to the generator failing. It has only been a few minutes since that happened. Although the cold of the temps outside will catch up to the supernatural one fast."

His brow furrowing, Ben snatched a thermometer off the cluttered desk and tested the temperature in the trailer.

Russell took off his jacket and waddled over to a closet and took out a bright yellow hoodie and slipped it on. He zippered it up to his chin and pulled on the hood, before slipping his jacket back on and zippering that, too.

"Maybe we should have gone to the Arctic and investigated there. Bet it feels tropical in that location." But he shut up when Ben flashed a pained look, and he sat down at a table loaded with books and candy wrappers. He picked up a wrapper and Neri saw it still held a half-eaten candy bar. With a flick of his wrist, he tossed it into the garbage bag.

"The temp has dropped ten degrees in here." Ben looked at her. "Of course, with the generator down, that means the heat isn't working in here."

Neri crossed over to him. "Ben, it's paranormal, not due to the generator failing."

He put down the thermometer and crossed his arms. "Look, I know you're able to communicate with the ghosts, and that's why I want you here. But not everything is paranormal. And if neither Russel nor I can get that generator working, then I will have to call off the investigation."

"I agree, but the cold in here has nothing to do with the weather for the moment or two. It's still warmish in here." Her breath came out in little clouds, and she knew not because of the cold weather outside. "Use that thermometer and see how much has dropped within the past couple of minutes. You can see our breaths in the air."

Ben checked again, and his eyes widened. "The temps dropped twenty more."

Suddenly, all three heard the whispering. Low at first, it grew louder until it sounded as if someone stood right by Neri. Chills ran up her spine and she saw a pair of lips in the air. Not a solid form or color, but like colorless jelly. She could see through it to Ben.

She demanded, "Who's here with us?"

Ben grabbed a recorder and turned it on.

The lips kept moving. Her psychic hearing told her the whispers came from masculine lips.

"I'm Neri, and this is Ben. That's Russell sitting over there."

Russell waved.

"Can you tell us your name?"

As if carried as on a breeze, a whisper uttered loud enough for all three to hear. "Achak."

Ben grew excited. "Sounds foreign."

Neri grew thoughtful. "Or maybe Native American. Possibly Algonquin due to the area."

"I am surprised the spirit understood you asked for its name—in English."

"Maybe it can read my thoughts." Her words punched out in thick frozen clouds. "Or maybe me being a medium helps. I wish I knew whether that's its name, or something else."

Ben lay his recorder on the desk holding his computer and crossed over to the door. "I think Silas might have a book with some Algonquin language in it." He flung the door open and bolted out but managed to close the door quietly.

Neri flinched and apologized to the ghost. "I'm sorry, but Ben is anxious."

She realized that she could see more of the entity as a face—still transparent—etched out of the freezing air. High cheekbones, sharp features, and the eyes, even with no color, deep and piercing. Hawk-like.

She rubbed her shoulders as the cold worsened. "Talk to me."

It spat each word at her. "Ikwe, ininì, not belong on the land of evil. Be gone before Kicikaw pisimw falls and let his wife, Tipiskaw pisimw, rise to the makadewà night. Okee will not protect wàbà People. Màdjà or Nagadàn!"

Some English, but not enough. Well, enough for her to understand it wanted them gone from here.

Ben busted in and handed Russell a hardback book with a dark blue cover. Russell opened it. Ben spoke the first word it said to them.

Russell flipped page until he found something. He looked up with surprise in his dark eyes. "Achak is the Algonquin word for spirit. Not sure if it gave us its name or just told us exactly what it is."

Neri turned back to the ghost and saw more of it, this time as a full body. Still translucent. "Achak said more words to me in that language. It doesn't help that I don't understand what he said to me. Though I can tell you he doesn't look happy, and he spat out the words, as if in anger." Neri played back what the entity told her on Ben's recorder.

Once the recording finished, Russell shut off the reorder, then opened the book and tried a few words in Algonquin. Achak didn't reply, but the spirit only flashed an arrogant look at Russell.

Neri said, "Achak?"

He turned back to her and put out a hand and touched her hair, and let his fingers fall against her cheek. His touch burned with an ice-coldness, but she fought the urge to flinch or break away.

Achak spoke, surprising her in English. "Woman with hair of sunlight and your sad, sad, pale warriors must go. Now. The dark one will take you as he has done for many moons. Like he did to my family. Only I escaped, by death, but here I remain, unable to leave the cursed land, always fleeing one step ahead of the monster so he will not take me. The only lone Achak. Sometimes, I want to let him take me so that I can be with my family."

He faded. The cold air grew warmer. Everyone jumped when the generator started back up, unusually loud in the stillness.

Neri asked, "Did you hear that? He spoke in English."

Russell shook his head. "I never heard him speaking in an English tongue. It was Algonquin I heard, but he spoke too fast. I'm not even sure on the spelling of the words." He lifted the book, and it opened, its pages flipping. "Silas just got this from an online dealer last week."

Neri looked at Ben, but he shrugged. "I only heard him speaking in a language, not English. Somehow, I guess, being a medium, you can interpret what he said."

Neri fell into a nearby chair. "I think he was warning us, telling us to go."

Ben snorted. "Hell, no. I fought hard to get permission for this investigation."

Neri shook her head. "I hope Hell is not what will happen to us. That spirit feels like the only one in this area. I can't get a lock on any other." Ben opened his mouth, and she held up a hand. "Oh, there's something paranormal in the air here, but it's not due to ghosts. I think our visitor is the only one."

Russell asked, "Is this other thing demonic?"

Neri tried to get a feel on it, but she realized it too had left. "I don't think so, but again, it disappeared too quick for me to get a complete read on it."

Ben snorted. "All right, Ms. Phelan. What makes this land cursed? Why do the people vanish? The stories make it sound almost like Roanoke."

Russell said, "You mean that lost colony on Roanoke Island, which is now Hatteras, in North Carolina?"

Ben gave him a disgruntled look. "There are several theories, but the one most prominent theory tells that local Indians took those colonists and assimilated them into the tribe."

Russell spoke, his voice sounding eager. "I heard the Croatoan themselves believed that the island had a spirit and, if angered, this spirit had the power to change those who offended it into the form of animals, trees, and rocks."

"Poppycock, Russell."

Neri chided her friend. "Ben, no one knows the real truth about that colony. Though what that colony and Burkett share in common are that the people vanished. Except it only happened to the colony that one time; here, it has been going on for centuries." She stood. "I just hope we don't find out to our sorrow where they went, for we might be joining them." She crossed over to the door, but she stopped long enough to look over her shoulder at the two men. "That scares me."

She walked out the door.

CHAPTER TWENTY

Parker loaded his car with his sleeping bag, and warm clothing he would need for the next few days, plus other things he figured he might need. He stood beside the driver's door, ready to get in and head to the pizza place to pick up the pizza he ordered when he blacked out.

Parker hissed when he came to, as he stood in front of his front door. *God, how did I get here from my car?* Somehow, he'd lost five minutes when he checked his smartphone. He'd never done that before, ever.

Stuffing the phone back in its leather case on his belt, he double-checked his door and found it still locked. Thank God, he had done nothing more than walking from the car to here. He made his way back to his car, and his fingers on the car door handle, a vision of the kid came to him. The boy looked at him, imploring, "Help me." The voice was different this time, not Terry's voice he'd heard come out of the boy he had possessed. The real kid's spirit?

"No!" He gave a hard yank, and his driver's door opened. "Get out of my head."

He crawled into his car and shut the door, but he didn't move, just sat behind the wheel. Breathing deeply until his lungs ached, he closed his eyes. When his breathing was slowing back to normal, he drew the seatbelt over his right shoulder and snapped himself in and started the engine.

He growled to himself, "There is no way I'm letting that damn piece of dirt I own get to me."

Parker backed out of his driveway onto the street. First stop, Migilio's Pizza Joint.

The visions didn't return.

Parker picked up the pizza he'd ordered, along with two orders of garlic breadsticks. From there, he took the nearest exit and hit I-95 around 4 o'clock in the afternoon, getting to I-64 fifteen minutes later. In an hour he should be at Burkett.

Music blared from the car radio. Not as busy as summer, when people used I-64 to head for Virginia Beach, he noticed still quite a few vehicles on the highway. Although gray clouds had covered the skies a few minutes ago, the news on his car's radio promised no rain. The weatherman said no rain or snow at all that weekend and that there would be none until the following one. It would be freezing though— dropping to the 30s that night. He could handle that, just as long there was no precipitation.

A shiver passed through him, and he felt confused as if that meant it was due to thoughts of the cold weather or maybe something else. He turned up the heat in the car. Better to blame the shiver on the climate than on the paranormal.

Hitting the signal for the right, he took the 220 exit that led to West Point. Everything appeared ordinary. The occasional car passed him on the opposite side of the road. A semi chugged up ahead. He rolled through what was the business section of West Point and only gave a cursory glance at the factory where smoke rose to merge with the clouds. The wheels of his car hit the bridge, and he passed over the river, slipping back onto the road. After about a mile down the road, he made a right turn, and bypassed farms and streets that led into subdivisions and more country before he arrived at the cement road that led to his property.

Nothing but brush and trees lined each side, and unlike the dead-end street, this one became a broad, private dirt road with scattered gravel. The grit crunched beneath the wheels and dust rose like smoke behind his car's rear end, blinding him to what lay behind when he glanced in the rear-view mirror. It felt like a symbol; he was cut off from civilization and safety. Another shiver hit him, and he reached out to turn up the heat, pausing on the button.

You're not cold. Admit it. You're scared shitless.

His headlights lit up something at the end of the road. His foot jammed on the brake, and the car screeched to a halt, barely touching the gate. What looked like a large buck bounded away, turning to leap over the fence and head into woods, vanishing. With a shaking hand, he shut off the engine and sat back, taking deep breaths. Not so easy when it hit him how sweltering it felt inside the vehicle and those shivers that he kept having had nothing to do with the chill. He almost cried out when, like a hand, the fear clutched his heart and squeezed. The pain of his fear almost had him restart the car, turn around, and head back home.

Okay, calm down, Burkett, be logical. Nothing but a deer, a big buck. Funny thing,, first deer I've seen this close to my property. Especially as that animal had leaped over the fence and went into the woods on the land.

He mumbled to himself, "I'm not a coward."

He hit the lock on the driver's door, and it unlocked. After unbuckling his seat belt, he swung his booted feet to step out of the car. Two vehicles were parked on the inside of his property, while a truck was parked outside of the gate. The investigators' vehicles, obviously.

The gravel announced his presence as he walked up to the gate and unlocked it, throwing it open. Back in his car, he drove through, only to get out to shut the gate, before he climbed back in to continue.

One thing confused Parker and almost made him wonder, but he refused to go that route yet: it felt colder on the Burkett side of the gate than on the other side. That, and how quiet it seemed. Not even the gravel beneath his vehicle's wheels made a sound.

He parked next to a station wagon, shut off the engine, and got out.

CHAPTER TWENTY-ONE

Parker balanced the six boxes of freshly made, hot pizzas and a large box with two dozen breadsticks inside and carried them from his vehicle. He set them down on a plastic table near a campfire blazing in the center of the half-moon circle of the buildings. Both of his gloved hands stuffed in his jacket pockets, Parker headed back to his car to grab his tent and everything else. There was an empty tent already set up in a spot nearby. The one Ben promised him?

"Hi."

Parker turned and saw Neri.

She flashed him a smile. A dimple at one end of her rosebud mouth winked at him. At least it appeared to him that it did. "Ben said that is supposed to be your tent."

He grinned back, feeling good for the first time since coming back to Burkett. "Hi there."

Ben joined them. "Need any help? No dinner until everyone is done."

He unrolled his sleeping bag and shoved what else he'd brought inside before he sat down before the campfire with a paper plate loaded with three slices of pizza and a breadstick. Neri handed him a 16-ounce bottle of orange soda he asked for when she had told him what they had. She settled beside him with her pizza and a cup of instant hot cocoa.

No one said anything, just ate and drank. After Parker, Neri, and the others thrust their trash inside a trash bag, everyone huddled around the fire to be able to hear well and to draw the warmth from the flames as the temperature had dropped even more in the past hour.

Ben tossed a thin stick in the fire, and the flames flickered and snapped at it. "Now that we are all here and our bellies filled, let's talk about the first investigation tonight.

Silas spoke up. "Anyone else felt something was off about this place as soon as we arrived?" He looked at Parker. "Sorry, Mr. Burkett, but the creep factor about this property is a 10 to me."

Parker acknowledged, "Oh, I agreed."

Regan said, "Other than the temperature growing colder?"

Russell wrapped his arms around himself, even though he wore sweats, a thick coat, and a knit cap. "Damn, I could have stayed home and watched a good movie on TV in a warm apartment."

Kendra snickered. "And miss all this?"

Russell retorted, "Spirits don't feel the cold like the living do. Are we in Alaska instead of Virginia?"

Zack laughed and gave the other a slight smack on his arm. "So instead of ghosts, you're afraid of the cold?"

Russell glared at him. "Maybe you're hoping someone will share your tent tonight."

Maybe it was the trick of the firelight, but Neri thought she saw red creep up the back of Zack's neck. She looked at Kendra, but the woman was whispering something to Regan.

Ben said, "Enough." Then he went into stories about the spot and stories told by the few survivors of Nowhere Land over the years. Others told what they knew. Zack mentioned the tree rotting nearest to the buildings. He thought he might get a sample to take to a lab to test.

Ben said, "Maybe you ought to get a sample tomorrow and either contact someone from your landscaping company to come to get it or I can drive you to give it to them yourself. I think getting information about that rot as soon as possible might be good when we've collected everything we can by the end of this investigation."

Zach agreed. "Okay, Ben."

They talked next about what Neri and Regan had gotten, about the EVP, too. Even about the Indigenous spirit.

Neri thought Ben was being smart about getting that information of the sickly tree. She stood and wandered over to it, touched its bark with her fingertips. Something like a mild electric shock from it stung her fingers, and Neri drew back with a curse. An offensive odor drifted to her nostrils from the tree, and she backed away.

Foul. Not just rot as Zack thought, but worse. She wished she'd never touched the bark. Not looking back at the tree, she hustled back to her spot before the fire and snatched a napkin and scrubbed at her fingers over and over.

Ben noticed. "What's wrong?"

"I went to touch the tree..." She couldn't explain, but she knew she had to try. "It felt as if more than rot is in the bark of it. That the whole insides of that tree... Oh, I don't know what to call it, but it's the rot of wrongness. Filth."

Zack broke in. "Guess I don't need to get that test done."

She whirled on him. "I am not joking, Zack! Whatever's wrong with this place has infiltrated that tree. Maybe everything here."

He threw up his hands. "Sorry."

"You should be. Plus, you need to be wary." She cast her gaze at each person. "We all should be. Want my opinion?"

No one answered her, but she took it as an affirmative. "We should pack up while it is still light enough and get the hell away from here. While we still can. Or we might become as rotted as that tree." She wrapped her arms around herself as a chill struck her from the inside out. "Nothing good hangs around this place. Even the entity I talked to, Achak, has a sort of stain from whatever killed him, enough to make him stay here." She twisted her lips. She untwisted them enough to add, "Even survivors who escaped really didn't escape entirely from the stain of this place."

The cold feeling inside frosted all of her and she understood the reason. Something wanted to use her, use her as a medium for communication. Maybe worse than that. Maybe, it even wanted her soul. She fought it, as her vision grew dim, and she lost all cognitive awareness. The few spirits that had used her in the past allowed her to know what was going on. This time proved different, and she gasped, tried to get to her feet, but she fell into the encroaching darkness.

***

Parker and Ben jumped to their feet and ran over to Neri; Parker reached her first.

He shook her shoulder. "Neri." When she didn't answer him, he grabbed her by both of her shoulders and shook harder. "Neri!"

She opened her eyes, and he flinched. No longer green, instead, they'd become pools of whirling shadows. Even her face had changed, the skin tautened, thin skin over bone and gray as pale ash. Ben dropped into a crouch beside Parker and her. He'd grabbed a ghost box and his recorder from a hard case near him and switched them on.

Ben demanded, "Who are you?"

Whatever had a hold of her, cocked her head and a dark grin formed on her lips.

Parker flinched. It reminded him of a death head grin he seen as a child on a Halloween mask at a costume shop. That mask had scared him enough to bolt from the place. When his mother forced him to go back to the shop to face up to his fear, the mask no longer hung on the wall. Someone had bought it. He'd refused to go trick-or-treating that Halloween or even answer the door to hand out candy, afraid he would see that mask on someone's face.

By the next Halloween, he'd convinced himself he'd imagined what was surely a stupid mask, that it was evil and went trick-or-treating. He never saw anyone wearing that mask that night or again. Until today.

A voice came out of the ghost box. "Souls. Need souls. You all look like candidates. Maybe it'd finally be enough this time." The voice sounded male and held an edge of cruelty in its lilt. It snickered. "Parker, did you like my version of that Halloween mask you encountered as a child?"

Parker fell back, his heart pounding. *How did the being know about the mask?*

Ben hooked a hand on Neri's arm and said, "Enough for what? Tell us who you are!"

The puppeteer jerked Neri's arm out of his grasp and shook a finger at him like he was a naughty boy as the same voice taunted him. "No, not going to tell you. You did not say the magic words."

Parker asked, "What, please and thank you?"

It mocked. "Really? No, not those words. But I figure you know the words I mean. Now, I have to go."

It lowered Neri's chin to her chest and closed her eyes. Next moment, Neri awoke with a gasp. She had her normal green eyes once more.

"Oh God, Oh God. My head." She grabbed her head and winced. "What happened?"

"Something took hold of you and wanted to play games with us," said Ben.

She flashed him an irritated look. "Tell me what it said."

Parker said, "It said souls at first, and that we looked like candidates, maybe enough for this time. It wouldn't tell us who it was. Or what it was. That we did not say the magic words."

She nodded. "I'm pretty sure it didn't mean please or thank you." She shook her head. "I can't think what it meant, but perhaps later it'll come to me. Can someone get me a painkiller? I have a bottle of them in my first aid kit in my tent."

Ben jogged over to her tent to grab her a couple of pills. Kendra handed her a bottle of water, and when Ben came back with the tablets, she took them with a shaking hand, tossed them in her mouth, and chased them down with water from the bottle.

Parker sat with her while the others got up and went to the trailer where Ben uploaded what he'd recorded to his laptop,

CHAPTER TWENTY-TWO

Neri stared into the fire as Regan added more wood, toasting marshmallows at the young woman's suggestion. The young woman had brought out two bags of marshmallows and gave each person a stick to use to toast the sweet confections. Only Neri and Parker ended up doing it. Everyone else began planning the investigation for that night.

Toasting the marshmallow made her feel like they were on a camping trip. Except, the marshmallows reminded her of ghosts. Just like the spirit that communicated earlier this afternoon and whatever took her over after dinner. Since the first one was the only ghost on the land, she did not doubt that whatever used her might never have been human, which Achak had been. She never told the others about how she felt slimy after its possession, wrong.

Neri took a fork and scraped the melted, sticky substance off the stick, and ate it.

Not too bad. Maybe Regan had it right. Make everyone forget that they were on cursed land, that they were only camping. Try to anyway.

The memories of the Powhatan ghost, her possession, and the marshmallow began to upset her stomach. No, not the marshmallow. Not the spirits, either. The dark entity.

The one who wanted souls. Could it be demonic? It could be a demon. And yet, her psychic Geiger counter insisted not.

She licked the stickiness off her fingers, and unable to toast marshmallows or eat any more, she set the stick aside and stood to head to her tent. She told Parker and Regan, "I'm going to my tent and lay down for a bit."

A half-hour nap might be the ticket. Neri needed some rest if she wanted to make it through tonight. If nothing else, she might rid herself of the pounding in her head and recharge her psychic powers.

Snuggled in her sleeping bag, she drifted off to sleep, something she thought wouldn't even happen. It didn't seem long before Kendra woke her up. The headache no longer plagued her, but she still felt tired.

It didn't matter.

Neri grabbed her flashlight and turned it on. Her bag of equipment slung over her right shoulder; she followed the petite girl to the trailer. A glance at the night sky revealed stars and a full moon. They said that the full moon made paranormal activity worse. She hoped not bad enough to have them all disappear like the last paranormal team.

Taking a deep breath, she followed Kendra inside the trailer.

CHAPTER TWENTY-THREE

Regan snapped pictures with the camera while she wandered around the room, while Silas asked questions. Her recorder lay beside his own and his Mel meter. He had set up a battery-operated LED candle and placed it on the floor beside the equipment, so he didn't have to use his flashlight to read the meter. She glanced down occasionally to check the lights on the KII meter she held, too.

The first light was the only thing lit up. The others remained off.

Silas thought his Mel was better than hers. He said it measured EMF, along with ambient temperature. It gave off sound besides the lights when tripped. It had made the noise just before they entered this building, not its usual squeal, but a more muted version. It had remained silent since.

Fingers of uneasiness tickled up Regan's spine; for her, that seemed too quiet.

Being close to winter, especially at night, one wouldn't hear birds or insects. Maybe owls, but now she thought about it, but she hadn't heard or seen any owl since they arrived on the property. Even her footsteps didn't make noise on the wooden floor. She couldn't blame cold weather on that.

Regan peeked out the doorway. Nothing. Only pitch blackness. Taking care, she stepped outside, flashing the light from her small LED flashlight around her. It barely broke through the darkness. She snapped a few pictures with the camera, its night vision on.

"Silas, it's dead out here," she called out.

No answer from him. He must be so deep into asking his questions that he hadn't heard.

Regan spoke louder this time.

"Silas, I said—"

That's when she lost her voice.

WTF?

She tried to speak again. Her voice barely rasped. It hurt, too. Like a sore throat.

Regan hoped that didn't mean she might be coming down with something. She'd had her checkup and had even gotten her flu and Covid shots back in October. The doctor assured her she'd passed the checkup with flying colors.

She stepped back inside. The LED candle no longer shined, and she didn't hear anything from Silas.

Freaking weird.

Worse, she couldn't call out to him. When she tried, her voice came out no more than a tiny squeak. She aimed her flashlight where she felt sure he had stood— by the equipment—when the light died.

Well, shit. Things couldn't get worse, could they?

The temperature began to drop. Goosebumps popped up along any of her bared skin. Buttoning up the jacket she wore, Regan felt along the walls as she took her time going around the room to where Silas might be. The cold penetrated through the thick material of her jacket, and she shivered. The woman wished she'd had the foresight to bring her gloves from her tent.

When Regan arrived at the spot where she believed she'd last seen Silas, her hands waved through empty air. She slid down to a crouch and felt along the floor, but her fingers didn't touch any of the recorders and Silas's Mel meter. Shaking, she rose to her feet.

Shit, shit, shit.

Where could he be? Along with the damn equipment? Had he sneaked out on her?

Dummy, you came back in through the only way he could have. You hadn't stepped far from the door even.

A breeze blew into her ear.

Her heart raced and she almost bit her tongue trying not to let out a gasp. There had been no breeze at all tonight. What just blew into her ear? She'd wished she had brought her phone or at least one of the radios Ben always had. He told both her and Silas to grab a radio, but no, they felt the shack was not that far away. F'ing idiots!

"Regan." Soft, the voice was low as it whispered her name.

She thought maybe it might be Silas playing a trick on her. A slow burn twisted in her gut, and she wanted to snap at him, tell him to cut it out, but with her voice gone, she couldn't. Her anger cooled as it came to her; she'd been on ghost hunts before with him, and Silas had always been serious, never acted like a trickster.

Who just whispered in her ear? God, where was Silas?

Fingers touched hers, though these felt freezer cold. Standing still, her breathing rattling in her chest and her heartbeat loud in her ears, she fought not to move, not to let it realize her fear. That bothered her, as she had never been scared on investigations before. First, with what happened earlier during the daytime, and now this.

"Regan." The voice curled into her ear. "Let me take your picture."

She didn't react.

"Regan."

She closed her eyes.

"Regan." The voice blew at wisps of her hair, tickling the back of her neck.

She thought, *Please, go away. Bring Silas back.*

The disembodied fingers squeezed her. Gentle at first, but the squeezing grew painful as they began to grip deep. Agonizing. She struggled to get free, but it wouldn't release her.

As sudden as they held her, the invisible fingers vanished. Not for long, as something grabbed her by her legs and with a hard yank, she hit the floor on her left side. Sharp pain agonized through the wrenched hip.

She found her voice was free, and she screamed and screamed, fighting, jerking like a fish on a hook. Whatever it was, it grabbed the other ankle and dragged her deeper into the shadows. Somewhere in the woods, the camera's strap was ripped from off her neck and flung away.

Regan's shrieks grew more frantic.

Until her screams cut off mid-scream.

∗

Silas jarred awake, as someone's screaming filled his hearing. He climbed to his feet and stared blurrily into the darkened room. It took his brain a second to understand, but it hit him that his LED candle no longer lit up the place. He dug his flashlight from his pocket and turned it on. His light swept over where he had been. The recorders lay there, his Mel meter too, but he didn't see the candle.

What? He rubbed at the side of his head. It hurt like hell. Had he fallen asleep? Maybe he'd hit his head on the floor or against the wall? Except that couldn't be possible. He slipped his cell phone from his flannel shirt pocket and saw the time: Midnight.

His breath hitched. He and Regan had begun at 10 p.m. Had he lost two hours, dropped off to sleep? In the middle of an investigation? *Where's Regan?*

"Regan?" Shocked, he realized for the first time tonight his voice boomed in the room. This place had an oddity about sound—something paranormal, though what, he couldn't figure.

Regan didn't reply to reassure him.

He called again. "Regan."

Silence. He followed the beam of light from his flashlight trailing along the floor to the closed door.

Wait a moment; he swore that it had been opened earlier when he and Regan began their investigation. *God.* Cold sweat slicked his skin, and he grew sick. The door creaked loud in the stillness as it opened.

Heart punching against his chest and his stomach cramping, he stumbled back. All his life, he wanted proof of ghosts and life beyond death, and here he stood, acting like a chicken shit.

Where's Regan? Why isn't she answering?

He gritted his teeth as resolution filled him. He went back to grab his meter and recorder, leaving Regan's recorder to keep recording. Then he walked outside.

The full moon hovered in the sky, its face peeking between the trees at the buildings. At him. No one else appeared to be outdoors. He saw a light through the window of another shack at the other end of the village. That must be Ben, Neri, and Parker Burkett. Russell and Keri were back at the trailer, watching the cameras onscreen. That reassured Silas. Somewhat.

Maybe he should get Ben and the others to help him find Regan. Yes, it sounded idiotic, as no doubt something had tricked her to leave the building. Or most likely, she went to use the bathroom in the trailer. She'd probably said something about it, but he hadn't heard her. Or maybe that was when he dozed off? He'd track her and get her back inside.

"Regan." His voice barely crawled above a whisper. He wondered what caused that and wished he had looked up reasons on the Internet before doing this week-long hunt. He didn't believe the paranormal was behind this phenomenon. It had to be something natural.

"Regan. Aw, quit playing around and answer me."

Nothing.

Silas's flashlight lit up buildings, trees, tents, and two vehicles, but no Regan. Growing worried, he picked his way through the dark and kept calling her name. He ended up back inside the shack.

What? How did he get back inside here? Had he never left the place, except in his mind? Had he awakened from a nightmare?

No Regan in the place with him. He still had his meter and recorder, and hers lay where he'd left it. He tucked his recorder in his jeans pocket, and just as he was going to do the same for the meter, its alarm went off. It became super-hot, and he cursed and dropped it. It hit the floor, its plastic face breaking. The noise stopped. He picked it up, tested it, but found it no longer worked. Had he imagined it had grown hot as it now felt cold as ice?

Laughter filled the room.

"Who are you?" demanded Silas, waving his meter around.

The dead meter squealed, and with a scream, he dropped it. It hit the floor, still shrieking. "That can't be, it doesn't work! It broke!" He yelled, though his voice barely rose above a hoarse whisper. "Who are you? Where's Regan?"

The meter went silent.

"Play a game with me." The deep voice came as an insidious whisper.

"No games. Where's Regan?"

"Here. There. Everywhere. Figure it out."

Silas tried to be patient. "Is everywhere in here?"

"Inside. Outside. Phantasmagoric."

"Great. Ha, ha." He crossed his arms. "I am tired of these games. Bring me, Regan."

The room appeared to move around and around like a merry-go-round. Cackling filled the air. "Around and around we go." His stomach grew upset and his head spun. Silas staggered to the doorway. A moaning packed the room. When his hand grasped the edge of the door frame, the door slammed shut on it.

Who's screaming? Damn, that's loud.

Then he understood it was him. Pain riveted through him, and he fought to open the door, but it remained fastened. The problem was, he couldn't find any doorknob on this door, meaning it shouldn't be able to be locked. It felt as if something held it barred from outside.

God, Regan vanishing, his hand, and now this. The fucking—

As if to escape the agony, his mind blacked out.

***

"Silas, wake up. Please, wake up. I don't want to go outside to get Ben. Please."

He opened his eyes. His eyes watered, and he saw someone standing over him through the blurry tears burning his eyeballs.

"Regan? His voice broadcasted raspy as if with disuse.

"Oh, thank God, Silas, you're all right."

"How's my hand?"

"What do you mean? Both of your hands look fine to me."

"I mean, my right hand got caught between the door and the door jam."

He blinked away the tears and saw her brows lowered as lines filled her forehead. She said, "No, you never left your spot here. I went outside and had gotten lost for a while—in the woods, for goodness sakes. Stumbled, fell a couple of times, and branches caught in my hair. It became downright frightening. I found my way back here and found you asleep. I tried shaking you, but damn, you wouldn't wake up, so I checked your pulse. You didn't have one! Then your eyes opened. Or maybe you came back from the dead. I don't know."

Silas rolled over and worked to stand on wobbly feet. "I never fell asleep. Honest. I thought you went missing and something...something began to play with me. My meter." He looked down at the floor but didn't see it. His recorder lay next to Regan's, though he swore he'd stuck it in his pocket, but nowhere did he see the meter. Something jiggled in his shirt pocket, and he thrust his hand in it. The former smashed hand. He drew out his meter, its face cracked. He held it out to Regan, feeling his blood drain from his face.

"It couldn't have been a dream. My meter fractured for real."

Regan touched it, then jerked her hand back as if it burned her. "It's cold."

She and Silas stared at each other in helpless bewilderment, along with each other's growing fear.

Silas said, "How can it manipulate reality with nightmares?"

"I don't know. Maybe it broke your meter when you slept. Let's get out of here and join Ben and the others."

He nodded and gathered up their recorders. He shut hers off and just before he did his own, a laughing voice rose from it.

"Play a game?"

Although his hand shook, he managed to shut it off. They bolted from the shack, not looking back to see if the door closed behind them when they heard a loud creak.

Silas saw the fire had died out, but lights were on in the trailer. He stopped and turned to Regan. She wasn't there.

Oh God, oh God. Where is she? Although scared, he traced back, calling her name. "Regan!"

"Silas?"

She stumbled out of the woods and almost fell into his arms. Sticks tangled in her hair, and with his flashlight, he saw bruises and bleeding scratches on her face, her jacket torn, and dirt on her clothing, hair, and skin.

Silas shook his head in denial. "You were perfectly fine when we ran from the building. What the hell happened?"

She blinked back tears. "You and the recorders and your Mel meter had vanished, and something got hold of me when I ran outside, dragged me into the woods to hurt me and left me there alone. It even took the camera, tossed it away."

He frowned. "I was still in the building."

She narrowed her eyes. "Maybe you're not Silas. Maybe you're that thing out to hurt me again."

He shook his head. "No, it's truly me, Silas." He put his arms around her. "You're right though, something did this to you, and the same thing did something to me. It even pretended to be you until I got close to the trailer, then the false you vanished."

She sagged against him, and he urged her to let him lead her to her tent. "Let's get you cleaned up. I want to get out of the dark and to where there's warmth and light."

"Yes, Silas." It wasn't Regan's voice, but some deep masculine one. It began laughing.

Silas realized he didn't hold Regan at all. Although dark, he could see the tall shadow that rose over her, darker than the night. He yelled and bolted, making for the trailer.

Dark laughter followed him.

CHAPTER TWENTY-FOUR

en sat on a chair at the other end of the shack, watching Neri and Parker laughing over the man's mishap at slipping the laser grid holder over her laser grid to keep it open and focused. When she did it, and the green lights covered Ben's body as much as the rest of the room they all were in, he tightened his gaze when Parker laid his hand over Neri's.

Ben thought, *Okay, admit it, you're jealous.* There was no John in her life. He'd hoped that she would see him for the one man in her life worth knowing. It hadn't happened.

Say it, Neilson, Parker Burkett happened instead.

Maybe he and Neri weren't meant to get together, other than as friends. Then again, he should tell her his feelings. When she knew the truth, she might give him a chance. After all, it wasn't as if she and Parker had become an exclusive couple in the short time since they met. Right?

Ben looked over his equipment on the camping table he set up by his chair, noticed that everything seemed fine, and got up to wander over to Neri and Parker.

Both grew silent as he drew near. He grinned.

"What? Am I stopping you from your conversation?"

Neri said, "No. Honestly, I don't know why I went quiet." Her eyes flashed uneasiness as they traveled along the walls, floor, and up at the rafters, pausing at the loft. The same area Parker had discovered John's finger.

Her gaze met Ben's. She licked her lips. "It's not you. It's this place. Nowhere Land—I mean Burkett—has been fooling with my inner psychic alarm since I stepped on the path to it."

Parker stuck his hands in his pants pockets. "And I'll be honest, I don't know why I shut up."

Ben frowned. "Yes, you do."

Parker kept his gaze on the floor as he negatively shook his head. "Sorry, I don't."

Heat boiled in Ben as he fisted his hands by his hips. "Don't give me that crap, Burkett. It's because you have been laughing with Neri. You aren't taking this investigation seriously, just as I bet you didn't when John Peters and VGT investigated. They all vanished, except for one finger of John's found in this very building. Did you take them seriously then?"

"Ben!" protested Neri.

Ben flinched, knowing that was low to mention John and his team, but damn.

Parker withdrew his hands from the pockets and stared straight at Ben. "I admit at first, I didn't think the problems with this property had anything to do with ghosts or crap like that and even after the weird stuff concerning the disappearances of people that the police still can't locate. I'm still not sure what happened has anything to do with the paranormal. But I did let you come here for the week to try and change my mind."

Ben swept his gaze from Parker to Neri. "It's not due to me, my team, or anything," he sneered, "paranormal, but most likely because of Neri."

"Exactly what are you insinuating, Neilson?"

Neri stepped in front of Parker as she looked at Ben. "Ben—"

Ben's lips thinned. "What? That I might have feelings for you, Neri? No, not good old buddy Ben. Ben makes a perfect big brother, nothing for romantic entanglements. Honestly, I am pretty sure you always suspected. You ignored it. Until we got here."

Neri's face whitened. Most people would think she was upset, but Ben knew this only meant that anger burned inside her. Except he was so out of it, angry himself, that he ignored the tell-tale sign.

She marched up to him and stopped, began to poke his chest each time she said a word. "Look here, Mr. Ben-says-Neri-only-thinks-I'm-big-brother-material Neilson, I never gave you any reason to think I had any romantic thoughts about you. To me, you were the best friend and yes, big brother, I never had, the person I could talk to, and who liked many of the same things I liked, like the paranormal. If you didn't get the message that we couldn't be anything more than we are, then I'm sorry. And I can laugh with any guy I want to."

Both stood toe-to-toe, breathing deep, one red-faced from anger, the other whose skin had gone so pale, it could be mistaken for porcelain if one didn't know the truth.

Parker got between them, and each backed up a few inches.

"What's going on here?" he asked. "I mean, is this you two, or something else?"

Neri's face lost the pallor. "Ben..."

Still red-faced and eyes flashing daggers, he bit out, "Is lover boy worried that your paranormal partner might hit you?"

"No, Ben, he's right, this is not me, and this is not you."

"Sure, it isn't..." His voice held sarcasm.

She reached around Parker and lay a hand on Ben's shoulder. "I'm sorry. I never realized you felt something for me, or maybe I did but turned a blind eye to it, but this isn't me getting this angry. Something else is pushing my buttons, and I know it did the same to you."

Ben didn't answer, but his breathing lessened. She pressed again, and after nodding at Parker who then moved aside to let her pass him so that she got closer to Ben. "Yes, you might feel hurt and maybe even anger, but I think you wouldn't use that now to bring it all out in the open. Now is not a good time for airing grievances and things. Be honest, can't you feel it? The air inside this room is growing dense as pea soup fog. Something wants us to fight. Something else is causing this."

The red faded until only Ben's normal flesh tone remained. He heard her words and let his mind open to what she said was happening. His labored breathing slowed. The room felt as if a thousand-people crowded it, not only the three of them. Feeling feverishly hot despite the cold, he began to feel sick and fought the urge to throw up.

She nodded. "Yes, I feel sick too."

They turned to Parker, who shrugged. "My stomach has been churning like butter for the last few minutes."

The sensation in the room thickened, like a thunderstorm about to unleash, and all three grew green at the gills. A horrible odor filled the room.

The door flew open, hitting the wall. The bang it made not more than a whimper instead of a resounding punch to the wood.

Silas ran in.

"Oh God, it feels and smells horrible in here."

Ben asked, "What are you doing here? And where is Regan?"

"I am not going back to that other building, at least, not tonight. It's just as bad here, so you know what, I'm going to the trailer. Who's with me?" Silas looked at each of them, one at a time.

Ben asked again. "Where's Regan?"

"I think that thing took her. The tall shadow."

Parker said, "What?"

Silas drew a shaky breath. "Regan goes outside, gets lost, I fall asleep for no reason, wake up, and my hand gets smashed by the door. It's all a nightmare. Plus, some creepy voice keeps asking me to play a game. I think it belongs to the tall, thin shadow that appeared to me. Pretty sure it took Regan."

Ben's radio beeped, and Zack's voice came over it. "Hey, Kendra and I see mist all over the room in your building, Ben. You guys hardly show on the cameras."

Neri walked away from the others, her hands crisscrossing to rub at her arms. "I can see it all. Hear it." She paused below the loft and looked up. "The voices are strongest up there."

Ben joined her. "But you said that Native American spirit was the only ghost here."

Her forehead furrowed. "That's what is bugging me. If I keep hearing voices and there is only one spirit stuck here, who do those other voices belong to?"

Ben stared with narrowed eyes at her. "Demons?"

"Maybe," her eyes met his, "and yet, maybe not?" She rubbed her arms more and her breath came out of her mouth as icy clouds. "This place confuses me. It throws my senses off balance."

"At least so far, it hasn't made any of us disappear, except Regan, if Silas is telling the truth." Ben grimaced. He crossed the room to pick up his recorder. He checked the camcorder on its tripod, then the camera that he had set to snap a shot every two minutes. He took out the disk from the camera.

"This disk claims it's full. Which is impossible as the disk is a new empty one I bought two days ago. It's a big enough file to hold up to a hundred photos." He turned to Silas. "Help me take this equipment down, and we'll head to the trailer."

Silas asked, "What about the building I was in?"

When Ben looked at him, he said, "Just letting you know you couldn't pay me to back inside it."

"You took pictures with your camera, right?" asked Ben.

"Regan did, but I never saw her camera in the shack or outside."

Another voice spoke, sounding like Regan. "I lost my camera in the woods when something yanked me away. And I think it killed me, Ben. If you saw what I looked like, you'd understand."

"Oh, fuck. Are you real? Are you okay?" Silas' whisper came out strangled.

Ben turned to look at what sounded like Regan and saw her. She looked fine to him. He opened his mouth to chew her out about losing it, but her frightened face and what was still happening in the room told him to keep quiet.

He laid a hand on her shoulder. It felt solidly like a living person's shoulder. Regan lifted her gaze to meet his, and he said, "We'll search for the camera when it's daylight. But we will stop by the other building on the way to see if the equipment is all right." He eyeballed the full-spectrum, night-vision video camera by the door. They were put there to cover the whole room and it was high enough to get the loft, too. Not the whole loft, but the front of it. It looked fine. "Let's go."

The five of them walked outside. As the last person to leave, when Ben walked out, the doors slammed shut. His lips twisted in a crooked grin that did not meet in his eyes, he said, "Guess that was this place's version of 'don't let the door hit you on the way out'."

Regan mumbled, "If I had my way, I wouldn't mind if it hit me on my way out of this land of insanity."

She shut up when Ben glowered at her.

Zack's voice crackled over Ben's radio. "The picture from the camera we set up in Regan's and Silas's shack just went out."

Ben replied, "Thanks, Zack. We'll stop there on our way back to the trailer."

When they arrived at the cabin, Ben opened the door, and they all peered inside. No feeling of oppression jammed the room. The cold air inside was nothing more than the 20-degree weather. But the full-spectrum night-vision camera lay on the floor, broken in two pieces. One piece by the door, the other at the far end of the room.

Silas leaned over to snatch up the piece by the door. But Ben decided to be the one to cross to the other side of the room to get the other one. He knew neither Regan nor Silas would feel comfortable enough to do it, and after his freakiness back in the other building, he wouldn't push Neri or Parker to do it.

He made it across the room without any incident. Paranormal or otherwise.

"The night is young, Neilson," he muttered under his breath, bending to pick up the camera piece.

Not taking any chances, he hastened to join the others at the door. Cold air touched like fingers along the back of his neck, causing the hair there to rise.

"Like to play a game?" curled a whisper into his ear.

He broke into a trot and caught up to the others. They all darted out the door.

The voice broke into a roar. "You won't play with me?" The door slammed shut, almost catching Ben by his buttocks, and a crack ran down the wood from top to bottom.

Regan giggled. "Don't let the door smack you in the ass."

Ben snarled. "That's not funny."

Tears welled up in her eyes. "I'm sorry. I don't know why I even said that. That's stupid of me." Tears rolled down her cheeks. "I want to go home."

"Well, you can't," said Ben. "Look, Regan, what did you expect from paranormal investigating?"

Regan sniffed. "The occasional EVP, a sight of a shadow person, something in a photograph, heck, even communication by lights on the EMF meter.

Simple, plain old ghost stuff. Not this drop-me-in-the middle-of-hell-where-things-are-out-to-get-you crap."

Ben sighed. "Anyway, it's still dark, and we all agreed to make it through the week." He nodded at Parker. "Excepting for Mr. Burkett here. He can leave in the morning, if he likes. After daytime arrives, how about I let Silas run you to the store to get more supplies. Maybe a trip away from here will make you feel better."

Silas grumbled. "You know, Ben, I hadn't seen anything on the cameras tonight I couldn't prove isn't real."

Ben shook his head. "Well, you're entitled to your opinion, but let's wait until we complete the investigation, and we go over all evidence, Silas. All right?"

Regan wiped her tears away and stopped crying. She narrowed her eyes when Neri walked over and whispered something in his ear. When the other woman went to join Parker, she said, "You're right, Ben. I want to stay. Not letting some ghost scare me off."

They reached the trailer and Ben flashed her a smile that made her feel good inside before he walked away to talk to a waiting Russell.

Regan whipped around to Silas, chewing him out. "Really? Telling Ben to his face that what happened in that building was fake?"

"Well, someone had to set him straight. I mean, I like to believe it was real, but what happened can be done by any living person. Having that psychic here proves what side of paranormal investigating he's on."

Regan crossed her arms and tattooed a foot against the dirt. "The EVPs. Are you saying one of us was off somewhere and used a mike or something? We all were there."

"That Parker dude could have arranged someone offsite, got things set up before we all arrived." Silas grew sullen.

"What about that Indian spirit earlier today? And whatever that was tonight?"

"That medium, Neri, is in on it. She's probably a good ventriloquist—threw her voice or something. And projectors can show movies. There are those special-effects DVDs sold by haunt companies around Halloween time. Halloween was last month, you know."

Regan threw up her hands. "Oh, Silas. Yes, I agree, not everything happens to be paranormal, and we are glad to have you on the team as the skeptic we need to keep us on the straight and narrow. But...oh, I don't know. I may not trust Neri on a lot of things, but when she's investigating, I admit she has never done anything wrong."

Silas blew air out of his nostrils. "You know what? You guys don't need me for this investigation. Glad I rode my motorcycle here. Let me pack up tomorrow morning and leave. I'll stove my tent with you and pick it up when you guys are all done and back home. I'm missing Jason anyway. We just got married last month."

Ben came back to them. "What's going on here?"

Regan said, "Silas wants to leave."

Silas said, "Tomorrow morning."

Ben stared at the other man. He let loose a sigh. "You sure? We just started this hunt."

"I'm sure." Silas thought to impart what he believed about the truth behind all the activity tonight, but he decided not to. Ben would never believe ill of Neri, and as for Parker, the man let him investigate. "Look, I've been doing soul searching on doing investigations lately, as being a skeptic, nothing has happened on any investigations we've done that's changed my mind about the paranormal, so I think it's time I quit the team and do other things. Like, focus more on my college classes in biology and on my marriage."

Ben agreed. "We'll miss you on the team, but I understand. If you change your mind..."

"I won't. I'm heading to bed now. Goodnight, see you in the morning."

"'Night," said Regan.

Ben said, "Good night, Silas."

Silas left them and headed for his tent. Closest to the woods than the others, he'd set it up there as it seemed a good choice at the time. He paused at the entrance.

Had he heard a noise from the woods nearby?

He walked over to the tree line, but he couldn't see anything due to the darkness of the night. There was no sound, either. The silence began to bother him. Worse, he swore the cold night touched him with its frozen fingers, and even with his jacket, knitted hat, and gloves; it felt as if they couldn't keep him warm. His sleeping bag and zipped-up tent lured him back and he crawled inside.

Except he didn't feel warm inside, either.

Silas slipped off his boots and decided to leave his jacket on, zippered, plus his hat and gloves, and he wiggled into his sleeping bag. Just when he thought he might never get to sleep due to the cold, he dropped off and right into a dream. An erotic fantasy with Tom, a guy from his biology class in college. They were in Tom's dorm room. It shocked his dream self, as he never felt attracted to the other man in real life, and he'd been in Tom's dorm room countless times, and nothing ever happened. Besides, Tom had a boyfriend, and he had Jason! Jason whom he'd only been married to for a month. It didn't seem to matter in the dream, something about Tom drew him.

It felt real, too. Rose petals in a path from the doorway to the bed, the silky coolness of the red satin sheets on the bed, and the dimmed light. Even Tom's naked skin felt like silk against his own. Seductive. Sultry. Just like his dream self, Silas hardened to sweet agony.

The dream faded out to whiteness, with only himself alone in it. In the real world, he shuddered in his sleep and tossed and turned in his sleeping bag.

In the dream, he walked and found that the white ground appeared stable enough.

He called out, "Tom!"

No answer. No Tom. Nothing. Just the damnable washed-out like bleach everywhere. Hands becoming fists, he kept them at his sides, and his nostrils flared, anger ready to erupt from him like molten lava. For some reason, his erotic dream with Tom ended, and he'd been left in this nowhere land, and he'd like to know what the fuck was going on.

Nowhere land. Like where—

The anger drained, replaced by icy tentacles of fear. Silas bit his lip and stood still, uncertain where he should go.

Wait. It's a dream, and he would wake up. Escape this. Instead, the fear took hold of his heart, squeezing with a gentle, invisible hand. It didn't last though, the squeezing morphing into crushing.

God, it hurt. Hurt like hell.

He dropped to his knees, as if heavy hands hammered his shoulders, forcing him down. The ground must be cement, and not dirt; he felt his knees crack and he screamed, although no sound came out. The constriction on his heart grew more agonizing, and he worried it would explode like a tomato losing its pulp.

"Does that hurt, Silas Jennings? Is that real? Or is it as unreal as a nightmare? Like you called me fake?"

He raised his head and considered the face above him. If evil could be something, then that face provided the sculpture of the Devil made flesh.

Humor lit up its dark eyes. "Oh, I am not the Devil, or what you think is the fallen angel. Though many have assumed that is what I am. Just as where I am from might be considered Hell to the souls of this world. That world is where I plan to take you."

"No. I don't want to go anywhere with you. Just let me wake up from this nightmare." Silas nodded. "Yes, that's what this is. Nothing more than the pizza I ate tonight, the investigation, and being tired of doing all this crap when I really hadn't found anything to make me believe the paranormal is real. That's it. You're badly digested pepperoni."

"Ah, you think you're Scrooge, and I'm Marley."

Silas blinked, frowning. "No...yeah, that does sound like something from *A Christmas Carol*. So—"

It finished for him. "—hackneyed?" It snickered.

The squashing of his heart had not dissipated, nor had the heaviness stopped pressing down on his shoulders. Worse, now his lungs seem to be expelling air like a deflated balloon and breathing grew difficult. He struggled, but he couldn't move.

Oh God, I'm dying. Dying in his dream.

The tall thing drew closer and whispered, "Yes, you are." It sent a gray elongated, thin part of itself inside his chest. If Silas believed his lungs and heart had endured torture up to that moment, it paled in comparison to the suffering he was experiencing now.

He managed to get the words out. "Where's the pain coming from?"

The voice roughened. "Your soul. I'm yanking it from your mortal body."

The distress degenerated. Silas finally woke up. Not in his sleeping bag in his tent but lying in the woods and staring straight up at the canopy of trees above.

Cold, it feels so cold, like the cold of the grave.

A growl vibrated against his ear. He couldn't move, though he wanted to. Silas got his wish granted, just not in the way he wanted, as sharp things sunk into his flesh. He barely had time to cry out from pain as he rose up, up, up, into the night air. Something flipped him around, and he saw a body on the ground. His body!

After that, his soul could see nothing, except the tops of trees that filled his vision. As he looked aside, he saw the darkness in the air like a harbinger. Agony tore at the ectoplasm of his soul, as whatever held him tossed him through the gloom like garbage, and he fell through a slit in the air, zippered shut after him.

CHAPTER TWENTY-FIVE

Regan twisted and turned in her sleeping bag. She needed to go to the bathroom, but the air inside her tent felt cold. Couldn't she get through what remained of the night without using the toilet in the trailer? The joys of camping in cold weather.

She gave up and slipped out of the bag, jerking on her hiking boots over her thick socks. She snatched her coat and shrugged it on, settled her dark blue knitted cap over her head and pulled thick gloves on, then grabbed her phone before darting outside. She trotted to the trailer, found the door unlocked, and entered. Amidst the undertone of electronics working, she walked into the small closet that held the toilet.

Minutes later, she left it, and just as she reached the door to go back to her tent, she heard an unusual sound coming from the monitor behind her. Regan turned and saw nothing out of the ordinary on its screen at first. Five cameras had been left running until morning to film while the investigators slept. Four held nothing, not even orbs. The fifth one, though, which had been set up to film all the tents and trailer, had a tall shadow in it.

"Oh God, oh God," moaned Regan, "It's heading for the trailer." *And I'm inside the trailer.*

Her heart slamming against her chest and her breath coming in short spurts, she bolted for the door. Her fingers fumbling, she tried locking it. After several mishaps, she got it locked and waited with a quiet hitch of her breathing, a throbbing in her temple.

Idiot. If it is a spirit, they can pass through walls.

"Regan." Dark, oily, whoever, whatever it could be, whispered her name from the other side of the door.

Shaking, she took a couple of steps back. *Dear God, it knew her!*

Spying a butter knife lying on a plate on a table, she fisted her hand around it, ready to stab.

Like you can slash at something that's not real flesh. The thought pushed its way into her brain, not unlike the dark, oily whisper on the other side of the door.

The door heaved inside, out, in, and out, like the heavy breathing of some great beast. Regan screamed in her head. A sharp crack hit the air, and the door swung open as if she'd never locked it. She fell on her rear when she tried to scramble away. Something jabbed into her skin there, sharp and painful. She struggled to get to her feet. The knife still gripped in her hand; she raised it.

"Come on, show yourself!" she called out. "Afraid?"

"No, but you should be...Regan."

This time the voice came from behind her. Stomach churning, fear squeezing her heart, her mouth dry, she whirled around, holding the knife before her. Like that would do any good.

She saw no one. The monitor had gone black though, and a mist rose from it, filling the air and changing from white to coal black. Two yellow eyes hung in the middle of all that darkness.

"Run, little sheep!" The voice boomed, shaking the trailer. "Run as if the big bad wolf is pursuing you." A giggle escaped it. "Which it will be."

Her voice captive inside her throat, Regan threw the butter knife at it, and it passed through, hitting a window. She turned and sprinted out into the night, slipping her flashlight out of a coat pocket and switching it on.

Not even thinking to stop and wake the others in the tents, not even to duck inside her own tent, fear made Regan bolted past it all and toward the trees. It was stupid, but still, she ran. She had darted onto the path when she tripped over something that lay across it and hit leaves, dirt, and rock. Her flashlight flew out of her hand. Pain exploded everywhere.

She crawled to her knees, flinched at the pain, and instead, lowered herself back onto her stomach and rolled onto her back. Bracing herself with her hands, she managed to sit up. She grabbed a thin, young tree nearby and hoisted herself to her feet. Her left ankle wouldn't hold up. So, she kept hold of the tree trunk, balancing on her right foot. *I hope I only sprained it.*

She looked around to see if she could find the flashlight. No such luck. It might have busted on impact, or the batteries died, as there was no sign of its light still shining. Turning around to figure out what tripped her, she felt something bang against her foot. A glance down, and she saw the flashlight, its light dimming.

I thought it flew out into the woods. Regan stared back over her shoulder at the path ahead but only saw darkness. She scrunched down to pick up the flashlight. Pressing it against her breasts, she flashed a wary look all around her. No sound. No movement.

An animal?

She whipped the beam of light back where she had fallen. Her breath caught heavy in her lungs, and her heart pounded as she saw a person. A dead person. Not just any person, either.

Silas.

The light revealed his slack mouth, grayish white flesh and—*God, his eyes.* Round and full of horror. If the eyes were the mirror to the soul, Silas must have screamed in fear at the last few minutes of his life. Just what had he seen that scared him?

A voice called to her. "Regan."

She hobbled away from the tree, heading back to camp. "What? Who's that? Ben? Is that you, Ben?"

No, not Ben. It didn't sound like his voice. She felt sure it wasn't one of the other guys, either.

"Ben. Ben. Ben. Always Ben." It sounded mocking.

She began to tremble as she then heard a feminine voice. Not Kendra or Neri, but it sounded like—

"It's Nana. How's my little apple dumpling?"

"Oh, God. Nana. It can't be you. You died when I was eight, had a heart attack after you caught me sneaking a cookie out of the cookie jar." The fear left her, and the heat of anger replaced it. "You grabbed your wooden spoon to beat me, but you fell to the kitchen floor. Dad came and took me home after the ambulance took you to the hospital. Aunt Sally called to tell us you died on the way."

"How could you kill your Nana, Regan? Your mother died at your birth, and your grandmother because you were naughty. Then your father died in that nursing home where you put him." The voice deepened, and her father's raspy voice rolled over her.

The fear returned. These couldn't be Nana and her father. And who called to her in that strange male voice earlier? *What about that shadow person on the monitor?*

This place. This damnable unholy spot. Whatever haunted it, it was playing tricks on her. She screamed. "Go away! Leave me alone!"

Her heart racing like a thoroughbred that had left the starting gate, she hopped away on the one foot back to camp. Her flashlight died. Darkness enclosed on her and not able to see what might be on the path; she fell a couple of times. Managing to find a broken branch after the second fall, she used it to help her.

She needed to tell them about Silas's body. When had he died and what had killed him? *Whatever is using the voices on you, dummy.*

"You better get your butt back here, my rotten little apple dumpling. Where's my wooden spoon?" Her grandmother's voice screeched like a harpy's, not at all familiar.

"I'll get it for you, Mama. Let's beat her ass together." Her father's voice sounded gleeful.

Just a little longer…Admittedly, Regan hadn't gotten that far from the camp. Being hurt made it hard to go any faster.

Wait! A light up ahead. That must be the light Ben kept outside the trailer. She reached the end of the path. Among the faint outlines of the buildings, and the shadows of the tents and the trailer, nothing stirred. That meant she must not have awoken anyone when she ran away.

"Hello?" she called out.

Just as she hopped off the path, something grabbed her from behind, cold against her back. Before she could scream, it yanked her and slammed her hard back against a tree.

The pain earlier had been nil prior, but now? She felt…broken. Every bone in her body shattered. She fought the darkness and stared up at the tall shadow hunched over her. It pressed a hand…paw…whatever, against her mouth.

"Shush," it said.

It took its hand away and jabbed what felt like long, sharp knives through her eyes. She let out a tiny shriek before it clenched her head and twisted it all the way around, snapping her neck with a crack that resounded in the night air.

CHAPTER TWENTY-SIX

Neri awoke with a start. Still sleepy, she sat up and shivered from the cold that found its way inside her tent even though she'd secured the flap. There had been a hint of a nightmare; no, it must be real. Her psychic sensitivity chimed like an insistent bell. Something had happened, and an uneasy feeling filled her. She slipped on her hiking boots, not even tying the laces, undid the flap and left her tent. Pausing for a minute, she stared at the woods, seeing nothing but a barely discernable line of trees. She went to Parker's tent.

She called out to him a low voice, not wanting to wake the others. "Parker."

"What?" He crawled out of his tent in stocking feet, yawning, and her torch revealed his eyes barely open and tousled hair. "What's wrong?"

"I don't know. Maybe it's only a bad dream, with the weird stuff that happened. But again, I thought I heard something. It woke me up, and whatever it could be, prodded me enough that I knew I should check it out."

Parker rubbed his hand through his hair. "Ghosts?"

She shook her head. "No, I can't tell if it's anything like that. And honestly, we only had that one spirit, and I don't think any more of those haunt this place," she pursed her lips and tried to consider what to say, "no, I assume it's a different kind of entity, a creature, a being, whatever, behind Burkett's problems for centuries. It did something. Something not good."

Not saying anything, Parker reached inside and grabbed his boots, his heavy jacket, and a flashlight.

Neri went back to her own and withdrew a jacket and zipped herself into it. She dug her small flashlight out of her paranormal equipment backpack and, as an afterthought, her EMF meter.

Parker 's forehead wrinkled as his gaze lit on her meter. "Why are you bringing that along?"

"Well, I know you think a flashlight might be the only thing we need, but my psychic senses are tingling, warning me, what if this is something supernatural? Plus, the meter can give us any heads up, and after what happened earlier tonight, I'd like to know if my senses fail." She stared into his eyes. "You do understand that not everything is ghost related? That there are worse things than phantoms. Something is wrong with Burkett, has always been wrong with it."

"You think it's demonic?"

"Could be," she said, frowning. "I'm not sure, although it feels...dark natured. Although, there's nothing of the demonic I'd encountered at other places." She looked at him. "So that you know, being a psychic medium isn't an exact science. Unless the ghost wants me to understand and is strong paranormally, it isn't a trick dog and pony show, where you get it to do what you want it to do. Or, sometimes, it can block you from obtaining information about it."

Parker glanced at the other tents as he clicked on his flashlight. "Should we wake the others?"

Neri shook her head. "No, not yet. Let's make sure there isn't anything wrong."

He nodded. "Okay. Let's go."

Neri pushed the on button, and her light cast a sharp glow along the ground. After, she pushed her EMF meter on and kept an eye on it to see if it reacted, they searched the village first. The buildings held no secrets. They headed toward the tree line, passing the dead tree.

Parker walked past it, but Neri stopped to flash her light at it. She saw nothing, at least not on initial contact. Drawing closer, Neri let the light slip over the bark and allowed her inner eye probe for a reason, any reason, she felt she had to stop. She pressed the EMF meter close, but its other four lights did not glow to red. Frustrated, she looked around.

Where's Parker?

Great, she'd lost him. She thrust out her extrasensory perception and detected living energy ahead of her, on the path between the trees crowding close enough on either side that it appeared like they held hands. Worried, she walked faster and stepped onto the trail, wondering if something had prompted her senses to react at the tree so she and Parker would be separated. Then she caught the flashing lights of her meter out of the corner of her eye. All of them blazed like Christmas lights in the obsidian night.

Oh God, I'm right! Isolated like a predator would its prey! Even knowing she could trip and fall, she broke into a trot as she flashed her light all around and called out his name.

"Parker! For God's sake, answer me!" she demanded, her voice came out harsh before rising to a shrill, shrieking tone. "Damn it, please say something!"

"Hey, what's going on?"

A hand grabbed her by a shoulder, and she whirled around, raising her flashlight as if to brain whatever had touched her.

Parker stood there. He had emerged from between two trees. She wrapped her arms around him and gave him a tight hug.

"Oh, thank the Lord! You're all right."

He disengaged from her and peered down at her, looking sheepish. "Yeah, I'm fine. Why wouldn't you think so, because I didn't stop to see if you were still behind me?"

She took a couple of gulps of freezing air before she felt she could talk. "Partially. Because my sense went nuts about the dead tree, and when I stopped to check it out, that's when I realized you were gone."

"I'm sorry, Neri," said Parker. "I thought I heard something off the path behind these trees, so I searched."

Neri said, "You found nothing, didn't you?"

He released a short breath of cold white mist. "Nothing but brush, dirt, and rocks. Must have been some small animal, maybe a fox or raccoon."

She snatched his hand. "Parker, we hardly heard sounds in this place, or haven't you noticed? Which I'm sure you do." She drew closer. "It wasn't a sound, but your psychic senses that led you to check it out. Am I right?"

Her light shone over his face. His lips thinned as he narrowed his eyes at her. "I don't have any... How did you guess?"

"Now. I realized it now when I should have before. You can see ghosts, too, can't you?"

He blew out a shaky breath. "Ever since I was a kid. I told my parents once about this shadow man coming into my bedroom and my sister's, but Dad threatened to take me to a shrink. I said I lied so he wouldn't. Kept my mouth shut. We moved from the house a couple of months later to another town in the Lost Angeles area. It didn't have phantoms there, but that didn't stop me from seeing other ones in different places over the years. Just as it didn't stop me from seeing Mom's when she died from cancer when I turned eighteen. Her wraith rose from her body on the bed in the hospital, and she looked directly at me. She knew I could see her, and her lips moved, but no words came out, not physically. I did hear them inside my head; she told me she was sorry for not believing me about the shadow man. She said Dad lied, as he believed me, but with the family history connected to Burkett, he wanted to deny me seeing the supernatural. Then her spirit passed through the hospital window. I never saw her again."

Neri squeezed his hand. "I'm sorry you had a worse time experiencing the dead than I did. Not that I didn't encounter people who thought me a fake, crazy lady."

He stared down at the ground, shrugging. "Yeah, well, now you know why I acted like I did that day in Carytown. I'm truly sorry for being an ass to you then."

She smiled but dropped it a second later. "It's all under the bridge, and one day, I hope we can talk about it over dinner, but tonight, we're out in the freezing night searching to see if what I felt might be real."

Parker spoke, "Yes, I will admit I felt 'something' off the track here, but as I said, I found nothing."

They did some more legwork, going all the way to the street before they headed back to camp after coming across zilch.

Neri said, "Let's get back to bed, and at breakfast tomorrow morning, when everyone is at the campfire, I'll tell them what I thought woke me up and how you helped me, but we didn't discover anything. In the light of day, in warmer conditions, and with more people, we can do an initial going-over of the whole land."

Wishing each other good night, they turned back toward their tents.

Neri snuggled in her warm sleeping bag and fell asleep. It didn't feel like she slept long enough, when she felt light on her face. She heaved a sigh and sat up. Her tent flap was open.

I thought I'd secure it. Again, maybe I didn't.

After she did it, her breath slipping out of her mouth in icy clouds, she struggled as quick as she could into her sweatshirt and pants over the black Heat 32 top and bottoms, she'd worn to bed. She had heard about the Heat 32s, how well they kept a person warm underneath clothing, even stopped sweat from staining fabric, and she'd purchased a pair of bottoms and tops for this investigation. Best investment ever. She jammed her sock-covered feet into her hiking boots, and after tying the shoestrings, clambered to her feet. Before she left her tent, she put on her thick, hooded coat, slipped her gloves into a pocket, and jammed her knitted cap with the words: "I'm Here for the Boos," onto her head, and walked outside.

She spied Ben at the fire, frying sausage patties and eggs. They sizzled and sent a tantalizing odor into the air. Her stomach rumbled.

She patted it, saying, "I know, I know, hungry," and wandered over to him.

Parker left his tent and met her and Ben at the fire. He smiled and said, "Good morning. Though it is brisk, isn't it?"

Ben looked up. "Not as bad as last night, still cold. Hopefully, this breakfast and fresh hot coffee will warm everyone up." He grinned when Zack tromped over. "And there's hot water and different kinds of teas or cocoa for those who prefer that instead."

"Thanks, Ben," said Zack in a low voice. "I hope there might be mint tea among those teas. I'm feeling a touch upset in the stomach this morning. I'm hoping it's not viral. When I called home last night before I went to sleep and mentioned feeling out of sorts, Mom wanted me to come home right then and there. I told her that if I felt any worse, Ben wouldn't have me stay. But I think it's just this place." He grimaced. "I admit I've been having an upset stomach ever since we arrived here. I don't know why—I never have before at any of the other investigations."

Kendra came out of the trailer, carrying a tray with a few Styrofoam cups on it, steam rising from them. She stopped next to Zack.

Pointing with her chin at one cup, she said, "Zack, your tea."

He picked up the cup, took a sip and wrinkled his nose. "Not mint. Earl Gray, and no sugar. I love Earl Gray, but I feel mint may be better this morning. Any in the trailer? And sugar? I know I don't take sugar on a normal basis, but today..."

Kendra nodded. "There's both mint tea and sugar."

He headed to the trailer.

Ben accepted his cup of black coffee. "Zack says he has an upset stomach, that he's been feeling it since we arrived here."

Kendra handed Neri a cup. "Flavored cream, right? It's peppermint—sorry. No sugar?"

Neri sipped and released a sigh. "This tastes like heaven, Kendra. I missed your coffee-making skills on investigations."

The other woman grinned. "Well, I do work for a coffee shop. It goes with the territory."

Parker took a cup filled to the brim with black coffee.

Kendra placed the tray on a nearby camp table, snatching one of the cups and leaving three cups: Russell's, Regan's and Silas's.

"Do I smell coffee?" asked the reedy voice that belonged to Russell, who joined them. He picked up a cup without asking if it was his or not and took a big drink. "God, I needed that."

Ben lifted slices of bacon from the pan to eight paper plates, adding an egg each afterward. He stood after taking the frying pan off the fire and while holding his cup with the other, he called out, "Hey, Regan and Silas, breakfast, you sleepyheads! If you're not out here in fifteen minutes, I'll eat yours myself!"

No one yelled at him from either tent.

He yelled, "Silas, I thought you wanted to leave here for good, be with your husband?"

Nothing.

Neri felt a chill not connected to the freezing air slither up her spine. Memories of the night before made her turn to Ben.

"Ben, check their tents."

He put the pan back on the fire and his coffee on the camp table. "I'm assuming they were still tired from the investigation last night. What's going on, Neri?"

"Last night, I awoke, thinking I heard something, not sure what—"

She never got to finish as Ben hurried over to the tents, raised the flaps, and found both empty. He turned a concerned face to the others.

"They're gone."

Neri glanced at Parker's concerned face. "I didn't want to wake you last night, Ben, figuring you and the others would be too tired, so I woke Parker up, and we did some exploring on a feeling I received. We found zip, but it was dark. We decided to wait until this morning when everyone was awake to do a look-see by daylight, but I never figured it had to do with any of our people." Her stomach began to cramp just like Zack's. "If they joined those other missing people..."

Ben swallowed his coffee and banged the cup down on the tray, causing the other two cups to spill, and, looking grim, said, "Everyone, forget breakfast, we need to go find our two compadres."

Neri's stomach worsened, and she poured her coffee out, losing her taste for it.

Parker drained his cup before he walked to his tent to grab a few things, most importantly his phone.

Neri bolted to hers to snatch her EMF meter and flashlight, tucking both into the pockets of her coat.

Kendra finished her cup and took it and the other cups on the tray back into the trailer to throw into the trash.

Standing at the opened doorway of the trailer, Zack finished his tea and tossed his cup in the trash bag, before running to his tent to grab his radio, flashlight, and yes, his EMF meter.

Everyone met by the fire.

Ben looked at Kendra. "Stay here. Otherwise, we'll need to put out the fire. Just keep your radio on, to hear from us, and if anything peculiar happens here, so you can call us, or if Silas and Regan return. Understand?"

Kendra nodded, her eyes wide, and the young woman sat down on one of the chairs close to the fire. Before the search party left, Neri saw her shiver, but she doubted it came from the cold that had grown steadily worse. Casting her eye to the sky, Neri noticed dark gray clouds clustered together.

Not a good sign. Not a good sign at all.

Neri's stomach gurgled, but not from hunger this time.

***

Kendra curled into herself, sipping her coffee and trying to keep warm. On occasion, she heard voices and knew it was the other investigators, but still, being here alone sent chills up her spine.

Both Regan and Silas vanishing. I can see Regan taking off, running scared. But Silas? No. She remembered some of the stories connected to this land. People went missing over the years. Like they just all fell into some portal.

She took another sip, not even noticing that her coffee had cooled. No doubt some people upped and took off on their own. The trouble was, there had been other disappearances no one could explain.

Like the last paranormal investigation team—The thought crawled into her head like some taunt.

She stood and tipped her cup, watching her coffee raining down on the dirt. Just as she turned to take it to the trashcan, she heard a ping. Small, but enough to catch her attention.

Her gloved fingers tightened, crushing the cup as she looked around. Nothing stirred. Deciding she imagined it, she turned to head to the trailer again, but the whisper reached her ear, bitter as ice.

"Kendra."

Kendra froze. It sounded like Regan.

She turned around, but she didn't see the other woman. She called out, "Regan?"

No answer.

She tried again. "Look, the others are looking for you and Silas. Are the two of you playing a game, or maybe just you?"

"Kendra."

Her name again, this time louder. Still holding the cup, she headed toward the dead tree, thinking the voice had come from that direction. Her stomach churning as she noticed she didn't hear any of the others, and how alone she indeed was. It hit her that she'd left her radio back on the table at the campfire. Plus, she'd left her cell phone in her tent. She clutched the cup between both of her hands like a lifeline. Like it might keep her safe.

Right. A styrofoam cup? What would I do with it— toss it?

She paused at the tree. An odor, liked something had died, filled the air. Her nose wrinkled and she gagged. Whatever it might be, it grew worse, overpowering. Her stomach rebelled, and she leaned over and threw up by the tree's rotting roots.

"Hello, Kendra. Don't like the way I smell?"

Not even wiping her mouth, Kendra straightened and looked right into the eyes of a bizarre version of Regan. Her form appeared to be shorting out like a television picture out of sync. Still, Kendra could see Regan's blackened lips, holes where her eyes should be, and skin as gray as ash and stretched so tight it almost looked like a skull.

Biting back a scream, Kendra squeaked out, "What's wrong with you, Regan?"

The weird, static movement halted, and, stable once more; the strange Regan flashed a wide grin, made more horrible by the absence of teeth. "I've never felt better." She leaned closer, and Kendra received a face full of rotting stink. "Unlike you, bitch."

Kendra's mouth dropped open, shocked. "Maybe we're not bosom buddies, but you never call me names like that!"

"About time I did. About time I call it like I know it. On the whole team."

Kendra dropped the cup and backed away, keeping her eyes on Regan. If she turned and ran, this fake Regan might give chase. If she ran, she knew that, like any prey, she wouldn't make it.

Regan snarled, "Hey, where are you going, twit? I didn't permit you to leave!" Her voice roughened, and she stalked Kendra, grounding the cup into the ground. "Run, little piggy." Her mouth curved into a grin and where before Kendra saw no teeth, this time rows of sharp fangs overfilled it.

Kendra broke into a sprint. Not back to camp: heedless of any thought but escape, she barreled toward the woods. Her chest complained in misery as her lungs filled full of freezing shards of air, cutting them. The thick winter boots she wore did not make for speed, but she kept at it as best as she could. Not daring to look back to see if false Regan still hounded her, she hoped she ran into one of the others.

Two of our team disappeared last night while we slept in our tents. One of them, the real Regan. They probably ran from whatever the hell rules this place.

Still, this was daylight. Even if the woods were shadow-ridden, she didn't need a flashlight to see her way to the dead-end street. She might not see the other investigators, but if she could get to the road, and head to one of the houses that lined it and find someone home, she could make a call to her cousin, Danny, to come to pick her up. Ben could pack her tent, cell phone, and everything else of hers, and drop it off at her apartment later. No way, she would go back and become another AWOL statistic.

Someone barred her way off the path and to the street. It stood tall, more shadow than substance.

Hoping it might be one of the others, she skittered to a stop, slip-sliding on an icy patch. "Ben? Neri? Russell, Zack?"

The shape drew closer and bent. It had no face!

Oh, God! She tried to scream, but her throat choked up as she found herself lifted into the air, face-to-face with the thing. She thrashed, kicking her legs and swinging her arms, her heart racing, her one thought: *I'm going to die.*

Then it vanished, and she hit the ground. Voices surrounded her, and she looked up at someone's face over her. Her vision was shaky at first, gradually it cleared, and she saw Ben. Tears sprang out to her eyes, blurring his features once more.

CHAPTER TWENTY-SEVEN

en helped the trembling Kendra to her feet. Her face had gone ghost pale, and her eyes appeared bruised.

Neri believed her form had shrunk, as if she had curled into herself, trying to make herself as small as possible. As if maybe, something wouldn't see her.

"Are you okay?" Ben asked.

Kendra hung onto him like a lifeline, staring at the other members of the team before her gaze traveled beyond them, to the darkened woods.

Neri could feel sheer terror pulsing off the young woman, and she fought her own fear from taking command. Something else had been here mere seconds before they had heard Kendra's screams, thankfully screams not muted, and they'd rushed to her aid. It hit her that if they hadn't reached her when they had, they wouldn't have found her at all, but another statistic for Nowhere Land.

"No, I'm not okay," Kendra finally said something, her voice rough, as if raw from the screaming. "I saw Regan."

Ben frowned and walked over to the dead tree. He stared at the ground before looking back up as the others joined him. "Regan? Here? I don't see any footprints, except yours, and I can tell they belong to you as you're wearing snow boots. Regan wore hiking boots if I remember from yesterday."

Kendra straightened her spine, and her chin thrust out as if to prove she wasn't as scared as her pale flesh and wide, teary eyes told otherwise, though her shaking didn't stop. "No. She was here. At that dead loblolly. Except, it wasn't her, but something else. She changed—fangs filled her mouth and all. No, now that I think about it, it couldn't have been the real Regan."

Ben narrowed his eyes. "I see...Regan, but not Regan."

Neri nodded. "She's right. I can't feel Regan. She's no longer here on this plane. Neither is Silas."

Ben stared at her, his eyebrows meeting together. "Not on this plane...look, their spirits may be gone, but their corpses must be somewhere on this land, or nearby. Flesh can't travel to the other side."

Russell chimed in, "I agree. I mean, bodies don't up and vanish. Maybe in the movies, but not in real life."

Neri tucked her hands into her jacket's pockets. They felt cold, despite the gloves she had jammed on. "I agree. These aren't normal circumstances. Whatever got them took every part of them. I can't figure out why. All these people and yes, even animals, vanishing over the centuries."

Zack chimed in, "It's like those fairy stories."

They all turned to him, and he continued. "You know, where fairies steal humans or find a way into their world. The very few who do find their way back to the mortal realm end up years later, still the same age as when they disappeared. Heck, people used to believe orbs or lights were fairies." He rubbed the back of his neck. "The UFO abductions use the same legends, too."

Kendra burst out, "I think we should pack up and leave." She looked to Parker, who had been quiet all this time. "I'm sorry, Mr. Burkett, but this place is getting to me and being honest, I don't want to be the next person to disappear. If you guys hadn't come when you did, it would have taken me like it did to Regan and Silas. I could feel the evilness of it when it stood over me, picked me up."

Ben clamped a hand on her shoulder. "Listen, come back to the fire, eat some breakfast—I'll make fresh eggs and sausage—and we'll talk about what happened to you."

Kendra shrugged his hand off her, her eyes burning with anger as she snarled, "Hell, no! If you think we should still stay here and investigate, despite two people gone missing off the face of this planet, well I'm not doing it any further! I'm packing my things, and I'm leaving this hellhole. If you won't take me home, at least take me to that McDonalds in West Point that we passed on the way here yesterday, and I'll call my brother and tell him to come pick me up there." Her breathing had sped up, and her face had grown beet red. "I wished I'd driven my car here now, instead of leaving it back at the apartment complex."

Parker spoke up. "I'll take her home. The rest of you can investigate while I do that. Kendra, go pack."

Kendra shook her head. "I'm not going back to my tent alone. Please, come with me, Mr. Burkett?"

He nodded, and they walked back to camp.

Russell looked disapproving, "We're staying, Ben? After all, that's happened?"

Ben heaved a sigh. "Yeah, we are. Kendra's right though, we should call the police. They might end the investigation, but I think that is the right thing to do."

Russell raised an eyebrow. "Maybe like Kendra, both Regan and Silas had been frightened away. I believe Kendra imagined what happened to her." He looked at Neri. "Sorry, Neri, I know you believe that you get these sixth sense impressions and all, but still, to be logical, shouldn't we make calls, see if they might be back home. Something like that?"

Zack rebuked Russell. "Russell! That's uncalled for."

Of course. I'm the woo-woo girl in Russell's and Zack's estimation, and I always have been. They were like John. Feeling ashamed at comparing the two men to her ex-fiancée, Neri said, "Ben, he's right. It's what a good investigator would do. Don't depend on my abilities—"

Russell opened his mouth, but Neri continued, "I know you didn't really mean that Russell, but you're right, we need to cover all bases. We should make phone calls, and if neither of them is home, then we need to call the police."

Ben agreed. "Yeah, lets head back to camp and I'll make some calls on my cell."

Neri, Ben, Russell, and Zack trudged back to camp. They found Kendra tearing down her tent, her stuff already packed and set aside. Parker stood nearby, his car keys in hand, while he finished eating his plate of cold sausage and egg.

He saw Neri glancing at him and shrugged. "Might as well not waste Ben's cooking. Besides, I doubt I'll get a chance to eat otherwise." He turned to Ben. "If you like, I can make a call to the Gloucester's sheriff department? Get someone out here."

Ben agreed. "Go ahead. I assume you're putting me in charge of talking to whomever they will send out. Until you get back?"

"Yes. Thanks. I will let them know that, too."

Ben and Parker helped Kendra carry her tent and other things to Parker's vehicle. Fifteen minutes later, Parker and Kendra drove away in a cloud of dust. Neri noted that the wheels didn't make a sound.

Nowhere Land making its statement.

Ben made a call on his smartphone. First to Regan, then to Silas. His face went through a gamut of expressions, from nothing to worry. He put down the phone, saying, "Silas's husband said he's not there. I think I got the poor guy worried now. As for Regan, her home phone rings and rings, and her answering service on her cell is the only thing I get from that. Is her cell in her tent?"

Russell ran to Regan's tent and searched, but at the end stepped outside and shook his head.

Neri looked around, a feeling prodding at her inner eye, but she didn't see anything with her normal ones. No shadows, nothing, but a sense of evil watching them. It emulated an overwhelming sense of distress....no, something more like...ruffled, upset?

"Not quite what you wanted," she whispered. "Thought you could snatch us, one by one. Except we're not primitives, nor people who are superstitious and afraid of the dark. Not children, but logical adults who brave the monster in the closet."

Ben asked, "What did you say, Neri?"

"Not to you, Zack, or Russell. I'm letting our watcher know how I feel, telling it can't scare us all."

Ben narrowed his eyes as he looked around. "It's watching us?"

"Yes. I'm not sure exactly where, but it's not happy with Kendra leaving and the plan to call the police. We took its control out of its hands,"

Zack piped up, "Maybe that's good?"

Russell huddled in his coat. "Should we pack? I mean, with Mr. Burkett calling in the cops and all, it's not like we'll be able to finish our investigation once they arrive."

Zack said, "I can tell you who'll be happy about this."

Russell retorted, "Yeah, your mother. Back home, safe and sound."

Zack flashed the other man a shocked look. "Hey, I never said she's unhappy about me investigating. She still lets me do it."

Russell retorted, "Hey, be honest, you can't wait to leave here, can you?"

"Mom can't help it if she's thinks the paranormal is malarkey. But she says I'm an adult and can still do it if it makes me happy."

Russell made kissy noises with his lips. "Your mother is fine, but that fat pug of hers? You know, the one that always growls at me if I come over? She thrusts that smelly thing at me, saying, "Pooka wants a hug from you. Shit, that mutt's good for nothing but pooping and sleeping, and let's not forget, stuffing his plump, ugly face."

Zack clenched his hands into fists and shot out, "Animal hater! You didn't think I knew you couldn't stand animals! Your place is pristine, and you have white furniture and rugs."

"Better than a house full of dog hair."

Neri stood there in shock, not believing what she was hearing. Both men who never once snapped at each other, even in the worst of conditions, suddenly ready to tear each other's throats out.

"Maybe you should leave now," suggested Zack. "Since you're better than the rest of us."

Russell's voice grew shriller. "Away from this woo-woo stuff? Never wanted a psychic on the team."

Ben broke in, "Russell! Apologize to Neri, then to Zack. And Zack, what's wrong with you? The both of you are the best of friends, but now you're acting like enemies."

Zack never answered Ben. Instead, he whirled on Russell. "You heard Ben! Say you're sorry to Neri and me. Nothing wrong with a medium!"

Russell got in the other's face. "Yeah, so what? We're supposed to be all scientific about this. Nothing science about some person saying ghosts talk to them." He clamped a hand partially around the other man's throat. "As for an idiot white guy..."

Both looked close to fighting and Ben stepped between them. "Hey, Russell, that's terrible. You know the rules here—what you just said, is uncalled for and wrong, you know that. What's the fuck's wrong with you two? Stop it!"

Neri could feel that a cloud of darkness had settled over both men arguing. "Ben, be careful. This isn't them."

Ben's face paled. He tried again, hoping to get past their anger. "Come on, guys. You two have never been like this before."

Zack growled, "I should have. This nerd needs to back off. What's the matter, you can't handle me? Jealous?"

Russell ranted, "Hell, no! I'm comfortable as a black man who lives on his own. I am not a pansy hiding behind Mama's skirts!

Ben remonstrated, "Cut it out! None of that from either of you! This team has never been about prejudices. Ever."

Neri called out, "Leave them alone, Ben! It'll go after you next."

Both bickering men stiffened, then toppled to the ground.

Ben kneeled beside them, laid a finger at their throats where their pulses would be, and showed worried eyes at Neri.

"They're still alive."

Neri opened her mouth, when a gust of heavy wind rampaged through the camp, yanking the stakes out of the ground and gathering up the tents. The campfire danced into the air over to the dead tree, sparks setting it afire.

Ben raced to the trailer and grabbed a fire extinguisher. He ran to the burning tree with it, but the wind proved strong enough to rip the container from his hands and fling it away from the burning tree.

Russell and Zack opened their eyes, moaning, but sat up.

Neri could tell that both men had returned to normal. She dropped beside them, shaking first one man, then the other, yelling at them. "Russell, Zack! Come on! We need to put the fire out! The dead tree is burning! Someone needs to go get the fire extinguisher, now!

Both men were confused still, until they saw the tree on fire and Ben running to get the extinguisher on the ground.

Neri saw the tents flying in a circle in the air like horses on a carousel. The wind hovered them closer to the fire. She worked to make her voice be heard over the wind as its roar had grown worse. "Zack and Russell, grab those tents before they catch on fire!"

Zack and Russell tottered over to snatch four of the tents and threw them inside the trailer, but the other two ended up on top of the roofs of a couple of the buildings. At least for now, they were not near the flames.

Neri ran to Ben, yelling over the roar of the wind. "Isn't there another extinguisher or two inside the trailer? Don't you have shovels, too? Maybe with shovels, we can also toss dirt up at the fire?"

Ben replied, "Yeah, I do—on both. Zack and Russell can snag the other two fire extinguishers I have in the trailer, both are attached to a wall, and you can get one of the shovels and use it to dig up dirt to fling at the tree. The shovels are in the large green tote near the door. None of those are big, but they get the job done. Especially if we use the extinguishers, too. "

Neri slipped inside, unearthed one of three shovels in a jumble with other tools in the tote, bolted out the door with it to a spot near the tree where she used it to try and break the frozen ground. Though it was hard to do, she worked at it until she collected enough dirt that might be worth throwing on the flames while the three male investigators sprayed the flames with their extinguishers. As Neri straightened and tossed the dirt, screaming erupted inside her head. Shrieking, she dropped the shovel and crumpled, the noise inside her head hurting her brain so much that blood trickled from her ears.

Ben didn't stop to help her but kept spraying foam on the conflagration. The foam doused some of the orange and yellow flames, sizzling. With Zack and Russell helping, the men finally got the fire out.

The screaming in Neri's head decreased down to a whisper. Somehow, she'd picked up the agonized psychic impressions from the tree itself. A tree that was supposed to be dead.

"Not as dead as we all thought."

Ben reached down to help her up, "Are you all right, Neri? What did you say?"

She met his gaze with her own, blurry one. "My head hurts, but not from me. The tree's not dead. It cried out in torment while burning." She tapped her head. "I heard it, inside my noggin." She winched as a shade of the pain hit her again, causing her to close her eyes.

Ben stole a look at the blackened timber and returned to her. "The tree? Not dead and able to communicate?"

Neri reopened her eyes and cupped her hand against her head, zoning into blocking out the misery she still felt. Finally, a wall set in place inside her head, she breathed in a gulp of air and let it back out before she felt ready to talk to Ben.

"I got it cut off from me. Zack's wrong. We all are. It's not a dead shell. It's still alive. Although, I think this time, it is truly dead." She added, "I'm not ready to let down my guard at this moment to test it. My brain still feels like a bell had rung inside it for an hour."

Ben brought her into his embrace, laying her head against his shoulder. "No, I won't ask you to do that, Neri."

Russell came over. "The fire's completely out. No embers, nothing." A charcoal streak arrowed across one cheek. He acted like his old self again.

Ben told him, "Russell, you and Zack grab a couple of axes from the trailer, chop the tree down into pieces. To be sure."

Russell frowned. "It's dead—"

Ben glared at the other man. "Neri said the tree let her know it was in agony in her head. I believe her; the tree might still be alive. It might not be any more, but she put up a psychic barrier to keep it out as it was harming her. Best to make sure this time that it is gone. Unless you're a tree hugger, or it's against your religion or something?"

Russell shook his head. "Hell, no. To me, it's nothing more than firewood for a fireplace. Zack and I'll take it down."

Russell told Zack what Ben asked them to do, then trotted off to the trailer, taking the fire extinguishers with him. Zack stood by the tree, guarding it.

Neri heard something and realized it came from a vehicle. *The land's allowing sounds again*, she thought. A figure in the distance grew more prominent as it drew nearer, and she realized Parker had returned. She saw him glance at Ben and her, and feeling uncomfortable, she untangled herself from Ben's arms.

She grimaced. No way should she feel like that. It's not like she and Ben, or even Parker and her.... Shocked, she pointed her eyes down at the terrain as if it'd grown fascinating. Best to gather her composure than to reveal her conflicting emotions on her face.

It slammed into her that the weird crap must have kept her from the truth about the personal stuff. Until now. Something she had been denying. Two men, one woman. Triangle. Hard to choose, both being good men.

I know I had been attracted to Parker the first time we met in Carytown. But Ben—he's always been like my brother.

She'd been refusing to look further at Ben's and her relationship. Maybe deep down, her feelings had been more than sisterly.

Nothing like forbidden fruit. A deep, dark voice snickered in Neri's head.

"Who said that?" she blurted out.

Parker and Ben looked at her like she'd lost it, both of their foreheads filled with frown lines.

She swallowed, looking around. Something found its way past the barricade in her head. Not from the tree, now dead for real. But she knew the voice never came from it. This voice sounded dark and…male?

Russell ambled from the trailer, carrying an axe in each hand. He handed one to Zack before walking over to Ben. *No, not him. It's not Zack, either.*

That's when she saw them. Silas and Regan. Except, both looked wrong. They grinned, their teeth overfilling their mouths, their eyes seemed—

Cold chills rushed up her spine, and she yelled, "Zack, run! RUN!"

Zack turned to her, bewildered. "What?" he questioned.

"Behind you!" she shrieked, "they're behind you. Looks like Regan and Silas, but they're not!"

Blinking, he looked over his shoulder. "I don't see anything."

Both 'things' no longer stood there.

When Zack looked forward again, they reappeared, face-to-face with him. He raised his axe, but never struck out, confused as they looked like the people he'd investigated with and knew.

Neri saw the realization in his eyes, but it was too late.

Regan snatched the axe out of his hands and in a movement that defied belief, she chopped off each of his arms with it. It was if he didn't have bones beneath his flesh, that his flesh consisted of tissue.

Zack howled in fear and pain, his blood spurting from the holes where his arms had been.

Neri screeched, "Oh my God, Ben, guys, help!"

Russell, Ben, and Parker ran to assist Zack, but too late, the bogus Silas's mouth jutted out and grew and grew until it was a snout full of jagged teeth. He opened and bit into Zack's horrified face, cutting off the wailing.

Neri felt the blood draining from her face and her heart thumping against her chest like a bird trying to escape its cage, but she didn't move. She watched in horrid fascination as both fake people merged into one tall, thin, dark shadow that reached into the remainder of Zack and ripped a glowing orb out of his flesh. His soul. A dark line appeared in the air beside it, and the shadow slid through it, forcing Zack's shade to go with it. The line zippered up without a sound and disappeared.

Parker shouted, "What the hell was that?"

Ben stopped by what remained of Zack. He lowered himself, not even noticing that his knees sank into puddles of dirty blood, and reached out with a shaking hand as if to lay a finger against the obviously dead man's neck to check for a pulse. He halted; not much remained of the man above his shoulders, including a throat, to perform that.

He cut his eyes at Neri, oblivious to the other men who'd reached him. "Neri, what killed Zack and what did it take out of his body? Why did it leave his remains here?"

"I don't know what it is, but whatever it is, it's strong enough to breach my defenses I put up against the tree and talk to me inside my head. As for what it withdrew from Zack—that was his soul. And remember, sometimes body parts have been left over the centuries."

Ben glanced at Parker. "Like that thumb found after the first investigation."

Parker stared at her. "I didn't hear anything. Didn't even sense it."

Ben rose to his feet and flashed Parker a strange look. "What do you mean?"

Neri could move her feet at last and joined them, not looking at the corpse. "Parker's like me. Able to see and hear the supernatural."

A dumbfounded look crossed Ben's face. "And you knew about it? You never thought to tell me?"

She shook her head. "I only learned last night, and no, I wouldn't have kept something like that from you. Though maybe deep down, I always suspected something since his and my first meeting. But we have more important matters."

Ben looked glum. "Like, we need to get out of here now, before it comes back for its next victim."

Parker asked, "Demonic?"

Neri shrugged. "I can't get a handle on it, but it could be. Heck, in the paranormal community, many argue that demons aren't from Hell, that what people believe are Hell and Heaven are nothing more than other dimensions. Of course, that's all theories. I will say, it feels powerful."

Ben snorted, "Fuck the theories. Fuck the investigation. Let's get out of here, get somewhere safe, and think about what to do next." He flashed a look at Parker. "We need to call the cops, too, since I assume you didn't stop like you said you would, Burkett—at the very least we need to report the others' disappearances and Zack's death to the authorities and Silas's husband and Zack's mother." He withdrew his truck's keys out of his pants pocket and marched off to get the vehicle and drive it to the trailer to get it hitched.

Shaken and quiet, Russell followed him. No doubt, Zack's murder and all the bizarre paranormal proved too much for him. Neri didn't blame him if he decided he would never investigate ever again.

Parker and Neri went to see what they could salvage what was left of the camp and pack it up.

Parker asked, "If we get away from here, we'll be safe, right? Although now that I think about it, I wonder if this thing is behind what made my sister go crazy and kill her husband."

Neri gave him a sharp look. "You never said anything about that to any of us."

He looked away. "Yeah, I know. It only just happened. But at the time," he took a shuddering breath, continuing, "I thought Lisa had gone bonkers on her own, not that some entity possessed her and made her do it. Besides, if your sister lost it, would you tell strangers you didn't know?"

Neri shook her head, "I guess not. Except for friends that know, I didn't blurt out my sister died by lightning when we were on an investigation and I stopped investigating for a while."

Parker looked at her and placed a hand on her shoulder. "Oh, God, I'm sorry, Neri. That's terrible for you."

"It's all right; it's been a while." She looked into his eyes. "At least, I can say this thing did not cause her death. Although, it told me in my home when it appeared as my spirit guide, that it took my brother in Afghanistan."

Neither broke contact. Neri thought she should say something, do something. Heat burned as thoughts arose in her mind. Inconvenient thoughts that shouldn't surface now, at a time like this. She broke free of eye contact when she heard tires rolling over dirt and rocks.

Ben drove his truck close to the trailer and turned around, letting Russell jump from the passenger side to navigate as Ben backed it up to the trailer's hitch. Russell hitched the vehicle and trailer together, before Ben and he helped Parker started putting anything not already inside it into the trailer.

Russell pointed to the two tents on the rooftops of the shacks. "What about those?"

Ben took his key and headed for the driver's side. "Forget it. I'm not going to try and climb up to a roof. We've been here longer than we should. Want to see that entity again?"

"Hell, no! If any of these are mine, I can always buy another tent!" Russell hurried to climb in behind Ben. "Forget buying another one, as I'm never going camping ever again." He buckled his seatbelt and yelled, "Come on, Neri and Mr. Burkett, let's go!"

It hit Neri what Parker said about his sister and the entity. She remembered it getting her spirit guide. The entity didn't stay on the land. It had been collecting people for centuries, for some reason, and she knew deep inside herself it could get them anywhere, not just on Burkett.

It could go anywhere for a short time.

She ran over to Ben, frantic, holding the passenger door open after Parker climbed in the back seat. "Oh, God, Kendra! It can leave Burkett—at least for short periods. We should drive to Kendra's apartment to make sure she's safe!"

Ben frowned. "What do you mean that...that damn thing can leave Nowhere Land?"

"Yes, yes. It went after Kendra here, but we came back and thwarted it. It needs her like it captured the other three members of our team. If it wanted us, why hasn't it come back by now? I can't sense it at all. I think that's because it's gone after her to finish the job."

A half hour later, Ben's truck roared down I-64, heading for Richmond.

Neri sat in the passenger seat and stared through the windshield; she noted how late it'd grown. It would be another hour or hour-and-a-half before they arrived at Kendra's apartment. She closed her eyes and began

to pray, hoping God would hear her. For Kendra's
sake.

CHAPTER TWENTY-EIGHT

Kendra cooked the last package of ramen noodles she rifled from her cupboard, adding leftover rotisserie chicken she'd bought for dinner the night before she left for the Burkett investigation. Never liking to cook much, she hadn't left much in her fridge when she'd gone. Her kitchen cabinets were mostly bare of dry and canned goods, and there'd been only the ramen, a can of chili past its expiration date, and an opened bag of moldy cereal that had been in there for four months.

She'd tossed the chili and cereal into the trash can under the sink. For this evening's dinner, a bowl of ramen would be enough until she went grocery shopping tomorrow.

The microwave beeped, and she pressed the button, cutting the sound off. She gave it a minute before she opened the door and took out the steaming container. Pouring the noodles and chicken into a bowl and adding a couple of spices into the hot food, she grabbed a fork from the utensil drawer, plus a bottle of cola she still had left from the fridge and carried it all to the living room. Forget eating at the dining room table; she wanted comfort right now. Like her couch and watching a good movie on television could supply.

Curling beneath a green fuzzy throw she kept on her couch, she tucked into her food after turning on the flat screen. Not fancying the news, she surfed the channels until she came across a romantic comedy movie on *HBO*. After living the scary stuff for real the past day and a half, no way did she want to watch any paranormal or horror flicks. Not for a long while.

As she slurped the last noodle into her mouth, Kendra heard something that didn't come from the TV. She muted the movie and slipped off the couch, carrying the bowl and fork back to the kitchen. After putting both in the sink to be washed later, she paused in the entryway between the kitchen and living room and listened for any sound out of the ordinary.

Silence.

Well, except for the hum from the fridge and yells from kids that came from outside. Many of the apartment complex's children played in the large grassy area that lay in the center of the apartments, which all the apartment patios faced. The yard had a basketball court, a swing set, and monkey bars, the rest was covered in grass.

She headed back to the couch and picked up the remote to bring the movie sound back on when a pounding erupted from upstairs. Right above her, from her bedroom. Her body tensed; she gave a wary glance up at the ceiling. The noise stopped.

"Kendra Quinn, you're not losing it because of Nowhere Land," mumbled Kendra.

Maybe someone had broken into her apartment before she arrived back home. She shook her head; since she'd gotten back home, she'd been in every room and would have found a window unlatched or glass broken. Nothing had been touched or appeared out of the ordinary. For Christ's sake, she'd washed and dried her dirty clothes and hung them in her closet in her bedroom upstairs. The only thing she noticed inside were her clothes and boxes of various things she stored. Nothing out of the ordinary or anyone hiding in any nook and cranny, or elsewhere on the second floor. Maybe a mouse might be able to get in, but she didn't see evidence of that, either.

But a ghost can get in; ghosts don't need to break in.

She dismissed that first thought. *No, nothing followed me home. Nothing!*

Did you remember to tell any entities not to come home with you? Pfft, they don't have to listen to you telling them that? Free will, you know.

Another noise exploded from upstairs, this time much louder. It sounded like running footsteps, so heavy that they caused the chandelier over Kendra's dining table to swing back and forth.

"Shit!" she said with a hiss. Her heart hammered to the beat of the running footsteps as she swallowed a couple of gulps of frigid polar air.

A quick check of the thermostat on her wall revealed the setting at 70 degrees. That meant the heater was working and the coldness was not caused by it breaking down.

Ice-cold air can be paranormal related.

"Shut up," Kendra whispered at the traitorous thought. "No ghosts or anything like that in this apartment or the whole complex. I know, I checked it out when I moved in."

It was one thing to go somewhere else to investigate, another thing to live in a building with paranormal activity. Kendra never wanted to wake up in the middle of the night to some shadow-person staring down at her, have her things tossed around, or share space with an incorporeal roommate.

The dead can follow you home from investigations and denying it won't change it. You know that. Kendra wished her thoughts wouldn't give her opinions. Unwanted opinions.

The commotion went silent.

Kendra whispered, "I know it might be impossible at this point, but maybe someone could have broken in." The words tasted false to her.

Though, how? Since the racket came from the second floor of her place, and if it just occurred, no one could have gotten past her down here without her seeing them. Maybe if the person had a tall ladder or could scale the outside brick walls of the building like a freaking lizard and break her bathroom or bedroom window, she couldn't see a smart thief being able to do that. She looked for her cell but remembered that she'd left it on the bedside table in her bedroom, charging.

This was one of those times that she'd wished she had kept the house phone and not taken it off the Fios bill when she moved here. Maybe she used the cell more or got more calls on it, but still, a house phone would be good for emergencies. Like now.

Yeah-right, but a good thief or murderer would think of that, cut the line so I couldn't make a call out. Damn her watching those scary movies.

Not wanting to admit to herself she didn't want to go upstairs to check the rooms out, or even grab her phone, she decided it might be better to go to her next-door neighbor, Mrs. Jones's apartment. She could ask to borrow the woman's phone. If she happened not to be home, then she would run down to the rental office. A glance at her watch let her know she only had ten minutes before that place closed.

Snatching her apartment key off the nail on her front room wall, she headed for the door. Not looking up the stairs to the second floor, she seized the doorknob and turned it. The door opened a crack.

The doorknob jerked out of her hands and the door slammed shut. Kendra's blood drained from her face. Dear God, something had wrestled the doorknob out of her hand! Right?

The same unseen force that knocked her to the floor, where she landed on her left side. She screamed, and her key flew out of her hand and into the living room. The blow felt as if a fist had wielded it. An invisible fist.

Pain riveted in her hip. Kendra tried to ignore it, which proved hard as the twinge shot from there along her nerves to her brain. She rolled off it and, using the wall, she managed to stand. Her left ankle almost gave out on her, but at the last moment, she leaned against the wall and kept on her feet. Damn, but she must have twisted it. She hoped neither the hip nor the ankle had anything worse than bruises or a sprain.

Kendra decided to see if she could move and pushed away from the wall, and realized with joy that she could hobble without falling. *No, not broken.* It hit her that every part of her body ached, which meant she wouldn't be surprised if by morning black and blue bruises would paint her entire body.

See, Kendra, it's the supernatural.

Damn, foul thought. A possibly accurate, but scary thought. Trying to be logical about it—*that's right, let's be scientific*—someone could have broken in while Kendra was away, hid really well, but she couldn't think of who would or might have done that. Nobody she knew. Special effects. Look at horror movies over the years and how realistic they were these days. *That's with computers, dummy. Did a computer fling you from the door?* She tried the door again, but this time, the lever wouldn't turn.

Locked.

She had a key, but it had shot out of her hand and could be anywhere in the living room. Slow as a turtle, Kendra limped into the living room to search for it. She couldn't find it. Was it beneath the couch or chair, maybe even behind the wall unit? Doubts filled her, since where she'd been when the key sailed from her hand, that latter piece of furniture was not in that area. No way she could get down to her knees, and if she did, she feared she might not be able to get back up.

She looked over her shoulder at the bottom of the stairs and began to doubt it was anything living that harmed her. Something wanted her to stay inside. No way in hell would she give it what it wanted. And whatever it wanted, she imagined mercy would not be on its list of things to give her.

Turning her head forward again, she caught sight of the patio door in her kitchen/dining area. Good, she might be able to escape to the outdoors that way. She hobbled across the living room, gritting her teeth at the agony vibrating in her hip and ankle. She stepped from rug to linoleum and staggered to the patio glass door. Once she got there, she tried to unlatch it, but it didn't work.

A male voice spoke in her head. A nauseating odor accompanied it. *You're not getting out, Kendra. You'll find out how much it will be like the horror movies.*

Kendra flinched. The voice sounded like Silas's, except he'd vanished back at Burkett. No way could it be him talking inside her head, even if he had the telepathic ability to do that, which she doubted.

Unless I'm dead? Dead, dead, dead! Silas's voice sang inside her brain.

The tone felt like a fist punching each word.

Wincing, Kendra didn't turn around or look back over her shoulder. She said, "The dead don't talk to me. Maybe they talk to Neri, after all, she's a medium, but they never have to me. Except by ghost box or EVPs off a recorder."

"Why would I want to talk to that bitch? I'm more interested in you, not her, Kendra."

Oh, God, God, God! It's not speaking inside my head, but behind me! Fear curdled her stomach, and she fought the urge to throw up from the rancid smell that twisted around her and found its way up her nose. Kendra glanced back over her shoulder to see if anything stood behind her or in the living room. Nothing appeared out of the ordinary.

No, that's not right.

The black screen of her television mocked her. She'd left it on earlier, though she had muted the sound. But she'd never turned it off.

The lights back in the living room and the bulbs in the chandelier in the dining area grew dimmer and dimmer until they made a popping noise and died. All the rooms were dark now.

Kendra let out a low moan.

It shouldn't be dark. It's not evening yet.

She placed her palms against the glass door and stared out. Dark gray clouds, heavy with possible snow, crowded the sky. Unable to hold it back, fat white flakes began to fall. When she saw three preteen boys hurrying from the basketball court toward the apartments opposite hers, she banged on the patio door, yelling and praying they heard her. "Help me! Help!"

They continued as if they hadn't heard her and reaching one of the back patios, pushed aside the glass door and raced inside.

Maybe they didn't hear me. Maybe it controlled my sound so that they couldn't hear my calls. Just like at Nowhere Land. That voice in my head couldn't be Silas's. Silas is dead. He must be. Otherwise, we would have found his corpse. We never saw a sign of his or Regan's.

Nowhere Land had him forever. Kept him like it had done to all those others over the years.

"Oh, God, I'm going to die," she cried, as it struck her that she must be next in line.

She'd survived Burkett, but her luck had run out. There would be no second chances for her. She would discover where the entity took Silas.

"Kendra, you're right, your luck is gone, and I finally have you." The smell from earlier returned, only worse.

Feeling cold as ice, Kendra turned around to face the owner of the voice. A cartoonish version of Silas stood there. It no longer wanted to make her pretend she'd been hearing the real Silas. Whip-thin, he stretched until the top of his head touched the ceiling. That proved terrible enough, but his mouth horrified her. Jagged teeth crammed inside jaws unable to hold that much. Bizarre Silas mocked a grin at her. Not a real smile, but exactly like a predator baring its fangs at its prey before it struck.

"Silas, you look different," she said, managing to talk despite the terror, hoping to stave off the attack. "Not yourself."

"Do you like the new man? Bet you'd like to kiss my lips now, wouldn't you? I'm such a kissable guy." He laughed as if he'd told a joke that only he understood.

Kendra shook her head. "I like the old you, not this monstrosity. Besides, you're not Silas. The real Silas would never harm me. Silas would never want to kiss me, not when his husband was the true love of his life."

It leaned over. "Maybe not me, how about Zack? Zack's with me and Regan now. Would you kiss dead Zack's lips?" Surreal Silas straightened and cocked its head as he morphed into a dead Zack, one without arms and a head. "Maybe you preferred it rough and liked to be tied up and sawed in half before you let anyone take you. Is that it?"

Kendra reached behind her and grabbed the patio door lever again, spinning to jiggle it forcefully. The undead Zack must have developed arms with hands as she felt hands on her upper arms and she was twisted around, where something that was not Zack, but a tall shadow-person took her lips.

The kiss tasted disgusting, like rot. The being grew rougher, forcing his tongue inside her mouth. It wiggled around like a big, fat, slimy worm.

Kendra struggled, but his hands tightened on her arms so that she couldn't move them.

When he finally released her and dissipated, she felt something in her mouth, wiggling. Horrified, she threw up and watched in horror as live maggots hit the floor. She whined, shuddered, and whipped around, jerking at the latch in repeated attempts, hoping it would come undone. Fear made her bang on the glass, but she saw no one outside. There was no one to save her.

At that moment, someone—no, something, grabbed her by the ankles and yanked hard. She crashed to the floor, her forehead whacking the linoleum. Her throat tightened, making it hard for her to scream, hell, she couldn't even whisper. Whatever had taken her, lugged her along the floor from the kitchen to the stairs, and then bounced her up the steps. The pain was terrible. Finally, mercifully, she blacked out.

***

Kendra woke up with a shriek. She lay there, shuddering breaths hurting her lungs thinking she'd had an awful nightmare. One where something horrible had invaded her home and caught her. It looked like Silas at first, changing to Zack, minus a head and arms. *Stupid dream.* She sat up, but pain struck everywhere in her body. Worse of all, her left leg protested outright agony.

"What the..." She looked down where her leg would be. Nothing there, not even blood. Fear blasted her, and she screeched like a frightened bird. "My leg! Where's my leg?" Oh God, where is it?"

"Shut up, whore!" a male voice roared.

Flinching, not able to stop crying, she looked toward where the voice originated. A shadow stood there. She saw it had a white mouth beaming a razor smile. The shadow shifted and became a tall, thin one that reached the ceiling.

Her body lifted into the air. Nothing held her.

She struggled, screeching, fighting not to be taken, big, fat tears rolling down her cheeks. "Please, please, don't do this. Let me go. I promise never to never return to Burkett. I'll even give up ghost hunting."

She floated over to the shadow, and it embraced her in its arms. "Don't worry. It won't hurt long."

She stared at where she thought its face should be, but she only saw swirling darkness. "What are you going to do with me?"

"This!" It flung her at her bedroom window, and she smashed through the glass and into the snowstorm, falling straight down. She collided with the ground. Was she dead? The agony let her know she still lived. Dim awareness let her know when residents came out of their apartments. She wanted to cry out, call them to help her, dial 911, but she couldn't. When she tried to move her neck, it wouldn't shift, and she realized it might be broken. That she might have even damaged her back as feeling in her body began to leave her. Only her eyes could move.

I might as well be dead. Why haven't I died?

Someone stood over her, and she thought it might be one of her neighbors. Kendra looked. She didn't see a human, but her tormenter. The snowflakes avoided the entity, hitting everywhere but it.

Even the snowflakes know it's evil.

It leaned over, and she saw its true face for the first time and tried to scream but couldn't. Only a tiny wisp of sound slipped from her mouth.

"My neighbors will see you," she croaked out in a tiny voice.

It said, "No, they won't. I can control their reality like I control your voice, which is why right now you cannot call out. For your voice box is still working. The stupid mortals only see a suicidal woman, a broken mess. Not me." It pressed against her. "Never me, unless I want them to." It grinned. "They can't even see the falling snow avoid me."

"Monster."

"Nope, not that."

"Demon."

It chuckled. "Do you think every bad thing done on a paranormal level is by a demon? The Devil made me do it—such a stupid quote."

It dug inside her chest, and she felt its fingers burrow pass her ribs until it grasped something and yanked it free of her body. Her last sight showed it held a glowing orb

The entity snickered. "Your soul. One more soul for my freedom."

Her soul floated up and morphed, turning into a specter of her living form that had just expired. Her ghost stared down at her snow-covered corpse. The unclean smell of its captor wafted to her, and she wrinkled her nose. She turned to her murderer. "Now I understand that odor you give off. It's death. Are you Death?

The shadow yanked her against him. "No, I'm something much worse than all that you called me. Think god. A minor one to be sure, but once I am free of my prison, I will make this world mine. Now, it's time for us to go home."

Kendra's spirit cried out in revulsion, and they dissipated just as the first living person reached her body.

***

Kendra's next-door neighbor, Mrs. Jones, halted and turned to another neighbor who joined her. She shivered. The woman had forgotten to slip into her boots but rushed outside into the snow wearing only her bedroom slippers. She took a few steps back as she found herself stepping not into snow, but blood from a broken body lying there.

God it's Kendra from next door!

"Do you hear that?" the other neighbor asked.

She frowned as she turned to the elderly woman, "Hear what?"

"I swear, someone shouted."

They both moved aside as paramedics burst from their emergency vehicle in the parking lot nearby, just as Ben parked his truck and trailer beside them in the parking lot.

CHAPTER TWENTY-NINE

The flashing LED lights of the emergency vehicle through the heavy, falling snow blinded Neri and the occupants of Ben's truck. Ben took time to maneuver into a parking spot, peering for anyone who might be standing nearby through a snowy windshield the wipers worked hard at pushing off. He turned off the wipers, then the engine, before switching on the overhead light in the ceiling, lighting up everyone.

"What's going on?" he asked.

Neri closed her eyes, sorrow a big solid ache in her heart. They'd been too late. She knew Ben looked at her and she reopened her eyes, saw the question in his eyes before he widened them, and she realized he knew the answer. She nodded at him.

"It's Kendra," he said, horror evident in his voice. "We got here too late."

A moan came from behind Ben.

Russell.

Neri looked back over the seat at him. His face was lined with strain and the evidence of fear lingered in his eyes. A gray aura washed over him. This final nail in what he'd been through since they'd gotten to Nowhere Land had driven him close to losing it, but she watched as he fought hard for control of himself. A man who always believed logic held the answers for him in the face of the paranormal found this time the paranormal laughing at his loss of discipline.

She said, "I'm sorry, Russell."

He accorded Parker a dark look as he spat out the bitter words to match it. "I wished you never okayed for our group to investigate your damned property. Zack, Regan, Silas, and Kendra would still be alive."

He unbuckled his seat belt. "Let me out. Let me see for myself. Maybe the paramedics have nothing to do with Kendra." But his tone said he didn't believe that.

Ben opened his mouth, but closed it, opened his door and stepped out. Russell shoved the seat forward and leaped out, sloshing through the snow drifts on the ground as he hurried toward the crowd of people.

Neri opened her door and slipped out, followed by Parker.

Ben pushed the button on his key and with a beep, locked his vehicle. Then he stuck his hands in his pockets and shuffled through the snow over to where people milled around a couple of paramedics loading something onto a stretcher.

Neri knew it had to be Kendra. Sometimes she hated being precognitive.

She peered over the shoulder of one woman dressed in a housecoat over pajamas and bedroom slippers.

The lady twisted around to look at Neri.

"It's horrible. I didn't know my neighbor well, just saw her here and there, but she seemed like a nice young woman. She never appeared to be the suicide type."

Neri raised an eyebrow. "Suicide?"

"Why yes, it sure looks like she leaped from her bedroom window." The woman pointed up, and Neri worked to see as best as she could through the thickening snow, noticing what might be a broken window. She looked down at the ground, saw something glinting by one of the stretcher's wheels. A piece of glass? The snow covered it as the paramedics rolled the gurney to their van.

Neri shook her head. "She didn't kill herself."

The woman narrowed her eyes. "What do you mean? Of course, it's evident that she did. Did you think someone pushed her through her window?"

Neri swept her gaze around the place. *The entity's here.* She felt it watching them. "No, no, you might be right. I'm sure the police won't find anything to suggest murder."

She walked away, feeling the woman's gaze on her and something else's, too. She joined Ben and Parker beneath a lamp, at the edge of the crowd. The light fought to glow over them, despite the snow. It was enough to let her know that Russell didn't stand with them.

"Where's Russell?"

Ben said, pointing at the crowd, most disappeared under the snowflakes growing worse, "He's over there."

Neri managed to see a shadow detached from the others and head their way. Once it reached them, she realized it was Russell. He stopped by Ben, hunched over and appearing drained, and when he looked at them, she saw dark shadows beneath his eyes, that mix of emotions, terror, pain, and even anger, swirling in them.

"That monster murdered her. But they all think she jumped, killed herself," said Russell in a biting tone. "Which one of us is next?"

Parker spoke, "Neri, what about an exorcism?"

She noticed he had gotten closer to her. "Exorcism? That's only performed for a possessed person. If we were on Nowhere Land right now, I'd suggest doing a blessing of it. But if you want my opinion, I don't think any normal stuff will work."

Ben asked, "Why not? It's a spirit of a kind, right?"

She blew out air through her nose and huddled deep into her coat, feeling chilled, but not just from the cold air. "Ben, drive us to my house. We'll talk more there." She passed her gaze over the forms of the apartment dwellers heading back to their places, to the hint of the darkened shadows that the playground equipment and snow hid from normal eyes, but not cognitive senses. They told her the entity watched it all from there. Particularly her and the others. "It's not safe here to talk."

Ben gave Neri a funny look. "It's...here?"

"Just get us to my house." She had warded her home before leaving for the investigation, figured that would be as safe as they could be against what had followed them from Parker's property.

Ben nodded and replied, "Sure."

They all piled into his truck and Ben drove away. No one looked back to see if the ambulance had left. More so, to catch sight of something watching them go.

Neri felt it though.

Suddenly, she found herself in its thoughts. Alien, terrible...evil. She struggled to free her mind from its thoughts. Finally, it let her go with a dark laugh. But she knew why it had let them go with no problem. That scared her even more.

Russell said, "Can you drop me off at my place?"

Ben said, "Russell, it's not safe to be alone. Kendra had been alone and look what happened to her."

Russell shrugged. "It doesn't matter if I'm alone or with you guys, the entity will get me if it wants me. If it gets me, I rather I'd be at my place."

Ben pulled over to the side of the road and turned to look behind him at the other man. "But, Russell, I..."

Russell glared at Ben. "I quit. And I want to go home."

Neri leaned over and placed a hand on Ben's upper arm. Tension knotted the muscles beneath his coat sleeve. "Take him home. Please. You can't make Russell come with us, even though I agree, he should."

Ben sighed and eased off the brake, merging back onto the street. The sound of the wipers swiping the snow off the windshield was the only sound made, as everyone remained silent.

At Russell's apartment, Parker assisted the ex-investigator with his tent and what else he'd brought into the man's duplex apartment. Once Parker stepped back outside, Russell shut the door on his face when he turned to say goodbye. His hands stuffed in his coat's pockets, he walked back to the car where Neri waited by the opened passenger door. He climbed into the back seat and buckled in, and Neri jumped in, doing the same. Ben started the engine and drove away.

Ben murmured, "He's dead."

Neri shook her head as she realized the truth. "Or maybe he won't. Our foe may not go after him, because it no longer cares about him. Although, I can't promise that." She looked at Ben before she swept her head around to the back where Parker sat. "I do know, it only needs Parker and me."

Ben jammed on the brakes, and the truck screeched to a halt, skidding into an arc before Ben worked on control of the steering wheel and the tires, letting the vehicle slow to a stop. He breathed heavy, shaking. He'd almost killed them in his shock. Made them ready spirits for the entity to snatch. Luckily, no other vehicles were moving along the street. The snow kept them indoors.

"Why are you saying this, Neri?" he demanded.

"It wants Parker because he owns the land and because he is psychic, too." She turned to Parker. "It got to your sister, didn't it?"

Ben sputtered, "Whoa! You never said a word about your sister, Parker Burkett."

Parker fisted his hands in his lap. "I'm not sure if it possessed her and made her kill her husband. I could be wrong about even thinking that after our own experiences with this thing. Maybe she just lost it, because she caught him cheating on her or something."

Neri spoke in a soft voice. "I'm sorry about your sister, Parker. Ben, it was back there at Kendra's apartment building. It let me into its thoughts. It wants him because of who he is and because he is a strong psychic medium—"

Ben turned his anger on Neri. "I see—it's because I'm just a paranormal investigator, not needed to keep in the loop as I can't hear ghosts all the time. Keep the ghost hunter from knowing that some dangerous demonic thing wants souls, so that it can take over the world or something! That it wants psychic souls now."

Neri knew she'd hurt Ben and laid a hand on his shoulder. His tension made him stiffen at her touch, almost drawing away. He did turn his head away from her.

"No, Ben, we need you. You're not dispensable."

He looked at her.

She continued, "It wants Parker, but it also wants me because it feels I have enough psychic power to add to his to help it finally be set free. The entity won't need any more souls if it takes us. We would be the final ingredients to what it has amassed over eons. That's why it may no longer care about Russell."

Ben's eyes narrowed. "Free it from what?"

"It's prison."

CHAPTER THIRTY

Neri unlocked the door and slipped inside, hitting the light switch on the wall nearby to turn on the light in the living room. Parker and Ben followed her in.

She pointed at the coatrack by the foyer. "Hang up your jackets and get warm. It shouldn't take me more than ten minutes to collect the crystals I need."

She flipped another switch at the beginning of the hallway and light flooded it.

Parker said, "Crystals?"

Neri paused and turned. "We'll need them if we hope to open a doorway to the entity's dimensional prison." She continued down the hallway, leaving the two men alone.

***

Parker slipped off his jacket; Ben didn't, but he lifted the edge of the blind on the window and looked out.

"You do know she's planning for us to head to Nowhere Land tonight and not wait for morning."

"But it's been snowing..."

Ben dropped the blind and turned around. "It doesn't matter. I know Neri. It's now or too late. Besides, the snow is tapering off." He shrugged. "Not that makes it any less safe, or easier to drive. I'm hoping that VDOT salted and sanded the highways at least. Can't promise about the secondary roads, though."

Parker stuck his arms through the sleeves of his jacket and put it back on. "Great. Death by slick roads or by some demon thing taking our souls in Hell."

"It's not a demon, Parker."

Neri had returned, carrying a cardboard box. She handed it to Ben. Both men peered inside and saw crystals of different sizes.

"The ones with the most power. Parker's and my psychic power will add to theirs, and we should be able to nudge open the doorway." She gave a wry twist of her lip. "It should, no, yes, I believe it will open it. Put the box in your truck. While you're at it, unhitch your trailer and leave it here. No need for it."

Ben grumbled, but he put his jacket back on and walked out the door after Neri opened it. Closing it with a soft click, she looked at Parker.

"It's not a demon, Parker. It's a god. Well, a minor one anyway. I managed to get in contact with the spirit world while in my office. The entity had taken my spirit guide, but my mother's spirit came through to me. She let me know it's Okee. That's what the Powhatans called it, although it's older than them, much older. It never had a name, but it took the one the natives called it. Took many of their souls, too."

He said, "I'm not sure how good I will be. I mean, I've never taken on a god before."

Neri smiled. "Neither have I. There's always a first time for anything."

She stuck her house key in her jeans pocket, threw on her jacket, slipped knitted gloves over her hands, and opened the door, setting the locks as she did so.

Parker sighed and followed her out the door.

"Maybe it's the first time, I just hope it's not the last time for us."

CHAPTER THIRTY-ONE

Russell had tossed his dirty clothes, including those he was wearing, into the hamper in the laundry area, before stepping into his bathroom to take a hot shower.

The water sluiced over him, and it felt good. Not that it might wash away the memories of this investigation and the death of people he knew. That might take a while, and he may even need to talk to a therapist.

Right. How do you tell someone that a ghost or demon killed your friends? No psychiatrist is going to believe that. Hell, if I hadn't been at Burkett and seen what I'd seen, I would consider them delusional.

Russell squirted shampoo out of the tube, rubbing the gel into his hair. His hands felt good, massaging it into his scalp. It made him feel drowsy, and his eyelids lowered...

Something brushed against his buttocks and jarred him awake. He craned his neck around to see what it was. The weather had been freezing, but that didn't mean some insect hadn't gotten in his apartment when the temperature had been warmer and not detected by him.

Nothing. Only him, the water, the—eyes? Freaking eyes! Staring at him through the thin, pale plastic shower curtain. Russell wrenched it open. But he didn't find anyone standing on the other side or elsewhere in the bathroom. The door was still closed, and the room was small, so there were no places someone or something could hide.

He yanked the curtain closed, snickering uneasily. *That's it.* No more paranormal investigating shows, no more books about the paranormal, all were off limits for him. Maybe he would drive down to Aquarian Bookshop in Carytown, see about finding a psychic who could smudge his place and even him. Just in case. Not that he believed in the supernatural still. What happened to them on Nowhere Land had to have logical—

What's that? Sounded like fingernails scratching on the linoleum wall in the shower stall. Maybe he might have done it accidentally.

"Keep telling yourself that, Russell buddy. Maybe you'll convince yourself." A giggle caused the hair on his body to rise. "NOT!"

Russell shrieked and almost fell out of the shower, the shower curtain tight in his hand. He ripped the plastic from its rings and he slip-slid on the linoleum floor, catching himself in time before slamming into the sink.

His heart knocking against his chest and shaking, Russell stared with wide eyes at the shower and the black cloud growing inside it. The water still ran, passing through the thing, steam rising as if it had hit something icy. The darkness rose and became thinner, until only a tall, slender shadow remained. The dark figure took hold of the shower head and yanked it out, water spraying. Instead of hot water filling the shower and into the bathroom, chunks of ice replaced it. Some pieces smacked Russell.

The creature laughed. "Oh, look at your face, Russell. You look almost white."

His paralysis broken, Russell bolted for the door, which he found locked and wouldn't budge, no matter how much he tried. Nasty laughter filled the bathroom, and he fell into a huddle, covering his face with his arms.

He thought, *Of course, Russell, did you think you would escape the fate the other team members had? And yeah, I said I didn't care if it got me, at least I would be in my own home. Well, I lied, because I want to live!*

Russell finally looked up and saw the swirling mass of black nothingness right above him. He couldn't stop screaming until the entity ripped his head from his neck and sucked his soul out of his body.

CHAPTER THIRTY-TWO

What took an hour to maybe an hour-and-a-half on a typical day driving from where Neri lived to get to Burkett, it took longer tonight.

Ben took his time, driving slowly and carefully.

Neri felt grateful that VDOT had salted and sanded I-64. It still didn't make for safe conditions on the highway. Plus, once they took the exit, it was hard to say what, if any secondary roads were prepared for the winter weather.

Yes, the snow had stopped falling, but due to the temperature dropping down close to the teens, the cement became a hazard, the truck making it a wild rollercoaster ride. Ben had put his vehicle into 4-wheel drive, and she hoped that it would help. Thank God, people had listened to stay off the road as it appeared empty of the usual traffic. They finally made it to Burkett twenty minutes to 3 a.m.

The witching hour.

People believed that midnight was the witching hour, but it was the time between 2:00 to 4:00 a.m. Folklore portrayed 3 a.m. being the Devil's hour when supernatural events happened the best. When spirits, demons, gremlins, and witches are at their most potent. That black magic is at its most effective around this time.

Happy hour for evil gods.

Neri hugged herself as chills after chills skittered along her nerves. Maybe that meant the crystals and Parker and she could get the doorway opened, but again, the time might make things worse. Help set Okee free.

Parker unlocked and pushed the gate open.

Ben drove past him, but stopped, so that Parker could climb back inside. No one complained that Parker had left the gate open. It might make escaping easier if they needed to do that. If things went south and Okee went after them.

If Okee comes after us, there'll be no escape.

Neri stopped thinking, as Ben parked as close as he could to their former campsite. Or what he thought could have been the spot, as thick drifts of snow had covered the entire area. He had turned the truck around, facing the way for fleeing.

Parker handed the box of crystals over to Neri who'd set it in back with him, and she took her time sloshing through the snow to what she hoped would be the middle of the village. She directed Ben and Parker to knock away as much of the white stuff, and she deposited each crystal, forming a pyramid. Stepping back, she took each man by the hand.

Neri called out, "Achak. Do you hear me?"

Silence. She tried again.

"Achak."

A gray image appeared.

Neri could see through it, but enough for her to see a man with long hair wearing a loincloth. He stood maybe no more than five feet tall.

Why do you call me? He didn't say them out loud, but the words filled her head.

"I need your help. I have my crystals set out on the ground; I am a psychic and the man to my right is one, too, but despite our abilities, we need to know how to get into Okee's prison."

No. I will not. Okee has not taken me to his dark world like many of my people. It took all my shaman powers to hide from him on this land I haunt.

Neri grew excited. If Achak had kept Okee from taking his spirit because he could hide from it, she suspected it was due to him being a psychic, too. A very powerful one, as he had managed to keep Okee from suspecting he haunted Burkett for centuries.

She pleaded, "Help us. It won't just be you anymore. Combine your abilities with ours to help us open the other world. I promise we won't ask you to travel to it. Hold it open for us, that way we'll be able to help all the lost souls Okee has taken—including your tribe—escape and find their way over to the other side, and it will enable us to come back to this world, too."

Achak didn't say anything, and as the minutes drew closer to three o'clock, Neri worried he would refuse.

His voice spoke softly inside her head. *I will do it. If you can free all the spirits, that will mean, my wife will be able to go, and I can finally leave this land and be with her.*

She smiled. "Yes, yes, you can. Thank you, Achak."

Ben cocked an eyebrow. "Is he going to help?"

Parker nodded. "Yes, Achak will." He flashed Neri a self-conscious grin. "I could hear him, too.

Ben grumbled, "Not fair being the only non-psychic here."

A radiant light flashed, and Achak no longer stood in front of them. The crystals shone with such brilliance that they hurt their eyes.

Neri squeezed her eyes shut, saying, "Ben, Parker, just keep holding my hands and don't look directly at the crystals."

A raw cold, worse than what filled the night, pierced through Neri. Wondering why, she popped open her eyes. A horizontal line as tall as the nearby shacks land illuminating with intense crimson light now hovered where the crystals had been. Besides the fierce bitterness, a rotten odor wafted to her. *It smells like death.* She squeezed Ben's and Parker's hands, only to realize she held nothing but air. A quick look at each side let her know that both had vanished. Oh God, had Okee taken them?

Achak's voice talked in her head, even though she didn't feel his presence. *They're gone and in that other world. You must enter, find them, and release all the souls Okee holds there.*

"All right, Achak. Wish me luck." Neri headed for the line.

No, I wish you more. I wish you a miracle.

Neri stopped just short of the pulsing thing. The awful smell from it rushed against her face. She flinched and tried to block it out, but the filth of evil infiltrated her nostrils anyway. The freezing air punched its way past the protective warmth of her outerwear to her skin. With no other choice but to go forward, Neri reached out with her gloved hands and the line thickened, spreading apart until it was large enough for her to step through. She did, laying her gloved hands on each side to steady herself.

The doorway's coldness burned Neri's fingertips through the material of the gloves. She couldn't be sure what the opening represented. Not anything earthly. Whatever it was, it felt truly alien.

Once she passed through it, she steadied herself as her body and even her mind fast forwarded in a version of a wormhole. An E-ticket ride of insanity. When it stopped, she leaned over and threw up.

She straightened, almost used her gloved hands to wipe her mouth, but not sure if holding onto the doorway might have fouled the material; she took them off before touching her mouth.

The skin on her hands and mouth felt knife cold. Neri stuffed her hands in her gloves again. Then she took stock of where she might be and saw a place where everything seemed to be colored blood-red. A very alien place.

Where's Ben and Parker? She didn't see either of the two men.

Hell? Am I in Hell? Or what could be interpreted as Hell?

Yes, maybe interpreted might be the right word. Some people with the Sight might have seen this world, this "other" place and thought it must be Hell. Neri always thought of Hell as a real place, but not here. If humanity's version of Hell was terrible, this place made that child's play. She let her inner eye send out feelers to figure it out. Maybe she would find Parker and Ben that way, too.

What is this place? Not Hell, though it is a hell made for Okee. What kind of being did this? God? Or something godlike? What crime did Okee commit?

Her blood chilled.

This dimension was where Okee had been locked up, at least most of the time, sharing the same spot metaphysically as Burkett. Aspects touching? Had the prison been here before the beginning of the Earth? Or had eons later, the land that is known today as Burkett connected to here at some point, or had Okee found a way to do it? So many questions and they began to hurt her head.

Neri leaned over to scrutinize the ground closer. It appeared to be...rotting? Did dirt decay? She straightened and wandered over to what looked like trees and on close inspection of one trunk saw that its bark had the same putrefaction problem as the rest of the terrain. Slipping a pen from her pants pocket, she prodded at it and found no rotting wood, but something else. A sort of disgusting gray spongy stuff.

Screams cut through her head. *Stop it! You're hurting us!*

She widened her eyes in horror and backed away. *Oh, God, that sounded human!*

More cries of torment jammed her head, begging her, some of them demanding her, all in different languages, to set them free. Modern and ancient words that she would never be able to understand back on Earth, except through her medium abilities? Otherwise, she would never have been able to communicate with Achak.

No, she sensed this wasn't due to her being a medium, but that this world changed the rules for its visitors. *Or prisoners.* It appeared that she had gotten a communication device in her head so that she heard everyone in English.

"Who or what are you?" she asked, spinning around and eying the forest.

One answered her in her head, *Souls. Spirits. The dead.*

"Trees made of souls. Did Okee do this to you?"

Not just trees—other things, too. Not just the one this time, but many voices shouted the words.

Her head was hammering and feeling ill in her stomach, she bent over and retched again. This time around, nothing but dry heaves came out of her mouth.

To think some being could do this to innocent souls. Reshape them for his world, imprison them.

But why?

"I'm sorry. I didn't mean to hurt you." She caressed one of the trees' trunks, fighting the revulsion overcoming her. It wasn't their fault. "Please, forgive me." She clenched her hands and made a promise. "I'll find a way to free you and then send you to the right place that you need to go. This world is not the Afterlife. Not the Other Side of the Veil. It may be a prison, but no one had shaped it for you." Burning anger swept through her. "I can see why they had locked up the bastard. Though if they thought themselves powerful gods, they should have made sure he couldn't escape it, even for a short time. Then no one's soul would have been torn from them and brought here."

Determination enveloped her, and she started walking through the macabre woods. Not knowing her destination, she only knew she had to find Ben and

Parker. Before their souls became part of this terrible world. And yes, before Okee made hers a permanent resident of it, too.

CHAPTER THIRTY-THREE

Parker regained consciousness. He blinked, and only seeing glowing red, sat up and held his aching head.

God. It feels like I've been drinking all night. Back when I was in college.

Parker remembered Neri, Ben and him getting ready to enter that strange strip of light. Now, after what felt like a minute, he woke up here. Wherever that was. And that crimson color of the doorway must have imprinted on his mind, as he saw the place bathed in it. Maybe it hadn't been only a minute. How long had he been here?

"Ah, Sleeping Beauty has awakened at last." Ben's voice sounded sarcastic.

"Ben?"

"Yep, right here with you. Did you think I would leave my new best friend?"

"Where are we? Is Neri all right?"

"Sad to report, it's just us boys. Not sure where Neri is or if she's okay or not. Wait a moment; I don't know where the fuck we are. It could be Hell. I haven't felt any heat in this place, so, thankfully, we're not roasting, but it stinks awful, and it feels frigid. Maybe Hell is like being stuck in the Antarctic."

Parker got to his feet. Still feeling shaky, he reached out, took a single step at a time, trying to find walls, Ben. Hell, anything. Well, maybe not anything, he did not want to run into Okee. "Where are you at in here?"

"Not leaning against any of the walls. I did it once and besides feeling disgusting, I think it jiggled. Guess it was a jiggle. Like gelatin."

Parker stopped. "It's dark in here, except for that red glow, so how could you tell I was awake?"

"Well, I did awake sooner than you did, and my eyes have adjusted to this weird light. Besides, I'm near you, and I heard you moan. Look down. If you give your eyes time, you can see me. We're like dark, bloody figures in this place."

Parker peered down and saw first eyes looking back up at him, then bit by bit, he could see the red outline of someone on the ground. He lowered himself to join Ben.

Parker groaned as he grabbed his head. "Damn head feels like there are little guys inside it, pickaxing away at my brain."

"Yeah, like we woke up from an all-nighter. I did the stupid and stumbled to my feet after I came to, ended up tossing a few of my stomach contents in some corner. It didn't help that this cell or whatever we're in smells like dead bodies and dog piss combined and touching that nasty wall, well, it just did it for me. I managed to find you still lying out cold and sat down to wait until you woke up. Which you eventually did, otherwise we wouldn't be having this conversation."

Parker asked, "How'd we get here?"

Ben snorted. "You think I know? Let's see; I'm assuming the devil god swept us up before we could walk through that thing hanging in the air. At least, he left us all in one piece and didn't rip our souls from our bodies."

Parker said, "We're the bait."

"What?"

"Figure out the math; it's simple. Okee wanted not only to lure Neri into his world but have her enter it alone. The monster knows she'll try and find us."

"Shit. We need to get out of here. Neri might need our help." Parker watched as Ben tried once, twice, before it took a third time for him to heave himself to his feet.

Parker climbed to his feet, only needing the one time.

"Great, it takes him one time to get up, me, three," grumbled Ben in a whisper. "No wonder Neri doesn't see me as a man."

Pretending he never heard that, Parker said, "Maybe if we feel around the walls, we might find a door?"

"Before I found you, I did that. Just stumbled around in a circle. No door or any opening that I could find."

"There has to be a way out. If nothing else, maybe we can kick and punch at the walls and yell, until someone comes to check on us."

"Thinking more a something than a someone. And that fiend doesn't need a door; the god can make an opening and close it afterward. I think it comes with being a god or something like that."

"Whatever," remarked Parker moving slow and steady until his hands found a wall. It didn't feel like wood or stone, more gelatinous. Maybe he could dig into it?

He shoved fingers into the stuff, trying not to think of its contents. Otherwise, he might do what Ben mentioned he did earlier: throw up. The odor worsened the more he clawed his hands into the gelatin stuff, managing to scoop out pieces and tossing them aside. The wall began to tremble. A disembodied shriek tore into his mind.

"Ben, get over here!" yelled Parker. "The damn wall doesn't like me tearing at it."

The other man joined him, and both worked on the strange material. The more they burrow into the wall, the more movement and yelling and moaning it did.

Before they knew it, the noise filled the room. They sounded like the cries of the tortured damned.

Parker stopped scooping and yelled himself.

"Hear them?"

Ben asked, "Hear who? What are you talking about?"

"Voices. So many voices. All are crying out as if someone is hurting them." He understood. "Stop it, Ben! It's the wall. We're doing the harm. Oh, my God, the walls of this room are made of—"

Ben finished for him. "People?" He stepped away, his face lining with revulsion as he shook out his hands. "Am I ripping souls apart? Oh, fricking hell!"

Parker shook the stuff out of his hands, too. "Yeah, hell for them." He thought of something and approached the wall. "Hey, guys, look, ah, we don't want to hurt you, but if you can part from each other, make us a way out, we can escape. We think a friend of ours is in this world and once we hook up with her, we have a plan to stop Okee. We would be able to free you all, get you out of this place and back to Earth or somewhere else. You can find your way to where all the dead go. I bet even if some of you end up in the real Hell, but it's got to be better than this prison. Will you help us? Kick a bad god in the ass?"

Silence. The voices didn't answer him, not at first.

Finally, one voice did. It sounded male, familiar. Parker couldn't think of who it might be.

"We'll help you, Parker. There may be some who won't, not at first, but I will. We all agree."

Chris? His brother-in-law? "Chris, is that you?"

"Yeah, it's me. Okee got me, by using Lisa. Guess this will teach me I shouldn't have cheated on her or smacked her around. I know it's rather late to say it. But I am sorry."

Parker didn't know how to answer that. He admitted a small portion of him thought the guy deserved what he got. And yet—

"I have to think about that, Chris. It was my sister. If you and the others get us out of here, maybe by the time all of us leave this dimension or wherever the fuck we are, I might thank you. It won't be a 'forgive you' deal, but a step toward healing."

"I understand."

The wall undulated, shifting until it parted.

Parker said, "Ben, we have our way out."

Ben walked over to him, and the pair of them slipped through the opening.

Parker paused and looked back.

"If you could do this, I think all of you can come apart, become individuals again. I don't know for sure but try it."

Ben and he moved away as it looked like a circular building began to jerk and sway before it exploded, and pieces flew everywhere. Those pieces became smaller pieces until hundreds of orbs floated. Their glow diminished, until only sad-looking, red balls remained.

Ben stuck a hand into the pocket of his cargo pants and pulled out something small and gray.

Parker's eyes widened when he saw an EMF meter. It had all its lights lit and flashed in a continuous sequence.

Ben saw him looking and gave a self-conscious grin, shrugged.

"Yeah, yeah, I'm ever the ghost hunter. Figured I could take one piece of equipment with me, so I stuffed it in a pocket. I mean, it's an opportunity. Another dimension. Full of ghosts and heck, one god, even if a minor one."

Parker shook his head. "Come on, we've got to find Neri."

Ben and he took off at a run.

***

An orb followed the two men. Neither saw it trailing them, nor did Parker sense it.

I'm not worried about the ghost hunter, but with that psychic crap of his, the other mortal could get wind of me. If he does, Okee won't do as he promised and make me a living man again.

CHAPTER THIRTY-FOUR

So many voices were calling and pleading. Neri even heard threats. As if they could carry those out without Okee's permission.

How many entities made up this prison? Had the being behind this place used the first souls to make the metaphysical bars to imprison Okee? It didn't matter who was to blame, Okee alone or others. All the spirits would be freed. Gods be damned.

The voices continued, overwhelming her.

She shouted, "Stop it! I can only do what I can do. I'm only one medium."

The demands quieted. Her headache still throbbed. She could set up a block, but if she did that, she wouldn't sense an attack before it was too late.

She wished she had an army of mediums, paranormal investigators, and whoever else could help. Even the United States Army. They had weapons. All she had was her psychic powers. Not sure if that would help when one went up against a god, even a minor one. Look at Achak; he still had died. Now having one of those military weapons combined with her ability to summon or exorcise ghosts, demons and angels? That'd be sweet.

Neri sagged in defeat. She wouldn't know how to lock and load that gun. Unless she could summon the ghost of someone who just died fighting in a current war. Her brother came to mind, but she shook her head. There would be no way she would bring her brother here. That would finally get Okee's hands on the boy he almost had gotten once.

He died in Afghanistan. So, how do you know that Okee didn't cause that and already has Mike here? He did say he'd killed Mike when he took your guide's shape, remember?

Okee might be able to get out on occasion and hit nearby spots in Virginia, but she doubted the god could take a quick jaunt overseas. She hoped his leash happened to be that short, anyway. Besides, she didn't sense Mike.

There's a lot of souls here, too many, so how can you be sure he isn't?

She halted at the edge of the fake forest. Her jaw dropped, and her eyes widened, as she saw the skyscrapers and other buildings of the city, everything full of the crimson sparkling light. It held an eerie, otherworld beauty. It terrified her.

Is this a trap set for me?

It's an attractive one. The spider quote came to mind.

Come to my web, said the spider to the stupid psychic medium fly.

Some poisonous spiders looked beautiful, too, but a smart person still didn't pick one up to pet it. Problem for Neri, smart or not, something told her if she wanted to find Parker and Ben, she needed to enter that place.

She just wished she had venom for evil gods. One that killed them.

***

Parker felt like they'd walked for miles. Although how could they tell, since the soul trees, as Parker called them, all look exactly the same. They hadn't even found Neri yet.

"Maybe she never made it to this dimension," said Ben.

Parker shook his head. "Ben, she's here."

Ben halted and turned. "You're in attuned with her, due to the both of you being psychic mediums."

"Ah, yeah." Parker continued, "I'm sorry—"

Ben didn't let him finish. "Not your fault, or hers." He sighed. "It's just the first time I met Neri, I knew she was the one for me. We both were interested in the paranormal, she handled my wisecracks with no bother, and we were..." He stopped, staring in the distance, before he looked at Parker. "Connected. I thought we were connected. When she started dating John, I realized I was the only one who felt a connection. Dumb guy."

"No, you're not."

"Yes, I was and still am, because here it is all over again, when I thought maybe we'd get together after the 'John' episode, she meets you." He chuckled, though it held a hint of melancholy. "Maybe after this, I should join the priesthood, give up on women."

Parker pointed. "We can talk about this once we get out of this hellhole. Hey, look! See that?"

Ben narrowed his eyes. "Does that look like a city?"

"Yes, it does. A bloody city for a bloody world. Come on."

As Ben trotted after Parker, he mumbled, "Yeah, where a bloody god is probably the mayor of it.

***

Neri entered the city, keeping close to the buildings to remain hidden. As if that would help. The souls knew she was walking on its road and no doubt, Okee knew she was here. Most likely, it waited for her, too, at whichever building made up as its castle.

At that moment, she felt it; the beginning of the thread Okee sent her. More and more like a spider, drawing the fly to its web. She shuddered.

Though she knew it to be a foolish move, she followed it through streets and through buildings, where souls cried out to her. Warning her.

"I know, I know. But I need to face Okee, or you'll be a part of his world forever, while he escapes to my dimension."

If he gets her soul and Parker's, too, then it would be a foregone conclusion that Okee leaves here. She didn't tell the others that though.

Not sure how long it took, Neri arrived at where Okee holed up. She didn't feel Parker in there. Did that mean Okee didn't have him, or had the demi-god concealed him from her psychic feelers?

The only way to know for sure is to enter the monster's den.

Neri reached out to grab the doorknob, when the door opened wide on its own. Seeing only darkness beyond and not feeling anything, she stepped through. The door slammed behind her, enclosing her in the weird crimson light.

"Welcome, welcome," said a familiar nasty voice. "Once the other two get here, may the games begin."

An orb with a dirtied glow appeared. "They are almost here. Remember your promise to make me alive again. I can't wait to punch that bitch, Lisa, for letting you possess her, so you could kill me. She needs a good beating from her hubby. Then I will let you have her soul."

Neri peered at the orb, trying to get a fix on its thoughts. She understood who it was in life.

"You're Chris Polivka? Married to Parker's sister?"

The orb whirled around her, snickering. "I am Chris Polivka! As for Lisa, that bitch is going to pay for my death and me being stuck in this place. Okee promised."

She shook her head. "He's lying to you. You're trusting something that killed you. Think about that. Whatever Okee means to do, it's not bringing you back to life. Maybe he doesn't even have the power to do that."

The orb screeched. "Is that true? Did you lie to me?"

Okee moved like smoke over to it, swirled around the former person. "Of course, I will make you alive. I'm a god and with her and Parker, I won't need one little soul like yours. Now, go pretend you found out where I am and lead the two mortal men here."

The orb dissipated.

Okee snickered. "You're right. Such a stupid soul. His was tarnished before I ever took it. He deserves to be in this dimension forever. Dead, dead, dead, dead..."

The word filled the room as Okee vanished from her sight.

Neri dropped to her knees and tears welled up in her eyes. Not for Parker's brother-in-law, but for her, Parker, and Ben, and the other souls who weren't 'tarnished' when Okee killed them.

CHAPTER THIRTY-FIVE

i, Parker.

Parker stopped as he heard Chris's voice in his head. "Chris?"

It's me. I discovered where Okee is. He's captured Neri, too.

The orb whipped around Parker and Ben.

Ben asked, "What's going on?"

Parker replied, "It's my brother-in-law again. He claims he knows where Okee is, says he has Neri."

Chris's voice yelled inside Parker's head. He sounded like a spoiled child. *I do, I do! Okee is in his place in the city!*

Parker said, "He says it's true."

"So, we take the word of a dead man and go?"

"It's Neri. Chris was awful to my sister, but if he can get us to Neri..."

Ben nodded. "Well, for Neri, I like to live dangerously. Why else would I do this?" He looked at Parker. "Well, tell the orb to get a move on and take us there."

The orb spun off as if in answer, and Parker joined Ben, and they both broke into a run to keep up with it.

***

The orb snickered. *A dead man, was he? He'd show that stupid man. Of course, Parker would blame him over his bitch sister. Soon, it will be that Ben creep and asshole Parker that will be dead and he alive.*

***

Neri sat Indian style on the floor, hoping she didn't hurt some poor soul. She'd tried earlier to see if she could make her getaway, but there had been no doors and windows. Okee had sealed the room until the others came to rescue her.

There had to be a way to get away from Okee. To defeat him and imprison him here forever.

The only way to lock him in this dimension for good is through the being or beings that put him here in the first place. It'd been their mistake not sealing it to ensure Okee stayed in it permanently.

It hit Neri how to do it, but she needed to wait until Parker and Ben got here, so all three of them could break out and head back to the spot where the doorway was between worlds.

She quickly cleared her mind as Okee had returned.

"The males are here," said the tall creature, drawing close to her.

"Neri!"

That was Ben.

Okee laughed.

The sound sent a chill up her spine.

"Go ahead. Let your males know you are here," said Okee.

It didn't matter if she didn't do it, they would be herded here by the traitor Chris.

"I'm here, Ben."

The room lightened, and she saw them come up to her. She stood and went to hug first Ben, then Parker.

Ben searched Neri's face. "Are you all right?"

Neri nodded. "Yes. I'm just sorry that you and Parker are here." She looked at Parker. "I'm sorry about Chris."

Understanding filled his eyes, and he turned to the orb who no longer was an orb, but the shade of Chris standing behind the two men. "I should have known. Cheat on your wife, beat her, being a turncoat isn't that far behind."

Chris sneered. "Yes, you should have 'used' your psychic powers. But they're as lame as you are."

Ben asked, "Why?"

Neri answered, "Because Okee promised to make him alive again."

Ben's eyes widened. "You said Okee is a god of a kind. Can he do that?"

Neri wrinkled her nose. "No, I know he can't. He only said what Chris wanted to hear."

Chris's ghost looked up at the god who'd been quiet. "What's she saying? Make me alive, now. Then send me back home."

Okee towered over the smaller spirit. "No. You know what happens to those who believe what they want to believe?" The shadow man bent over until its face of whirling shadows was close to Chris's frightened one. "You'll become a part of me. I planned for all the souls to become a part of me; you'll do it sooner."

Once more an orb, it sailed away, shrieking, until it ran into a wall, merging with it.

Okee turned his attention to them. "Now, it's your turn."

Neri said, "You wanted Parker and me, as the final souls to bypass this dimension and go to ours, to stay there for good. Let Ben go. Send him back to Earth."

"Oh, no. Yes, all I need is the two of you as psychic mediums that are powerful, so I can finally leave. But it won't hurt to add your other hero, call him added insurance."

Neri snatched Parker's hand. "Parker, time to talk to ghosts."

He stared at her and nodded. "Sure."

Neri called out, "All the lost spirits here, in this corrupt city, in this world, hear me! You have the power to set yourselves free. Use this man whose hand I hold and me, and join us to stop Okee and take down this city and the surrounding forest Okee made!"

"NO!" Okee's voice shouted and he grew taller, the ceiling beginning to shatter.

Not only the ceiling, but the walls and the floor separated. Neri felt this happening also in the city and the woods nearby. Okee's imprisoned souls fought to be free, using her and Parker as psychic conduits.

She dropped Parker's hand and yelled, "It's time to leave. Now!"

The trio fled, passing through ectoplasm of many spirits. The giant roar of Okee followed them as they bolted down what had been a street, heading toward where Neri hoped would be where the portal would be.

"Okee sounds pissed off," said Parker.

"You think so?" retorted Ben.

Another earth-shaking roar came out of Okee's mouth as the reality of the world completely went down. The false buildings crumbled, red crystals shards tumbling to the ground, piling all around them as they kept running.

They saw for the first time the weird things that had lived inside them. These things stumbled and screamed, surging out into the streets, only to have the earth become giant pits and swallow them. No longer confined to structures, roads, and more, spirits fled as whatever power held them came undone. The city vanished in seconds. Emptiness replaced it, glowing red.

Okee shook a sharp finger at the tiny humans. "It does not matter. Once I tear your souls from you, I will flee this prison. Maybe the souls no longer are shaped to my delight, but they're still in this prison with me. I like what I see of your world. A place full of non-believers, insane religious fanatics, evil, depraved humans, and as for the rest: fodder for my darkness. I will be worshipped. And I will search for the other minor gods imprisoned like me and free them to come here."

Neri, Ben, and Parker looked at each other. There are more like Okee in dimensional prisons?

Neri thought, *We must stop him.*

Dodging metaphysical trees and stones that Okee made appear to stop them, they barreled past what remained of the end of the city and into a forest coming apart.

Neri's lungs screamed from the fetid air. Her chest burned. The air grew denser, less oxygenated. Out of the corner of her eye, she noticed that Parker struggled, too. As for Ben, his running slowed. If they didn't find the doorway that led back to Burkett, sooner than later, Okee would catch them. Worse, they would perish due to lack of oxygen.

Okee only needed their souls; get those, and he would be free. Free to ravage their planet, free to control and gain followers. Free to have those followers cause mayhem.

Something of immense power slammed into Neri's solar plexus, and she tripped.

Parker gripped her by the arm to keep her from falling.

She stared ahead and saw a glimmer, one that grew bigger as they drew closer. Behind them, her senses told her that Okee had stepped up his game to stop them.

"Look." Neri's breathing labored as she pointed ahead. "It's the doorway."

A shimmer wavered at what might be a tunnel, though Neri doubted that. It was just the way her third eye saw it. Or a comfortable way of seeing it.

Ben grabbed her other arm, and both men forced her to head toward it. Just as they came upon the opening, the shimmer began to shrink, until it was nothing more than a ball of fire floating in the atmosphere.

Neri screeched. "No! This can't be happening!"

Parker, Ben, and she whipped around.

Her heart in her mouth, she quaked as Okee towered over them. He had hellish, mad things dancing with glee around his feet. The same things she'd seen in the false city earlier. Were they the actual residents of this dimension? Or something he made with his magic? On noticing they shone with the same crimson light, she believed them to be Okee's manifestations.

Ben dropped Neri's arm. "Neri, you got us in here with Achak's help. Can you summon him? I mean, with him, can the both of you reopen the portal? Parker and I will keep the god who thinks he's big shit, and whatever the fuck those are, busy."

"God, no, Ben. Parker. No, he'll..."

Both men left her alone. She needed to call Achak and bring back the opening to full force, or both men would die and forfeit their souls to this hellhole. Hers, too.

She wondered if she could do what Ben suggested. *I may not be strong enough.* She closed her eyes and shuddered.

If she did nothing, they would die. If she tried, they might still perish, but it was better to try her best. She reopened her eyes.

The damn dark entity had his way for eons. Now, it's our turn.

Neri drew as close as she could get to the heat rising off the fireball. It hurt.

"Achak."

Nothing. The medium inched closer to the ball. Its temperature scorched her skin. Any closer and she would be set alight.

"Please, Achak. I need you to come and help me, to call for those who made this prison. Help the other spirits finally be set free and give them and us a way home. It's time to stop Okee."

A soft female voice added its plea to Neri's. "My love, yes, help us all. Or we will never be together."

Neri saw an Algonquian woman standing near her, naked except for a deerskin skirt, and a few tattoos etched into the skin of both arms. One didn't need to be a psychic to understand that this must be Achak's wife.

Another shimmer formed in front of her.

Achak?

A face formed in the pale shimmer. High cheekbones. Piercing black eyes. It was Achak. Wearing a breechcloth, leggings, and moccasins of buckskin and a feathered cloak settled upon his shoulder, he'd become fully formed.

His wife drifted over to him and stopped. She turned her head away.

Neri understood as waves of shame at what Okee had done with her over the centuries hit Neri. The woman no longer felt worthy of her husband.

Neri bowed her head and said, "Thank you for appearing in this place, my friend."

He glowered. "I can be caught by the devil god. Made to help free him at last, something I fought not to let him do."

"I'm sorry, but my two friends and I'll become residents of this world, plus your wife and so many other unless you and I can get that way out opened again. Bring back the beings who imprisoned Okee here."

The ghost floated closer to her. "Devil god has much power here. Okee would need to be distracted, so we can open it up, call the gods who put him here."

"Oh."

She turned and tried to run over to Parker, but a gale appeared, its winds making it difficult to make it to him. Finally, she managed to get to him.

Parker turned to her and frowned.

"What are you doing here—"

She shouted over the roar of the growing wind, Okee, and the others. "I got Achak, but he says we need to get Okee's mind busy while he and I call Okee's jailers and reopen the portal."

Ben fell against Parker. "Why's Neri here?"

Parker's voice carried over the wind, as he hoped that Okee didn't hear him. "We need Okee distracted enough to get his mind control over the vortex, so that she and that Indian spirit can get it to reopen, so we can go home."

Okee's roar shook the ground.

Neri saw orbs darting at him, surrounding him. The giant god swung at them, before speaking words in a language she'd never heard. One by one, the orbs screamed and fell into him. He grew taller and stronger as he sucked them in. As for the creatures that were with him, they shrieked and merged with Okee.

Neri cried out. "Okee is gaining power. He's planning to escape this dimension for good. If Achak and I can't get the doorway to reform, he, you, Parker, and I will be the final souls he needs. We need him occupied."

Neri ran back to the fireball and Achak.

Achak chanted in Powhatan, while Neri used English. The fireball began spinning in place, sparking off like fireworks. It grew and grew until it filled its spot.

Achak flashed a look at her, then slipped into the shimmering light. One by one, those souls not already sucked into Okee, flowed through it. Neri darted aside before they pushed her into it. She needed to wait until the last moment and make sure Parker and Ben joined her before she slipped through.

"Parker. Ben. Come on; we need to escape." The combined winds of Okee's powers and the vortex minimized her voice.

But they saw it, as did Okee.

Both men stumbled, but the winds helped them along until they found themselves with Neri.

Neri took their hands, and the three of them moved toward the light. Parker passed through first.

Ben gestured to Neri go ahead of him when suddenly, the winds swept her up into the air. He tried to leap up to grab hold of one of her dangling feet but had no success. Neri rose higher, her arms stretching out until she looked like someone nailed to a cross, minus the cross. She cried out in agony.

Okee laughed as he stepped nearer.

Ben whipped around and shouted. "Let her go, you filthy beast!"

Okee gave his answer by stretching Neri's arms some more.

Tears welled up in her eyes.

Ben yelled, spittle flying from his lips. "You hurt her, kill her, and I'll escape and let my world know the truth about you. Maybe getting an army from my world to blow up Burkett will stop you." Ben rushed the giant.

Long shadowy tentacles appeared out of Okee's body. They snaked around Ben.

Okee's hold on her gone, Neri fell to the ground. She rolled over to her hands and knees and slowly got to her feet as pain riveted through her body and her breath knocked out of her. Finally on her feet, she looked up and saw Ben wrapped up in the slender god's tentacles.

Her legs still felt shaky, but Neri staggered closer.

Ben called out. "No, Neri. No. Get away."

She replied, "No, I can't leave you."

"Yes, you can. I love you enough to let you flee this awful place. Get out and find a way to block this monster from ever getting to our world ever again."

Tears rolled down her cheeks. "Oh God, Ben. I love you."

The tentacles squeezed tighter around Ben's body, and he cried out.

Neri flinched.

Ben managed to spit out, "I know, as a brother or friend."

She shook her head as she turned back to the vortex. "No, I always loved you as a woman for a man. I always have. I just never saw it."

He didn't answer her, so she turned to the entrance to her world. Before she had turned fully, she saw Okee dash Ben to the ground and stomp on him.

Neri screamed, tears almost blinding her. Suddenly, the winds stopped. The souls grown quiet. Shadows bigger than Okee formed on each side of him. Tentacles whipped out of them and circled him, forcing him to the ground.

A voice echoed in her head. *Go, leave. We have him. This time, we promise he won't be able to come to your world, even for a temporary visit.*

Neri turned back to the doorway, but before she stepped through the same voice curled inside her mind. *Sorry about your friend, but we will make sure his soul is set free.*

Tears in her eyes, she stopped at the edge of the pulsing light. The owner of the voice never said that Ben's spirit would be allowed to go to the other side or return to her world. Neri turned, determined to go back for his spirit, when something she couldn't see shoved her and she fell into the light.

***

Neri tumbled to the dirt in the village green.

Parker stood nearby and helped her up.

"Neri, where's Ben?"

She shook her head as she looked at him, crying.

His face fell. "Oh. I'm sorry."

She turned to the shimmer that reached its finger to the night sky. It shrunk and shrunk until it vanished.

The gods or whatever they were, had sealed Okee's prison from Earth completely.

Achak and his wife appeared before Parker and Neri. "We leave now. To go where our tribe waits for us. Once we made it here, it was I who called for the gods who imprisoned Okee."

Neri said, "Thank you, Achak. Without you at the last moment, I'm not sure if we could have stopped Okee for good." She grew sad.

Achak gave her a gentle smile. "You will see your warrior again."

Both vanished.

Neri knew who Achak meant. She began crying again.

Parker took her into his arms and let her release her pain. It took her a while, but at last, she withdrew and dried her face.

Parker said, "Let's get out of here. I think Ben left the keys in the ignition of his truck."

Once he got her inside the vehicle, Neri curled into a ball. It didn't matter that the heater blasted her with warmth, she still felt icy inside. She wanted Ben here to keep her warm.

Thank you again, shaman lady, my wife and I are with our tribe and many other spirits you have saved.

Neri stopped crying at Achak's voice. She didn't know what to say, as the misery in her own heart blocked all thought.

Like I told you earlier, your warrior must have escaped, too. For I feel no other soul back in that place. Goodbye.

She knew that Achak had left for good. She scrubbed at her tear-stained cheeks as she sat up and frowned. What did he mean about not sensing Ben in Okee's prison?

She sat up and closed her eyes, sending out psychic feelers. She sensed nothing but peace. Wherever Ben was, maybe Achak was right, he wasn't with Okee.

EPILOGUE

A month had passed. Christmas loomed not far away and earlier that morning, Neri had Parker drag her artificial tree down from her attic and set it up in one corner of her living room. They had just finished decorating it and Parker had plugged in the lights.

"It's beautiful," said Neri. "We did a fine job." She turned to Parker. "Aren't you going to visit your sister this afternoon?"

He nodded. "Yes. I'm going to let Lisa know her psychiatrist is permitting me to visit her and have a sort of gift exchange Christmas Eve morning. He thinks it will be good for her." He smiled. "He told me she's making my gift in the crafts class she takes Friday mornings there." A sigh escaped him. "Maybe one day she can finally come home, although, with the murder of her husband, it'll be years. As you know, possession by some god and made to kill Chris would never hold up in any court."

She let out a breath. "That's a shame. You're right, no court on Earth would believe her, and she would be locked away on insanity." A thought hit her. "Maybe they might give her a lighter sentence due to spousal abuse?" She patted his shoulder. "Anyway, go and sit at the kitchen table, Parker. I baked and decorated Christmas cookies last night, and I'm going to make a fresh pot of coffee to go with them." She frowned. "Unless you prefer milk to coffee with them?"

"No, coffee is fine."

Neri carried the cups of hot coffee and plate of cookies over to the table. She placed one cup in front of Parker and after setting the plate in the middle, sat across from him. Before taking a sip from her cup, Neri took a reindeer cookie and bit into it. As she swallowed the last crumb and drank several sips of her coffee, she could feel Parker's intent gaze on her. She wiped her mouth with a napkin and looked at him. His eyes looked sad.

Parker said, "Here, you let me go on about my sister, and it hit me, that it's not been that long since we lost Ben. I should say, you lost him since he'd been a friend of yours for a long time. I'm sorry about him." He stretched out his arm and covered her hand with his.

She realized she'd clenched her hand, her nails digging through the napkin she still held and into her palm. It hurt, but she didn't care. At least she could feel something. Ben would never....*Oh, God.* She shook Parker's hand off hers and dropped the napkin on the table.

Her eyes settled on the cream-filled liquid of her coffee, its steam rising. She lifted the cup to her lips and drank it down to the last drop. It had cooled enough not to be hot, just warm, but she doubted she would have noticed if a fire had roared down her throat.

"So many people lost their lives to that...thing, to Okee or whatever it was, but Ben," she caught back a sob, "we left him in that terrible world, knowing there wouldn't be any escape for him like the other souls. He'll never be able to cross over, to find everlasting peace. Just be in hell with that monster god for eternity."

Parker reached out and retook Neri's hand, gave it a light squeeze. "He knew what would happen, but he cared for you. He wanted you to live. He wanted us to escape, plus all those entities, too."

"Yes, I know." Her voice sounded dull to her ears. "It still doesn't make me feel any better, knowing he died a hero."

Her eyes closed, a slight headache thrumming behind her eyes, she tried not to think, but couldn't stop. Ben in various scenes flittered through her mind like an ever-shifting kaleidoscope. Her life with him passed before her. Until the last view of him, back in that dimension.

She understood at that moment that she did love him. Not as a brother or a best friend, but as a woman for a man. She recognized the truth at last, but it was too late. She may have been psychic, able to talk to phantoms and even fight gods—at least minor ones— but she didn't have a grasp of the understanding of relationships. Neri could help the dead get closure, but when it came to her own heart, she couldn't help herself.

Psychic or not, she couldn't have a relationship with a ghost, even if Ben's spirit had escaped that terrible place. When whatever that other thing that came and chained Okee for good and the rip in the air sealed, what happened to Ben's soul on the other side? Was he stuck forever in whatever hell was reserved for Okee?

Unable to handle her emotions any longer, she bolted from her table and ran outdoors. She stopped in front of the apple tree that Ben had helped her plant in her backyard and dropped into a boneless heap on the grass. Her fingers tugged, ripping out handfuls of the green.

When she felt the hand on her head, stroking, she said, "Go away, Parker."

"It's not Parker, Neri."

No longer sobbing, her heart pounding, she lifted her head to look over her shoulder. She saw a shadow of a man standing there, but the sun shone through him, almost blinding her. Then again, maybe it wasn't the sun.

"Ben?" Her voice cracked.

"Who else would it be?" Ben's laugh surprised her as it came, so rich, so easy.

The brightness dimmed until she saw him. Not solid, but not a complete see-through or even a shadow. A lop-sided grin on his lips and a tender, though mischievous, look in his eyes. He reached out and caressed her hair, stopping to pull out bits of grass and dirt from the strands.

Neri got to her feet. She fought the shakiness in her legs, refusing to collapse in front of him. There would never be this chance again.

Her hands found him. He felt solid under their touch. He bent and kissed her, touching her forehead with his.

"I love you, Neri. Always have. Always will. Death hasn't changed that."

"I should have seen you for who you were, Ben."

He shushed her. "It's all right. You finally did, didn't you?"

"But..."

He kissed her again, but before she could say anything else, he stepped back. "I had to say goodbye. But I have to go now."

Frantic, she moved toward him. "Don't go. We can..." She tried to grab his hand, but she found she couldn't. It seemed he stood inches away. Maybe even more than that—like the Veil stood between them.

"Can what? Communicate. I can become your spirit guide, help you when other spirits come to you?" His eyes darkened with sadness. "I don't want that kind of relationship. Be one of many spirits hanging around you. Besides, it is time for me to go. Time for my next adventure on the other side." He looked at the house. She did, too.

Parker stood on the back porch.

Neri pleaded, "Don't go, Ben. Stay."

Ben said, "The dead should stay with the dead and the living with the living. I gather you won't be alone long, and you know what, I approve. I do not even know why I was ever jealous of Parker Burkett. He's a good man. Goodbye, Neri. I love you."

"Ben, no—"

The brightness returned, hurting her eyes, and she barely saw his form dissipate, not until she realized she was alone. Her cheeks felt wet and touching them, Neri realized they were tears.

"Goodbye, Ben."

A hand touched her, and for a moment she thought maybe Ben had returned, but her psychic senses told her it wasn't him, but someone alive. She turned.

"Parker."

"He's gone?"

"Yes. For good this time."

"I'm sorry, Neri."

She scrubbed the tears off her cheeks and from her eyes. "You don't have to say sorry. Ben's going to a better place. At least, a better spot than stuck in that prison of Okee's. I—" She faltered, unsure what to say or think. Was Ben in a better place? Or did she placate herself with that, as she had done with many lost souls who had come to her? Tears bubbling up in her eyes, she pressed herself to Parker, and he held her, letting her sob it out.

Neri sat down and Parker went to get her some tea. Before he got himself a cup of coffee, his cell phone rang. He withdrew his cell and put it to his ear.

The sorrow that lined his face lightened. "Is Lisa all right?"

He listened, nodding occasionally as if to the other person on the phone, even though they couldn't really see his movements. Neri heard him mutter "Yes," or "Okay," on occasion, but that was it.

"Thanks." He clicked his phone off and turned to her.

"It's my sister. She seems better, herself again. There is still the upcoming trial for the murder of her husband. She'll need a good lawyer, and there's still the jail time and whatever else she will be facing. No one is going to believe about Okee and an alternate world."

Neri said, "No, they won't. We can't even testify that he's the real murderer of her husband. They would lock us away, too." She stood. "Well, why are we standing here? Let's go visit her."

She took his hand, grabbed her purse, and they walked out of the house.

***

Neither of them saw Neri's teacup move as if by an invisible hand and drop over the edge, falling to the floor. It shattered, pieces flying everywhere, and the tea leaves spilled with the liquid onto the tiled floor. The liquid evaporated until the tea leaves remained in the shape of a handprint.

***

As they drove to the hospital, Neri looked back over her shoulder with a slight frown.

Parker asked, "Anything wrong?"

She swung her gaze to his. "I don't think so." She smiled. "For now, anyway."

ABOUT THE AUTHOR

Pamela K. Kinney gave up ignoring the voices in her head a long time ago, and has written horror, fantasy, and science fiction. Her horror short story, "Bottled Spirits," was runner-up for the 2013 WSFA Small Press Award and her poem, "Dementia," was in the *HWA Poetry Showcase Vol VII*, and got her a mention in Best Horror of the Years, Vol 13. She has a story and a poem in *The Haunted Zone,* a horror anthology with stories and poetry written by women military veterans, released in 2024. Her YA dark fantasy novel, first in the *Moon Ridge, Virginia* trilogy, *Demon Memories*, was released October 15, 2024; she is working on the second book in the *Moon Ridge, Virginia* trilogy.

Pamela and her husband live with one crazy black cat in Virginia. Along with writing, Pamela has acted on stage and film. She is a member of Horror Writers Association, Virginia Writers Club, and James River Writers.

Other Books by Pamela K. Kinney published by DreamPunk Press

How the Vortex Changed my Life
Demon Memories – first in a YA horror trilogy
Maverick Heart – a novella

These titles are available from your favorite bookseller, or from www.dreampunkpress.com.

Pamela has short stories published in fiction anthologies and magazines/ezines, plus an article in a nonfiction anthology, *Ghost on Every Corner*. Find out about these at her website: www.PamelaKKinney.com.